A
Cosmetic
Conspiracy

A Cosmetic Conspiracy

A Will and Betsy Black Adventure

David and Nancy Beckwith

ABSOLUTELY AMAZING eBOOKS

ABSOLUTELY AMAZING eBOOKS

Published by Whiz Bang LLC, 926 Truman Avenue, Key West, Florida 33040, USA.

For information contact:
Publisher@AbsolutelyAmazingEbooks.com

ISBN-13: 978-1945772085 (Absolutely Amazing Ebooks)
ISBN-10: 1945772085

We dedicate this book to our daughter Aimee (A/K/A Lexie) who has brought endless sunshine to our lives. This book is also dedicated to all of our friends in the Florida Keys who gave us the scuttlebutt which made this book possible.

A
Cosmetic
Conspiracy

PROLOGUE

People were streaming out of Jehovah's Witnesses' Kingdom Hall, now the home base for the Cosmic Ray Scientific Church of Prosperity on Little Torch Key. Some paused to talk; others headed straight for their cars. Walter Wanderley, Chief of Police for the city of Key West and Will and Betsy Black stood on the sidewalk and watched as the people scattered.

"It was a nice memorial service, wasn't it?" said Walter Wanderley.

"Yes, but I'll never get used to a young person dying prematurely," said Will Black. "Who would have ever thought a person could perish on a nudist sun worshiping excursion even in a third world country."

Will was the branch manager for the Key West office of Reynolds Smathers and Thompson Securities; his wife Betsy was the local area president for WB Bank. Even though they were now seasoned Floridians, Will was originally from the Mississippi Delta; Betsy was a native of Mobile, Alabama. Will and Betsy had originally met in Mobile when both were working in the financial district. They had moved to Vero Beach, Florida when Will was offered a promotion and transfer there. Their daughter Lexie was born in Vero. For many years in Vero Beach as Lexie grew up, graduated from a private school and was accepted by the University of Miami, Vero Beach was a great place to be. But when Lexie left for college and Betsy was offered the presidency of WB in Monroe County at the same time RST decided to open a branch office there, it seemed a no-brainer for the Blacks to move to the lower Keys. Just as it had worked out when they moved to Vero, the move to the Keys also turned out to be a marvelous decision. They had become friends with Key West Police Chief Walter Wanderley since Betsy handled all the banking for both the city and the county.

"You guys going to the scattering of the ashes?" Walter asked.

"We've planned to. After all, I was her banker, and Will was her broker," said Betsy.

"Why don't we catch a burger at Sloppy Joe's, and then go together?" suggested Walter.

"Good idea," said Will. "Sloppy's is right down the street from where we need to be."

Within thirty minutes they reassembled at Sloppy Joe's, and the waitress took their order.

"It was a pleasant surprise to hear Reverend Bootee conduct the memorial service with dignity and decorum," commented Betsy.

"Somewhat surprising since when we first met him, he was Dub Bootee, rap singer," Will said. "Remember, the first time we ever saw him he was part of Reverend LeRoy Cho-Arturo's entourage – with all their flashy cars, gaudy clothes and bimbos."

"And don't forget – drug connections," said Walter.

"How could I ever," said Will and laughed. "That bunch was quite a sight to behold."

"Just Key West funky monkeys. Reverend Bootee certainly seems to have cleaned up his act," Betsy said. "I wonder what happened to old LeRoy."

"We may never know. I'm sorry I didn't get to hear Dub's whole service this morning. As usual I had a situation I had to deal with, and it was a doozie. I've never seen such a repentant criminal in my entire career in law enforcement. I couldn't force myself to leave until I had heard the whole story," said Walter.

"Anything you can share?" Will asked.

"I thought you'd never ask," Walter said and grinned. "A 55-year-old woman bartender who works at night was trying to get some shut-eye this morning in Old Town when she heard someone walk into her bedroom. The intruder sat on top of her and began to threaten and curse her. At first she begged him not to harm her."

"How old was this guy?"

"Twenty-five. The man took off his clothes and demanded oral sex. The woman then realized he wasn't armed, grabbed his penis, and began to twist and yank it with one hand. With her other hand she grabbed his testicles. He began to bite and hit her.

"He told us he pleaded with her, 'Please, please, you're killing me.'

"Her response was, 'Die then!'

"He continued to scream, 'Woman, woman, you got me suffering,' to which she responded, 'Have you thought about how you were going to leave *me* suffering?'

"He begged her to call the police, but she refused. She somehow got him to the front porch where he fell down and curled up in a fetal position to keep her from grabbing him again. She ran back in the house and grabbed her pistol. He limped off the porch and started running. She got off two shots but missed him."

By this time Will and Betsy were doubled up with laughter.

"I guess that guy won't need a penis enlarger for a long time," Will said.

"I bet his flag will be hanging at half-mast," said Betsy.

"I guess Won Hung Lo was really hanging low," Will said.

"You clowns are going to love the finish," Walter went on. "When we got there we discovered he'd written his name in the waistband of the blue-jeans he left in her bedroom. We looked up his address and went to his house. We found him in bed in severe pain. He told us he regretted his actions."

"That has got to go down as the understatement of the year," Betsy said, as Will grimaced, forming a mental picture of the suffering criminal.

"We had a doctor examine him," Walter said. "The doctor reported he has no permanent damage, but he will definitely be hurting for several more days."

"I guess the iceman cometh," Betsy said.

"I can see why you didn't want to leave that kinky excitement for a dull conventional memorial service," said Will.

"As long as we're discussing the depressing topic of early demise, that was really a strange way for Sun Raye to die," said Betsy when she got her breath back at last. "She was reportedly killed in a hit-and-run accident in Runaway Bay Jamaica when a local tried to pass too closely and a goat stepped out on the road. Then Luis Bernstein went to Jamaica and ran into a nightmare trying to get through the third-world bureaucratic bullshit to try to get the body out.

So he had her cremated locally and brought back the ashes."

"That's an unusual story, but I guess in Jamaica anything can happen. For many years it's been ranked as one of the most dangerous places in the world to drive a car," said Will.

They finished their meal, paid the tab, and rushed to the Garden of Eden for the ash scattering ceremony.

The Garden of Eden was a clothing-optional rooftop bar. The Bull was the bar on the building's first floor, The Whistle was the second floor bar, and the Garden of Eden was on the roof.

This building was a massive, almost square brick structure that dominated the corner of Duval and Caroline Streets. It reminded Will and Betsy of buildings in the French Quarter of New Orleans since the second floor was encircled by a wrought iron balcony. An almost life-size, three-dimensional bull sprang from the white-painted brick on one side of the building.

They entered The Bull. The décor was dominated by murals of people who had played a part in Key West's history. Henry Flagler, Mel Fisher, Ernest Hemingway, Fidel Castro, Peter Audubon, Tennessee Williams and Jimmy Buffett peered down on the assembled drinkers. Elvis even blessed the bar's activities. Yankee Jack, a freshwater Conch from Boston, was just starting his afternoon gig. He was partially through playing a self-penned composition, "Manatee Woman", when Will, Betsy and Walter arrived. Patrons laughed at his satirical song of the woman who thought she was a mermaid but looked more like a manatee. Since they were in a hurry, they didn't stop to listen to Jack, just waved and headed for the second floor where the Whistle was located. The atmosphere was completely different than the Bull. The room was full of pool tables, Foosball tables, and dartboards. Some patrons sat on the stools out on the wrought-iron balcony watching the mass of humanity on Duval Street. A tourist on the balcony was pulling on his wife's sleeve, pointing at the snake man wending his way down from Mallory Square with his snake wrapped around his neck. He was parting the sidewalk crowd as he passed as if they were waves in the Red Sea. Will paused for a moment to watch the bartender's dog, Max, pick up a tip off the bar with his mouth and give it to the bartender before heading up the stairs once again to the Garden of Eden.

The room was already full of people when they got there. Some were dressed in business attire like Will, Betsy and Walter. Others were in various states of undress ranging from topless to nude. Some were body-painted. Foliage surrounded the edge of the building. A tent used for body-painting dominated one portion. There was an abundance of comfortable seating, all of which was occupied.

Reverend Dub Bootee, wearing only a g-string, was motioning for silence as they entered. Will tried to squeeze through the crowd and felt something bump into his chest. He looked down and saw it was the ample chest of a pudgy body-painted woman. She had an open Bible painted on her front which said EXODUS 20: 2-17. The Bible was emerging from a rainbow. He realized the bump he'd felt was from her stumbling into him. She was drinking champagne that had spilled down her front. The wet body paint had rubbed off on Will's shirt. He put his hands up instinctively and accidentally grabbed her by both painted boobs.

"I'm certainly glad you're a witness so I don't have to explain a 'lipstick smear' when I get home tonight," Will said to his wife.

"Yes," She said with a smile. "Would you say her life is an open book?"

"I think you could call it an incomplete book. I think she's down to nine commandments now."

"What's missing? Thou shalt not plagiarize scripture?"

When Dub Bootee had the crowd's attention the service began.

He opened with, "At the rising of the sun and at its going down..."

The crowd refrained, "We will forever remember Sun Raye."

Bootee continued, "At the blowing of the wind and in the heat of summer..."

The crowd: "We will forever remember Sun Raye."

Bootee continued eulogizing the remaining seasons and then moved on to messages about strength and accomplishment.

Dub Bootee: "When we have achievements that are based on her..."

The crowd: "We will forever remember Sun Raye.

For as long as we live, she too will live, for she is now a part of us as we remember her."

With those words Reverend Dub Bootee threw the ashes in the urn from the edge of the roof. A sudden gust of wind came from the opposite direction, sending the ashes back onto the roof. Everywhere Will and Betsy looked they saw ashes sticking to body paint, in people's hair, or on hors d'oeuvres and in cocktails.

Betsy looked at Dub. He merely looked embarrassed and gave her a "you can't win them all" shrug. The lady with the biblical chest chugalugged another drink.

Will punched Betsy and whispered, "So which of Sun Raye's body parts do you think the biblical boobie lady of Duval Street got sprinkled into her drink?"

Betsy whispered back, "If her drink turns tittie-pink, we'll know."

THE PAST

CHAPTER 1

It was a perfect Florida spring day, the kind of day that most Floridians would prefer to spend outdoors basking in the sunlight. Spring is an idyllic time in Florida. The summer heat has yet to arrive. It is still the dry season, so outings can be planned with a virtual assurance they can be finished without disruption. The days are getting longer. Most importantly, hurricane season seems light-years away. While much of the rest of the nation is preoccupied with outlasting another endless winter, Floridians guiltlessly enjoy feeling like God's chosen people.

Madelyn Koury, however, was virtually unaware of her surroundings as she went into the Orlando auditorium. She was preoccupied with her agenda for the day and the hope she had found the key to breaking the cycle of mediocrity that had been her fate until now.

Madelyn was a second-generation Conch born at the Lower Keys Medical Center in Key West. Her father had been a street performer known as 4S, which stood for Silent Screaming Silver Swabbie. He would dress in a naval uniform, paint himself silver and stand silently on the sidewalk until a mark passed. Then he would start screaming naval commands until the person either walked on or contributed money. 4S's ambition was to become a street performer on Mallory Square, but city officials considered him a nuisance and would never grant him the necessary permit.

Madelyn's mother was a bartender at the Bourbon Street Pub. One night after 4S finished that day's pursuits, he decided to visit his wife and have a drink at the pub to celebrate his good fortune. A drunken mark who found him entertaining had contributed $50. 4S's one drink soon turned into a celebration. An inebriated 4S climbed on the bar and began to bark orders to a drunken sailor from the Naval Air Station. The sailor took a swing at 4S but missed. He did not miss, however, with a bar glass that hit 4S in the forehead sending him careening into a chair, breaking his neck on the way down. He was dead by the time paramedics arrived. Madelyn's mother was fired.

4S's fellow performers chipped in to buy him a plot in the cemetery and properly prepare his body. On the day he was interred they visited his grave en mass and danced on his burial site. To make his grave stand out, his headstone was placed at his feet and marked accordingly.

Neither of Madelyn's parents had been especially good role models. Usually no one was home when she got out of school, and for all intents and purposes she was her own parent. After her father's death, Madelyn's mom had a series of boyfriends, most of whom had picked her up at whichever bar was currently employing her.

By the time she hit Key West High School, Madelyn was an out-of-control rebellious teenager on a variety of pills. She was knocked up by a school dropout named Kevin O'Dare before she could graduate. There was a quickie wedding, and she became Madelyn Koury-O'Dare. After instigating an embarrassing episode that was reported in the *Key West Citizen*, Kevin disappeared.

What A Drag

A local man who passed out and rolled under a car after a long night of drinking, was dragged nearly four blocks before the driver noticed, police say.

The 20-year-old victim, Kevin O'Dare, was "asleep or otherwise unconscious" under a 1989 Ford parked on the 300 block of Simonton Street.

The driver and a passenger got in the car without seeing the man and took off but stopped a short time later when they heard muffled screaming.

Police say the man was in a lot of pain and was very intoxicated.

Madelyn named the resulting twin girls Mary and Mildred. Madelyn soon left the Keys herself and moved to Orlando. There she got a job doing the only thing she knew how to do — bartend. Madelyn developed a gift for gab with her customers that served her tip-jar well.

Life was not easy for the single mother of two. She and her daughters barely scraped by. One day a big-tipping customer told her there was a better way to live. She could take charge of her life. Either she could be a loser all her life, or she could dare to be great. He told her he had once been a failure like her until he met Glenn W. Turner who had shown him the path to success. It was now his mission to show other people the secrets to success that Turner had taught him.

Madelyn's customer invited her to a meeting that would teach her the secrets to being successful. Madelyn was skeptical at first. She had little education; she had no job skills other than bartending or being a waitress; she had no technical skills; she had never sold anything in her life.

Night after night, Madelyn's customer continued extolling the virtues of the good life. His enthusiasm was boundless. With her knack for chat, the brass ring could be hers. All she had to do was grab it, the man said.

Now Madelyn was on her way to her first *Dare To Be Great* meeting. She was scared, but she was also desperate for a way out of her dead-end existence.

Madelyn was not prepared for the compelling scene she encountered in Orlando. Before anyone was let inside the auditorium, they had to wait outside in the heat for what seemed like an eternity. Once they were finally allowed inside, the excitement escalated beyond belief. She was awestruck as she watched the program unfold. The crowd was at an even more excited fever pitch than they would have been at a championship football game. It was like being in the throes of a true cult.

There seemed to be enthusiastic, self-confident people everywhere as she entered the Orlando auditorium. She wasn't sure whether to be intimidated or awed by the circus-like atmosphere. There were fireworks, laser lights, special effects from dry ice and spotlights shining in every direction. The décor and theme was highly patriotic. She found a place in the middle of the auditorium where she felt she might not stand out and waited to see what would happen next. People all around her talked excitedly about their big plans and high aspirations. Madelyn wondered if attending this event had been a mistake, and maybe she was out of her league. She had never felt so out of place.

When Madelyn heard Strauss' "Also Sprach Zarathustra" over the auditorium sound system, she recognized it as the music from "2001: A Space Odyssey". From the back of the auditorium a man in a suit ran down the aisle and bolted behind the podium. He was over-weight and Mediterranean looking. His weight was partially disguised by his expensive chalk-striped custom-made suit and vest and his perfectly styled hair. He introduced himself as Vince Bonati. The crowd was mute, waiting to hear his words. He enthusiastically welcomed the audience to a day he said would soon change their lives – just like Glenn Turner had changed his own life years ago.

"I had a three-thousand dollar a day coke habit when I met Glenn Turner," he began, "but he told me I could turn my life around."

The crowd was riveted by his words.

All of a sudden Bonati raised his voice, "You wanna know what 'Dare To Be Great' really did for me? I'm alive. That's what Glenn Turner did for me. Otherwise I would be dead."

He lowered his voice back to a normal volume.

"And he introduced me to the most beautiful people on earth - YOU. Now let's start to count down – a countdown to greatness. You are about to hear one of the greatest men of the 20th century, a man who has changed the lives of millions, a man who has risen over more adversity than any person in this room to become one of the dynamic leaders of this great country. Listen carefully because you too can rise to heights you've never dreamed you could reach. It is up to you. This is going to be the greatest day of your life, like the day *I* met Glenn Turner which became the greatest day of my life."

Another man in a white suit and vest ran down the aisle. People recognized him and began to cheer. Every eye in the building was on him as he raced like a bionic man toward the stage. The music got loud playing the song "Dare To Be Great". The crowd of 1,500 chanted, "GO-GO-GO-GO-GO!! Madelyn felt her heart beat loudly as she became caught up in the frenzy. She had been to meetings before but nothing like this. It reminded her of a revival meeting, and Glenn W. Turner was the evangelist preacher sent by God to rule his flock.

After bounding on the stage, he waved his fist and shouted "GO!" The crowd instantly became silent.

The voice that Madelyn heard was not what she expected. At first she thought Turner had a bad cold. He sounded nasal and slurred some of his words. The voice was southern and had a slight lisp.

"My name is Glenn W. Turner, and I have a message for you," the man said. "You can be whatever you want to be. You can be a winner."

The crowd went wild.

"*You* can take back your mind, because *you* lost it."

The crowd went wild once again.

Turner held up his fist and again shouted "GO!" The audience immediately became silent again. Now that Turner once more had their complete attention he continued; "In 1966 I grabbed a book entitled "Think and Grow Rich". It was printed in 1920. It said that anything that the mind of man can conceive, it can achieve.

"I didn't have enough sense and education to look at the copyright of that book. What the author wrote and what other people interpreted in that book and what I

6

interpreted in that book were different. He meant in the 1930's and the 1940's people could become multi-millionaires, and I thought he meant today. I didn't know the book was 20 or 30 years outdate. Therefore I believed it.

"Other people with more education and more ability than I had at that point in my life read that same book and didn't do anything with it because they glanced down and saw that single statement – printed 1920 – and they said 'no wonder, that was back when a person could still make it before 'taxes were too high', but all I seen was the meat and I grabbed it and I run with it and my belief was what made it true."

Madelyn found herself being drawn to this man who spoke poor grammar with a lisp.

Turner went on to tell the crowd how he was born to a sharecropper and had a harelip and cleft palate at birth because his mother had scarlet fever during her pregnancy since she could not afford proper prenatal care. He told of his surgery as an infant to correct his deformity and went on to talk about how he dropped out of school in the eighth grade because he was constantly teased by other children about his harelip. He described joining the Air Force at 17 only to be discharged a year later when it was discovered he had a perforated eardrum.

He told how he turned a $5,000 loan into $100 million in 36 short months despite his shortcomings and how he transformed himself from a loser having no self-confidence to a winner with the self-assurance and knowledge to become a master speaker and entrepreneur.

"A winner says I'm good but not as good as I ought to

be," said Turner. "A loser says I'm not as bad as a lot of other people."

By the time Turner had finished his talk, Madelyn was pumped. Kirby Grant from the television show "Sky King" now sang the "Dare To Be Great" theme song and the crowd resumed chanting. By God, he was right! She could leave her miserable existence behind and become whatever she desired. She could be a winner. Madelyn took what little money she had and bought as many of the motivational materials as she could afford before she left the auditorium. She would follow Glenn Turner's advice. She would focus and become a winner instead of continuing to be a dysfunctional loser.

CHAPTER 2

Glenn Turner's Koscot Interplanetary Inc. organization required that a person invest $5,000 in their distributorship. This left Madelyn with a dilemma. Where could she possibly get $5,000? Most months she was lucky to pay her bills, and when something unbudgeted came up, she couldn't do that. She investigated the possibility of borrowing the funds on a series of credit cards, but came up short. She even considered picking up men in the bar where she worked. Some of its patrons certainly had shown an interest in her. Each time Madelyn thought about this option, she remembered some of her mother's boyfriends she had called "uncles" and couldn't convince herself to go that route. She didn't want her twin girls to have their own "uncles" to remember when they got older. She thought about selling her car, but it was a clunker that would have still left her short of her objective. She even thought about embezzling from her employer but was afraid she'd get caught. Then who would raise her girls? She certainly didn't want them to be raised by their boozy Key West grandmother.

She listened to the "Dare To Be Great" motivational tapes over and over. All this did was to depress her because she wanted so badly to take her shot at the brass ring but the $5,000 requirement seemed like $5,000,000. There just didn't seem to be any way.

Then one day, Madelyn visited Radio Shack to window-shop computers for the girls. Her daughters were getting to the age when they would need to start learning computer fundamentals. But she sighed as she looked at the units. Maybe next month. The money simply wasn't there to purchase one on what she had coming in this month. Standing near her was a middle-aged man, enthusiastically looking through games. He kept excitedly reading the backs of the boxes, making comments like "Isn't it amazing what they are able to do these days?" and "Who knows where technology will be five years from now."

Madelyn sighed and told him that maybe next year she might be able to afford a computer. The man told her his name was Ted and he knew someone who had a very affordable used machine. Ted said if she gave him her phone number, he'd get back to her with the details. Although Madelyn was reluctant to give out personal information to a total stranger, she agreed to give him the phone number of the bar where she worked.

Madelyn was surprised the next evening when Ted walked in and ordered a Miller Lite. He gave her a lead on a $100 used computer and told her he would gladly set it up for her for free. Madelyn said she'd think about it. He gave her a big tip and left.

The next night Ted again returned. He seemed to be an affable, well-intentioned person. Madelyn agreed to buy the machine and agreed to let Ted hook it up for her on her next day off. When Ted came over, he asked Madelyn, "How would you like some personal help from trained professionals on how to start you own business?"

She responded that she'd love to but she didn't have money to invest.

"No problem," he said.

A few days later, her first audiocassette arrived. It had an innocuous, attention-grabbing title - "Building a Bright Future in the 21st Century." The speaker talked about the difficulty of getting money in the modern world and how hard it is for most people to budget their time so that they are poised to maximize their earnings and be successful. Then the tape shifted gears:

How would you like to hear about a business which can raise your income and shorten your workweek? Doesn't this sound wonderful? If you want to learn more, contact the person who gave you this tape.

At first Madelyn thought it was another *Dare To Be Great* tape and put it aside, thinking it was another dream beyond her means. Ted called and asked if he could show her another presentation. This time he showed her a videotape. It was just as vague as the cassette had been. Now Ted launched into a hard sell, pressuring Madelyn to come to an informational meeting and learn more.

"You're going to love the people there," Ted declared. "They are nice and friendly and helpful people who genuinely love and respect each other. People will actually put their wallets down on their seats to save their place and walk away. There has never been one stolen. People are more trusting there than they would be at church."

When Madelyn arrived, an older speaker had the crowd worked into a passionate frenzy. People hung on his every word and constantly applauded him wildly. The audience all wore cookie-cutter conservative business attire so alike it almost made them look like Hasidic Jews. Each had an identical black leather planner with identical yellow legal pads which they used to diligently take notes. The speaker ranted excitedly,

"There are two kinds of people in this world - people who have excuses, and people who have money. If you have an excuse, keep it to yourself. And do you know what I say to the excuse-maker? If you have all the answers, why aren't you rich?"

Every person in the room seemed to worship the ground that the speaker walked on. Why? Because he was rich. He left the podium to an ear-splitting standing ovation. For a few moments, Madelyn was the last person sitting, but she was soon drawn into the frenzy and found herself standing and cheering as loudly as anyone in the room. Ted located her and gave her a thumbs-up from across the room. He worked his way through the crowd until he was next to her. He whispered, "I have more information in my car for you, but before we leave, I want to introduce you to our speaker."

Madelyn was wowed. "Me? But what do I say to him?"

"Don't worry about that. This is your once-in-a-lifetime opportunity to meet someone really important. You'll be shocked at what a nice guy he is," Ted said.

A stranger on the other side of her added, "Trust me. It's all right. You can talk to him. I had the same awed reaction the first time I met him, but he's human, just like you and me. Welcome to the Ramway family." The man vigorously pumped Madelyn's hand.

All Madelyn could think was, "Yes! This is my way out. She still wasn't sure what she was expected to sell or to whom, but she was convinced, whatever it was, it was her ticket to raise her standing in life. She was convinced she too could be rich.

CHAPTER 3

Madelyn quickly became a workaholic. Every waking moment not working at the bar was used to promote Ramway. Every night at the bar she kept her ear to the ground trying to spot prospects. She started using Ramway products exclusively whenever possible in her apartment even though they were more expensive than similar items at Publix or Wal-Mart. Despite her fervor her business grew more slowly than she initially expected. Ted told her it was because she didn't attend enough rallies and didn't buy enough motivational tapes. Her rebuttal was that she was attending all the meetings she could since their times often conflicted with her working hours at the bar. Ted could eject tried, standard answers to every doubt she brought up. He seemed to have an innate ability to know when to talk and when to just say "Uh huh" to prove he was listening. He kept stressing following "The Plan" and told her if she hoped to achieve success she should never question him, her up-line, even when the going got tough.

Ted always seemed to have a pat but often nonsensical answer to every issue she brought up.

Madelyn: "If Ramway is so good, why isn't the whole world selling it?"

Ted: "Then everyone would be rich! There'd be no more wars."

Madelyn: "Yes, but how can everybody be rich when there's only a finite amount of money to go around?"

Ted: "There's not a finite amount of money; there's as much as there needs to be."

Madelyn: "How can everybody get rich if everyone on the planet is already signed up and there's no one left to sponsor?"

Ted: "Parents can sponsor their children. Quit asking questions and go to work. Your primary problem is your lack of commitment."

Ted seemed to have a comeback for everything.

Madelyn decided to prove her commitment to Ramway once and for all. She quit her night-job at the bar. Instead she got a part-time receptionist job at a temporary agency, even though she now made less. She reasoned this would leave her more time to study motivational books and go to meetings. And there were meetings several nights each week as well as larger meetings on weekends. A small event might cost her $10, a larger event might cost her $50, and then there were the large events that cost $100 or more to attend. Books and tapes cost additional money. Madelyn's life began to evolve more and more around Ramway.

Madelyn's business slowly began to grow. She became what was known in the business as a "Direct", signifying that she had achieved some measure of success. She hoped her next step would take her to the classification of "Pearl." But she still wasn't getting rich. In fact because of the constant expenditures, her Ramway income added to her receptionist' salary still left her with less money than she had had when she was only a bartender. What was wrong?

Her question was answered when Madelyn discovered

a new concept, pyramids. She first read the word in a crossword puzzle and Googled it to find out the meaning. What she would discover would finally truly change her life. More than Glenn W. Turner had. More than Ramway had.

She came across an article entitled "How Pyramid Schemes Work". She read it with interest. It described pyramids as being a gifting plan which could be presented through many formats. Approaches like dinner parties or dinner clubs, meetings about women empowering women, or creating a circle of friends were used as examples. It further instructed that *Recruits are to be promised a substantial lump sum once they reach the peak level.*

An article from the Skeptic's Dictionary was the one that mesmerized her as it made her visualize possibilities. It contained a diagram that stopped her in her tracks.

1
10
100
1,000
10,000
100,000
1,000,000
10,000,000
100,000,000
1,000,000,000

She looked at it and looked at it. Of course! Maybe one person could influence many people. She read on.

With the odds so stacked against a person, why would one gamble on a pyramid scheme? Greed is only part of the answer. Most pyramid people don't envision themselves anywhere near the bottom layer of the pyramid. Even the most greedy person on the planet would probably see that if one is near the bottom of recruits it will be very hard to get new recruits. They have position themselves near the top in order to envision the immense wealth from minimal effort that is going to come their way.

Concepts were starting to jell in her head. She read on.

... if you hope to get people involved in a pyramid scheme, the first thing you must do is convince them they are not getting involved in a pyramid scheme. Tell them they are joining a club.

Madelyn read that what separated legal from illegal organizations was that the business had to sell a product, not just distributorships – just like Koscot and Ramway did.

Madelyn saw she had had the right idea long ago. She had just been in the wrong position in the pyramid. She'd been in the right church, just sitting on the wrong pew. Maybe she could still be wealthy after all. She just needed to be number 1.

Madelyn replayed the number pyramid all night in her sleep. She kept seeing the number "1". It was like a song that had gotten caught in her brain. The following morning she opened her medicine cabinet and saw "One-A-Day" vitamins. As she left her apartment, she noted that she lived in apartment "1". As she drove to work Three Dog Night's *One* came on the radio. At work, she glanced at the sports section of the newspaper. There was an interview with several sports greats in tennis, golf, and football, all lauding how great it was to be number 1. On her way back home, Bob Marley sang *One Love* on her radio. She dreamed again that night about the number pyramid and being the one on top.

By the weekend Madelyn was convinced that all these "1's" were a divine sign on what her direction in life should be. She now firmly believed in numerology. If she hoped to succeed, she had to thrust herself into the number one position. She could never do that with Koscot or Ramway. She would have to start her own pyramid with herself already entrenched at the top, and she knew just what to sell in Florida to keep her business legal - sunscreen. And she wouldn't have to reinvent the wheel. She could structure her new business a lot like Ramway. She even knew what to call her new enterprise, the CANDO Corporation LLC.

CHAPTER 4

Conceiving CANDO and getting it off the ground were two different things. Madelyn's first efforts were to attract people she had met through Ramway. Her initial efforts were hampered by amateurish sales pitches, her limited credibility and the fact for the first six months she had no sunscreen product. Madelyn was finally able to convince a small sunscreen manufacturer in Rockledge Florida to private label a sunscreen product for her. The sunscreen was average, but it was better than nothing. At least it made CANDO legal.

Attracting distributors away from Ramway was not as easy as she had originally envisioned. Her product line only had one item - sunscreen. Her fledgling organization did not have the large bank of motivational materials her competitor relied so heavily on. The fight got dirty, with local upper-level Ramway distributors fighting back by spreading false rumors about her and CANDO.

After two years CANDO was barely afloat. Even Madelyn wondered if she was ever going to make it work. She was now deeply in debt. She had also lost weight and couldn't sleep. It had begun to look harder and harder to establish the pyramid which was going to make her a rich woman. The twins were teenagers by now, only adding to her pressures. She was behind on her rent and expected possible eviction in the near future. Madelyn began mixing Adderall and hydrocodone chased with vodka tonics to get through each long workday. Soon her addictions drove her even deeper into debt.

Orlando was obviously not working out for CANDO. Her depression increased. One day a car passed her with a U.S. 1 Mile Marker zero bumper sticker. Madelyn, still a numerologist, saw the "1" on the bumper sticker and interpreted it as a sign. "1's" had gotten her into her own business, and now they were speaking to her again. She should listen and follow U.S. 1 to Key West. It was time to return to her roots. The Keys would be where her future was, not Orlando.

That evening she announced her decision to Mary and Mildred. The family was moving to the Keys. The girls were not pleased about being uprooted, but Madelyn convinced them that the move was in all their best interests since they could live rent-free in a trailer Madelyn had recently inherited from her mother on Big Pine Key.

By the time Madelyn and the girls arrived in the Keys, Madelyn had worn herself to a frazzle and desperately felt she needed support from her drugs. She recalled where she used to buy them on Stock Island and found that her Colombian connection was still good.

Madelyn's pusher seemed glad to see her but was curious why she had returned to the Keys. She told him about CANDO and how she was trying to relocate the company from Orlando. The pusher seemed genuinely interested.

The following week while Madelyn was buying a new supply of pills, the pusher told her that he had a prospect for her, a local restaurateur named Miguel Valdes. Madelyn followed up and was invited to a meeting at

Valdes' office. Valdes' office was not what she expected. It was small and cramped with scarred wooden furniture.

Valdes was a short stocky man with acne scars. His hair was greasy, and his fingers were stained with nicotine. He wore a no-nonsense plaid shirt and dark pants. Madelyn winced when he stared sullenly at her. This look insinuated he could be either beating her up, raping her or slitting her throat, and it would not cause him to lose sleep.

"Take a fuckin' chair," he said brusquely, not bothering to stand up or shake hands when she entered.

Valdes listened to her sales pitch stoically, saying nothing. Then he made her a proposal, which was more like a thinly veiled demand. He told Madelyn he knew about her debts and her need for pills. Instead of continuing to use her current supplier for sunscreen, Valdes matter-of-factly said he would reformulate her sunscreen, take over the manufacturing and distribution and virtually guaranteed alternate outlets for the product. In return he would see that many of her debts were forgiven, that she would have an uninterrupted supply of pills at a reasonable price and that the cops would remain unaware of her habit.

She said she would think about his proposal.

He said, "Don't think too fuckin' long."

CHAPTER 5

Madelyn found her meeting with Miguel Valdes to be very upsetting. She was also furious that this gangster thought he could just dictate how she was to run her business. CANDO was her dream not his. This was the business she had slaved over to build from scratch, the business she had lost sleep over, prayed over. It had even taken her away from her daughters, and sent her into debt. Now Valdes thought he could just muscle in on her operation. The problem was he and his friends *could* muscle in on her operation, and she couldn't do a damn thing to stop him. She was a single mom with no money, a drug habit and no leverage.

Madelyn didn't see how she could keep Valdes from taking over manufacturing and distributing sunscreen. She was one woman against an organization of professional thugs. But why did he want to? She didn't sell enough sunscreen to interest someone like him. She didn't sell any more than the average outlet at a flea market. Was this possibly just a first step in the taking over of her whole life? Was the dream lost? Had it been a mistake to think she could dare to be great?

It bothered Madelyn that her dependence on uppers and downers had left her vulnerable to a creep like Valdes. She couldn't report his muscling activities to the police as long as he could turn her in for using illegal drugs. But then again, she rationalized she needed these stimulants to work the long hours she worked. She would quit taking them when the pressures subsided. For now she resigned herself to co-existing with her new partner.

There's a hackneyed old proverb that says "it's always darkest before the dawn." Madelyn didn't know it at that moment, but this statement was applicable to her.

She sorely needed a reliable income so she answered a help-wanted ad looking for a receptionist at the Green Rainbow Tattoo Parlor and Ashram in Key West. The people there seemed nice enough and the hours were flexible. The ashram's spiritual leader was the Highly Exalted Reverend LeRoy Cho-Arturo. One of the spiritual counselors was a Cuban Jew named Luis Bernstein.

Madelyn did not know when she met the affable boyish Luis that he was an ex-don of the digital underworld and an ex-con. He was a computer genius and accomplished hacker who had served five years in the Federal pen. As a teenager Luis had hacked for fun, but he turned his skill into a lucrative career when he worked as a computer consultant. He would break into private networks and steal credit card numbers. He finally got caught when he got greedy and began to steal from banks, credit unions, and even other hackers.

A few weeks after Madelyn took the job, she was sideswiped on North Roosevelt by a car as she was en route to work. The driver was a Cuban and, as it turned out, also an uninsured motorist. The damage to Madelyn's car was extensive. She was distraught. She did not have the $1,000 for the insurance deductible. This car was her only transportation. Her car had to be towed, and she was forced to take a pink taxi to work.

She said nothing about her problem at work but

instead stewed and doodled on a crossword puzzle. Luis paused as he stopped by her desk to pick up his phone messages.

"What's wrong, Madelyn? You look down," Luis said.

Madelyn told him about her accident, that the other motorist was uninsured, and how she didn't have the money to get her car repaired.

"Did you say he's Cuban?" Luis asked.

Madelyn nodded.

"I do have certain connections in the Cuban community," Luis said. "Give me his name and let me see what I can do."

The following day Luis came in and put $3,000 on her desk.

"Will this cover it?" he asked.

Madelyn was dumb-founded. "Where did you get this?"

"Let's just say Serge has assets he had forgotten about."

For the first time, Madelyn noticed Luis's bruised knuckles.

He said nothing more and put his hands in his pockets.

After that day Luis and Madelyn became friends. They would go out to lunch together at least once a week. As they got to know each other better, Madelyn confided in him about her background. She told him about her addiction to uppers and downers and how the pressures of trying to start a business had made her resort to taking them. She also told him about the pressures of being the single mom of two rebellious teenage girls and confided in him about her financial pressures but purposely did not mention Miguel Valdes. She did not want Luis to get hurt. Madelyn finally had found someone she could talk to.

Luis showed a genuine interest in CANDO. She showed him the number triangle for pyramids and explained to him the significance of her being on the top of it. As she explained the importance of her own position, he became even more intrigued. He said he could see that the business had vast untapped potential. Madelyn told him of her problems with recruiting distributors. He told her he had a solution. He would prove it by becoming one of her second-rung distributors. He put one condition on his participation. Madelyn had to give up the pills.

She agreed that she would try and she did indeed succeed. Soon other distributors, mostly Cuban, started to join. Luis recruited more distributors in one month than Madelyn had been able to recruit in a year. She was amazed.

"You don't know who I am, do you?" Luis asked one day.

Madelyn admitted she didn't even know his last name.

"My family owns Bernstein's Down Home Cuban Grocery Store," he said.

"That's an institution around here," Madelyn said.

Luis nodded, "And we Cubans stick together. When I showed them how close they could be to the top of your pyramid, everyone wanted aboard."

After that the participants in CANDO began to expand exponentially. Madelyn had renewed faith there was a rainbow where a pot of gold could be discovered. She finally began to feel that some of Glenn W. Turner's platitudes were on target.

A winner makes a commitment. A loser makes promises.

If we seem nutty to you, and if we seem like an oddball to you, just remember one thing; the mighty oak tree was once a nut like me.

CHAPTER 6

The next few years were good ones for Madelyn. She felt like she was finally starting to participate in the American dream. With Luis' Cuban contacts and street-smarts she developed a solid core of CANDO distributors in both the Cuban community and through Green Rainbow Ministries. Suntan lotion volume levels had risen to the point where operating leverage began to work in her favor, making it extremely profitable. Virtually all of the new sales seemed to be going through a company named Tango Products of Colombia. Madelyn thought her life was finally looking up. As unpleasant as Miguel Valdes was, he seemed to manufacture good products and did not seem to be interfering in her other business. He introduced new skin products from time to time that gradually expanded CANDO's product line. It did bother her that Valdes never suggested these new products but simply seemed to impose them, but no matter what the product Tango Products was always willing to buy it in quantity. She never was comfortable with her Colombian partner, but as long as things went well she didn't dwell on unpleasant matters.

Luis, as it turned out, had other talents that benefitted the organization. He had a degree from the University of Miami in communications. He helped her refine CANDO's structure and began to design motivational materials on his computer for CANDO to sell through its growing network. With his help CANDO established sales tiers and recognition clubs. They used the blueprint she had first seen at Ramway by establishing recognition clubs that started at Bronze and then graduated to Silver, Gold, Palladium and finally Platinum.

Madelyn continued to keep her promise to Luis. She stayed off of uppers and downers. She also honed her speaking skills at Green Rainbow religious meetings, which also motivated her to develop a personal interest in world religions.

Madelyn rented a meeting room from Green Rainbow to conduct training meetings and motivational rallies, but she could only use it when it was convenient for Green Rainbow. Madelyn dreamed of someday getting away from the retail and honky-tonkish atmosphere of Duval Street and have a facility she could set up permanently and use however and whenever she wanted to.

One day Luis came to her with an idea. The Jehovah's Witnesses Kingdom Hall on Little Torch Key was for sale and seemed to be priced right. Luis suggested that if Madelyn were willing to sell the trailer she had inherited from her mom she would have the necessary down payment to purchase the building. She and the girls could live in part of the building. The rest could be used as a meeting room which she could decorate and furnish permanently and the building would give her on-premise storage space to inventory sunscreen products and motivational materials. It had an office as well as a kitchen and public restrooms. She would also have adequate parking. Jehovah's Witnesses was even willing to leave behind the folding chairs and tables she would need for meetings. It seemed ideal. She could even continue to call it Kingdom Hall, a name that appealed to her. At last CANDO would have a permanent home and the stability it needed to grow. Valdes insisted that his associates could lend her the funds for the mortgage. She was shocked at how quickly her mother's trailer sold. A Colombian family paid her the full asking price. To Madelyn it was a dream come true. Many of her growth problems could now be solved. Glenn Turner's words came back to her:

A winner sees an answer for every problem. A loser sees a problem in every answer.

CHAPTER 7

Miguel Valdes was a little nervous as he drove to Adolfo Soltero's Key West office. As far as he knew everything was going fine, but he was nervous anyway. A person never knew when something might be amiss and he simply was not aware of it. Soltero was the type to delegate. He typically only got more involved in a project when there was a problem. His associates liked it that way. Miguel had found that it was best to keep his interactions with his superior as social as possible. So why had he gotten nervous when Al suggested they have lunch at the Pepe's Café on Caroline Street? Al always felt Pepe's wooden booths and lack of soundproofing gave him enough privacy to conduct a business luncheon.

Valdes picked Soltero up, and they headed toward the restaurant. Soltero kept the conversation to small talk along the way, asking about Valdes' wife and children. The closest parking place was several blocks away, requiring that they walk the remainder of the way to the restaurant. Pepe's wasn't elegant, but their food was consistently first-rate.

After their orders had been brought and the waiter had assured himself that things were satisfactory, Al gave Miguel a hint as to the real purpose of the meeting.

"How are things going with Tango?" he asked. "How about your new restaurant, Casa Camilio Sur?"

"Fine in both cases," Valdes said and took a bite of his fish.

Soltero waited patiently for him to elaborate.

"The sunscreen operation is going as scheduled. It has established a strong bond with Tango Trading," Valdes said.

"And CANDO is satisfied with the increase in volume?" asked Soltero.

"They are thrilled and have asked no questions."

"Your last report stated that the number of CANDO distributors has expanded nicely," said Soltero.

"CANDO has expanded to the point that Green Rainbow Ministries meeting room is inadequate for their purposes, and Duval Street is not a good address for them. With our help Ms. Koury-O'Dare was able to purchase the Jehovah's Witness building on Little Torch Key. It should help give the organization credibility and enable it to continue to expand," Valdes said.

"And Luis Bernstein does not suspect that you have helped him with his CANDO recruiting?" Al asked.

"The fucker thinks he's just a good salesman with good local connections," Miguel said.

"And I am sure he is. You have performed your mission well up until now. Señor Carlos will be pleased," Soltero said. "Now I want to place some of our people in the CANDO organization to protect our interests and to enhance future potential."

"Do you have a suggestion?" asked Miguel.

"It would certainly be nice to have our people in a policy making position in the inner circle," said Soltero. "I hear the daughter Mildred has shown an interest in our enforcer Bobby Perez."

"That's almost fuckin' kinky," said Valdes. "A twin

who's got the hots for another twin."

"Why don't you encourage Bobby to pursue Mildred?" Soltero said. "If he were to marry into the O'Dare family it would certainly be good for his career."

"I'll see he gets the fuckin' message," Miquel said.

"I knew I could depend on you," Soltero said.

CHAPTER 8

A cocky Bobby Perez sauntered into Casa Camilio Sur. The muscles he worked on in the gym every day strained the sleeves on the fitted shirt he was wearing. His jeans were too tight.

An eye-catching tattoo armband prominently encircled the bicep on Bobby's right arm. The design on the tattoo had a background of a continuous strand of barbed wire. The foreground consisted of an alternating pattern of a skull with a shark swimming on each side. His identical twin, Billy, had the same pattern tattooed on his *left* arm. This was the only way many people could tell them apart.

"Did you meet with the fish supplier?" Valdes asked.

Bobby nodded.

"Did you tell him to sharpen his fuckin' pencil before he sends me another invoice unless he wants me to stick a grouper up his ass?" Valdes asked.

"He got the message," Bobby said as he looked himself over in the reflection of a painting on the restaurant's wall and made sure his hair wasn't mussed.

"That's some fat ugly broads in these pictures," he continued. "I've never been sure what you see in those things."

"Too bad the muscles between your ears aren't as developed as the muscles in your arms," Valdes said. "You obviously don't know shit about fine art. That picture is fuckin' worth more than you are. Fernando Botero is one of the most famous painters Colombia has ever produced."

"I'll be goddamned if I know why," Bobby said. "Give me a picture of a broad with big tits and a small waist any day."

"Yeah, yeah. Everyone's an art critic. Come in my office, meathead. I want to talk to you in private," Valdes said. "And close the fuckin' door."

Bobby slammed the door

"Mr. Soltero tells me you're going out with one of the Koury-O'Dare girls at CANDO."

Bobby looked surprised. "How does he know that?"

"That's why he's the boss, and you're a fuckin' peon," Valdes said. "Yes or no?"

Bobby smiled boastfully and said, "She's one tight piece of pussy."

"She's not jail-bait, is she?" asked Valdes.

"She's legal and she's wild about my hunky Latin ass," Bobby said. "You gotta know how to stroke 'em, know how to poke 'em."

Bobby flexed his muscles and sang to the tune of the Kenny Rogers song, *The Gambler*. "You gotta know how to stroke 'em, know how to poke 'em. Not to brag, but she's so crazy about me that she wants me to line her sister up with my twin brother, Billy."

"Mr. Soltero would like that," Valdes said. "Pretty boy, how would you like to be something in our organization other than a low-end soldier? This could be your chance. Mr. Soltero would like to be a CANDO insider. That means he needs a center of influence in their business. Centers of influence command respect. Respect translates into power and money. You could be a person of respect if you play your cards right."

"You tryin' to say you want me to marry the cunt?" Bobby asked. "She'd marry me in a heartbeat."

"I'm not trying to tell you how to run your life, but men have succeeded with the right wife. You could do fuckin' worse," said Valdes. "Beats the hell out of some of the tattooed pierced whores I've seen you run with. Some people have been known to knock-up a bitch to accomplish their goal."

"Why's Mr. Soltero interested in CANDO?" Bobby asked.

"People like you don't ask people like Mr. Soltero questions," Valdes said. "Let's just say he sees investment potential there."

~ ~ ~

Within a year, Mary and Mildred Koury-O'Dare, attended by the CANDO family, became Mrs. William Perez and Mrs. Robert Perez in a double-ring ceremony held at the old Jehovah's Witnesses Kingdom Hall. Reverend LeRoy Cho-Arturo conducted the service. Adolfo Soltero silently observed the ceremony from the back of the room and nodded his approval. He gave both Bobby and Billy generous wedding gifts.

CHAPTER 9

"Bobby," Miguel Valdes said, "Make plans to be here this morning. Mr. Soltero wants to talk to you."

"Did I do something wrong?" Bobby asked.

"Why do you always think that when the boss wants to see you, something's wrong? Just fuckin' be here."

Adolfo Soltero warmly greeted the nervous Bobby Perez when he entered Casa Camilio Sur.

"How are things going with the newlyweds?" Soltero asked.

"Very well, with both Billy and myself," Bobby replied. "And we both thank you for your generous wedding gift."

"A wedding is a special occasion and should be treated as such," Al said. "I expect you young people to have a long and happy life together. May we speak about business?"

He took Bobby over to a table in the empty restaurant.

"As you know, CANDO's interests and my interests overlap," he began. "My associates and I believe that the business has much unexploited potential. That is why I am very pleased to have you two, friends and fellow countrymen, as part of the core management group going forward. This is a wonderful opportunity for a bright young man. I advise you and Billy to make every effort to learn as much about CANDO as you can. Miguel and I will be here as your mentors and resources. We can also provide from time to time other resources with expertise in the sophisticated financial disciplines that are needed to grow a modern business."

Boy, is this guy smooth, thought Bobby. *I'm not totally sure what he just said, but I get the message. He's telling me I fell in a honey-pot.*

Bobby told his brother about this conversation with Al Soltero. Then neither Bobby nor Billy heard from him again for six months until Valdes told Bobby that Mr. Soltero wished to meet with him once more.

After a few pleasantries meant to assess the twins' progress, Soltero got down to the business at hand.

"Would your mother-in-law be open-minded if she were presented with some constructive ways to grow CANDO?" he asked.

Bobby shrugged and scratched his underarm.

"Tell her Miguel Valdes has someone he wants her to meet. Since he has the mortgage on her building, she should be receptive. Tell her they are financial consultants," Soltero said.

"Are they really?" Bobby asked.

Soltero gave him a condescending look of disgust. "Are you questioning my integrity, young man? Just do as you are instructed and let me know when the meeting has been set up. We'll handle matters from that point forward."

On the appointed day, the consultants sent by Soltero, Chip Talbos and T. Rodney Chamberlain III, arrived. Their birth names were Charles "Charlie-horse" Romito and Tino "Fast Fingers" Marone, and they had both been raised in Newark, New Jersey. They now wore ivy-league suits, British shoes, each carrying a Gucci leather briefcase and spoke flawless English.

Madelyn felt at ease with them immediately. Before their meeting could begin Chamberlain asked that they take a moment and pray. He asked that they all get on their knees in a circle and then took Madelyn's and Chip's hand. In a melodic voice he invoked God's blessing for the success of their future ventures together and pledged that these successes would be used for the glorification of the all-mighty. When they arose again Madelyn felt cleansed and was becoming sure these were people she could trust.

Rod and Chip then easily name-dropped financial concepts such as coefficient of variations, acid test ratios, primary and secondary markets, holding companies, stock classes, NASDAQ versus listed securities, Black-Scholes models, cost of funds indexes and a multitude of other terms that had Madelyn's head spinning. Finally when she was totally confused they recommended that the company file to sell CANDO stock to the public. They would put together the investment banking team. They told her the advantages would be to release her equity in the company, give her working capital for growth, and tie her distributors to the company with stock awards with future vesting. They said the stock would enable her to buy the trailer park behind the former Jehovah's Witnesses Kingdom Hall owned by Spoonbill Partners. They conveniently failed to mention that Spoonbill was owned by Soltero and his partners. In essence, she'd be foolish if she didn't follow their advice. Bobby and Billy, as they had been instructed to do by Miguel Valdes, worked on their wives behind the scenes to approve the company's new thrust. Bobby and Billy weren't sure why, but they knew this is what Mr. Soltero wanted.

Madelyn remembered what Glenn Turner had said years ago about experts.

A winner respects those who are superior to him, and tries to learn something from them. A loser resents those who are superior to him and tries to find clinks in their armor.

Maybe it was time to accept their help and try to take CANDO to a new level.

CHAPTER 10

Madelyn's head was spinning after meeting with the business consultants. What they proposed sounded very compelling, but she was afraid to make a decision of this magnitude. She consulted Luis Bernstein about what the right thing to do would be. He agreed with her that being a public company might have its advantages. She was still uncertain. Luis hacked into Talbos' and Chamberlain's computers to learn more and filed away the new information for future use.

Madelyn needed time to think. She drove north toward Bahia Honda until she saw a small secluded beach. She was relieved to see she had the area completely to herself. As she sat on a rock overlooking the ocean, the sunlight began to fade. She looked up and saw no clouds. She saw a glimpse of what looked like a disk of pure blackness sliding across the face of the sun. Soon the blackness had almost completely covered the sun, and dusk began to fall over the water. The hot tropical air started to cool. The birds became silent and still. It was both frightening and beautiful at the same time.

As the eclipse's totality approached, the sky became darker and an eerie twilight began to descend just before total waves of shadow rushed rapidly from horizon to horizon. Then, in those final moments light shone through valleys in the moon's surface and gave the impression of beads on its periphery. The last flash of light from the surface of the sun as it disappeared behind the moon gave the appearance of a diamond ring. The solar corona blazed into view. Over the next hour the motion of the moon began to uncover the surface of the sun, and the eclipse proceeded through partial phases until the Sun was once again completely revealed.

To Madelyn this was a divine sign. She made up her mind right then that she would follow the consultants' recommendations. CANDO would become a public company.

She drove back to Little Torch Key and told Luis of her decision. Luis invited her to join him in thanking Ra, the ancient sun god, for sending her his message.

~ ~ ~

Over the next several months Madelyn met with a variety of financial consultants. They explained to her matters such as letters of intent, underwriting agreements, underwriting costs, how syndicates work and other matters.

The offering including a green shoe would consist of 1,700,000 units of CANDO stock that would be priced at $3.00 each. A unit would consist of three shares of stock and a warrant. Insiders would control another 2,000,000 shares of class B voting stock at $.50 per share. Another 10,000,000 shares of treasury stock would be authorized. They applied for and were assigned CNDO as the stock's over-the-counter trading symbol. As distributors rose from Bronze to Platinum they would be awarded five-year restricted shares in the company as part of their incentive program. CANDO's corporate board could designate the stock to either come from purchases in the open market or from the authorized treasury stock.

Madelyn would be Chairman of the Board and President. Her daughters, their husbands Billy and Bobby Perez, as well as both Adolfo Soltero and Miguel Valdes would be board members. Berrios & Aguinaga CPA's were hired at Soltero's suggestion to do the accounting and audit work. He also suggested a market-maker, 21st Century Securities.

The stock that came to market in April at $2.50 was stabilized by the investment banker during the early days of trading. It then climbed to a bid of $3, where it traded in a narrow trading range with low volume. After Berrios & Aguinaga issued a favorable earnings report, the stock began to slowly climb again. Madelyn did not know that the earnings growth resulted from some aggressive depreciation techniques. She got a rush each time she looked up the stock quotes and thought that this was a company *she* had started. Another thing she did not know was that the market-maker, 21st Century Securities, with the help of the Colombians was doing a carefully orchestrated pump-and-dump on the shares. In their barrage of financial terminology name-dropping meetings the business consultants had never exposed her to this illegal concept. Luis silently monitored market activities even though he wasn't sure exactly what was occurring.

Bobby Perez, at Soltero's suggestion, brought to the board's attention once more the availability of the property owned by Spoonbill Partners behind Kingdom Hall. The board voted to purchase the property with some of the funds brought in from the initial stock sale.

CHAPTER 11

Luis was in the office kitchen pouring a cup of coffee when Mary Koury-O'Dare Perez entered the room.

"Have you seen your mom?" he asked. "I need to go over some things with her."

"Not this morning, but I'm sure she'll be in," Mary said.

Madelyn was still not in the office by noon. Luis tried to call her on her cell phone but no one answered. He asked Mildred if she had seen her.

"Maybe she had to run some errands," Mildred said.

"Maybe so," said Luis, "but it's not like her not to check in."

No one heard from her that afternoon. By five o'clock, Madelyn's co-workers at CANDO were starting to be mildly concerned.

There was still no sign of Madelyn the following morning. The CANDO staff was starting to panic. Bobby Perez called Miguel Valdes and asked him to put the word out that they were looking for her. No word came back. Luis decided to call the sheriff's department. Despite the deputy's best efforts, Madelyn could not be found.

~ ~ ~

While all the panic over her disappearance was happening on Little Torch Key, Madelyn was sitting on a beach on a small offshore key eating a protein bar and watching a crab scurry along. She breathed the sea air while watching the cloud formations change. It was good to get away. She needed some time to think and sort things out. She had been listening to the gospel channel on television recently hoping for some guidance, but the diverse teachings only seemed to whet her appetite for more answers and raise new questions, instead of providing solutions to her dilemmas. She felt she needed, as she had once heard someone say, to have a joint meeting with herself. She knew she should have told someone where she was going, but she didn't plan on being gone that long. She had kayaked out to the island through some mangroves along the shore. The office had been starting to make her claustrophobic. It felt good just to sit here and commune with nature.

A few hours later Madelyn still felt like she needed more time to herself and decided to spend the night. She kayaked back to civilization, got the provisions she needed and returned to the island. This time she brought a Bible and other books as well as writing materials. Thoughts began to fall into place on how CANDO might be a springboard to ethereal spiritual planes. She wrote her musings down while they appeared organized and logical in her brain and gradually began to formulate a philosophy. The next few days became a blur as one lazily drifted into another. She even became accustomed to sleeping on the air mattress and rarely noticed the pesky insects.

She simply felt compelled to pursue this project and lost track of everything else. She read:

And the Lord answered me and said, 'Write the vision and make it plain. Habakkuk 2:2

She began to connect Bible passages to the building

blocks to self discovery she was creating.

It is written, man shall not live by bread alone, but by every word that proceeds out of the mouth of God. - Matthew 4:4

became

"You will never accomplish more than the ideas in your mind.

Therefore, only feed your mind with healthy ideas."

Do not conform any longer to the pattern of this world, but be transformed by the renewing of your mind. Then you will be able to test and approve what God's will is his good pleasing and perfect will. - Romans 12:2

became

"God wants you to have what you want as long as it is right and good."

My word that goes forth out of my mouth shall not return unto me void, but it shall accomplish that which I please and it shall prosper in the thing whereto I sent it. - Isaiah 55:11

became

"Your mind power will do anything for you that you make clear."

Madelyn's list grew and grew as she meditated. Time seemed to stand still. On the fourth day Madelyn named the list the Affirmations for the Cause of Prosperity. She then drew up a second list which she entitled What I've Learned. She swore to live by these maxims from that day on. She shed her clothes and announced as she stared naked at a perfect sky that her name from that point forward would not be Madelyn Koury-O'Dare but Sun Raye, the mistress of happiness, the mistress of money, and the mistress of life. It would be her mission to purvey the good things in life to her flock and CANDO would be the mechanism that would finance her efforts. As Glenn Turner had lectured years ago:

You can better your best. You can have everything you want in life, if you build belief in yourself and go after it.

Now it was time to return in triumph to Little Torch Key — not as Madelyn Koury-O'Dare, CEO of CANDO, but Sun Raye, the mistress of life and high priestess of the Cosmic Ray Scientific Church of Prosperity.

CHAPTER 12

T he prescheduled regular CANDO meeting was going strong at Kingdom Hall despite Madelyn's absence. Mary Perez had taken over and was speaking to a packed house. She welcomed new distributors and then launched into a motivational talk.

"My message today is entitled 'Life Is Hard' and how you can live a great life despite the fact that life is not easy," she began.

"Everyone in this room wants to live a happy life. What constitutes happiness is different to different people. You," she pointed to one member of the audience, "want to be married to Mr. Right. You want to have great kids." She pointed to another person. "We all want to have friends who will stick by us come rain or shine. And you wouldn't be here if you didn't want the material things life has to offer and have all your problems disappear."

The audience was receptive but far from worked up.

Mary continued, "Everybody wishes for the good life even though your wishes may have different levels. Some people in this room may define the good life a different way from another person sitting here. But I think I am safe in saying no one here defines the good life as simply three meals a day. I think I your definitions come closer to wanting a huge mansion or a couple of million dollars in the bank. That's why you are CANDO distributors. That's why you are attending this meeting instead of staying home watching TV."

Mary droned on to the somewhat attentive but somewhat bored gathering. Mildred, Bobby and Billy nodded their support. This was the first time Mary had run a meeting alone, and she was somewhat nervous. Madelyn usually conducted these meetings, but since Madelyn hadn't been seen for several days, Mary was chosen to take over the speech Madelyn had written before her mysterious disappearance.

Suddenly the back door to the meeting room opened. What Mary saw caused her to lose her composure completely. Standing in the doorway was the disheveled figure of her mother looking like a street person who'd been released from an asylum after suffering a beating. Madelyn's hair hadn't been combed since she left. She had on no makeup and her legs hadn't been shaved in days. Her body was covered with insect bites. There was an unwashed odor that emanated from her body. Her clothes were wrinkled and stained, and she was barefoot and braless.

Despite her rough appearance, Madelyn did not have the wild look of a whacked-out psychopath about to shoot up the room, but instead she had a dreamy, contented look that somehow made her look even crazier. Mary was so surprised she tripped and fell into the lap of an obese black Cuban woman. She accidentally ripped the microphone from its holder and fell forward with it. The folding-chair the woman was sitting in gave way with a loud snap, and they both ended up in a heap on the floor. The woman's print dress ended up over her head, and when Mary head-butted her in the crotch, she let out a loud fart as she peed. The microphone was still connected and carried the fart loudly throughout the room. People, thinking the sound was a gunshot, hit the deck or started to run. The Cuban woman's short, thin husband, who was sitting next to her, jumped up but then slipped on the urine and ended going over the bodies, taking out all the folding-chairs and people behind them.

Bobby and Billy Perez both instinctively whipped out their pistols and started to search around the room for the other weapon they thought they had heard. A man in the back of the room pulled out a .357 and probably would have gotten shot if a woman hadn't careened into Bobby after she skidded on a set of errant dentures.

Oblivious, Madelyn marched down the aisle towards the podium. She carried several legal pads. At first the shocked silent people shrank away as she walked to the front of the hall. An unwashed odor followed her. Mildred, Bobby and Billy now just stood with their mouths agape. The fat woman inadvertently kicked Mary in the head.

Finally Mildred called out, "Mother, thank God you're all right. Where have you been?"

Madelyn approached the front and simply said, "I have been on a mission of self-discovery."

Madelyn grabbed the microphone off the floor and spoke, "Tonight I will change your lives. Call me Sun Raye, the high priestess of the Cosmic Ray Scientific Church of Prosperity. You who have faith and believe my teachings are going to be blessed and become wealthy."

Some people were starting to pay attention again despite their inherent disgust and the general level of confusion still in the room.

Sun Raye raised her hands and continued. "God has

spoken to me over the last three days and told me to take you his message. I deeply believe that achieving success, prosperity and having money is a person's divine right. My goals are clear. I know what I want, and I know I can have all these things because of my enthusiasm, my persistence, and my belief that this is the law of God. I am not hung-up on how these good things will come about because God has instilled in me how to do what I have to do. And then he told me to teach you how to do it easily and effortlessly."

She now had the room's attention. People looked at the person next to them and nodded.

"You will soon release all your irritations and aggravations because you know I will love and forgive you for every mistake. You will not be afraid to make an error because you will understand each challenge is merely a learning situation. We will achieve success, prosperity and wealth because it is our divine right. It is God's will that we do these things with CANDO. With my guidance you will be blessed. I will drive the demon of negative thinking from your soul."

The fat Cuban woman had made it to her feet by now. She waved her chunky arms and yelled, "Glory hallelujah, sister! Show us the way!" She jumped in the air. When she came down she let out another ripper. Bobby and Billy again reached for their guns.

"Yes," said Sun Raye, turning toward her and shouting in return, "Sister, I will show you the way. You are going to be a blessed and prosperous person instead of continuing to walk in the counsel of ungodly sinners. Do you know what sin is, my friends? To sin is to miss the mark. We will expel the devil of negativity. Together we will change our world."

Suddenly Sun Raye broke out in song.

Let there be peace on earth

And let it begin with me

Emotional people began to hold hands and join in. Some started to sway in the aisles and hug their neighbors.

Let there be peace on earth

The peace that was meant to be

Mildred, Mary, Bobby and Billy simply stood there speechless. They weren't sure just what was happening, but it was apparent that a transformation was taking place at CANDO.

Sun Raye's voice soared and began to reverberate throughout the room.

"Are you ready to become a master of happiness?"

"YES!" came back in unison.

"Are you ready to become a master of money?"

"YES!"

"Are you ready to become the master of your life?"

"YES!"

"Do you want to discover how to harness your mind's God-given power to achieve good health ... happiness ... success ... prosperity ... and MONEY?"

As one man yelled "Yes!" He grabbed his head and then fell on the floor and looked like he was writhing in ecstasy or pain. He started to speak in a foreign tongue. He was answered by others.

Sun Raye's voice screeched higher and laryngitis started to take hold.

"Yes, my children, I will wash out doubt, fear and

worry. In their places I will implant self-esteem, success, and love into your subconscious.

"My flock, you will achieve these things and more if you believe in the Cosmic Ray Scientific Church of Prosperity. God sent me back to you with the way to make you into the person you want and deserve to be. We are God's chosen people! Kingdom Hall will be our Mecca!"

With those words Madelyn collapsed in a faint. Madelyn Koury-O'Dare was dead; Sun Raye had replaced her.

CHAPTER 13

Bobby Perez sipped his coffee as he ate a slice of key lime pie at Casa Camilio Sur before heading to the gym. He shook his head and said, "Mr. Valdes, you had to be there yesterday to appreciate what was happening at CANDO. That was the most surreal meeting I've ever been to in my life."

"What the fuck you rattlin' on about?" said Miguel Valdes.

Bobby proceeded to tell Valdes everything that had happened when Madelyn finally showed up.

"Has the broad lost her fuckin' mind?" Valdes asked.

"Billy and I thought so too at first," Bobby said. "She looked like something out of a living-dead movie and smelled like it too. I thought at first that this was the end of CANDO. Nobody will ever come back after this. But by the end of the meeting she had people in a trance. It had turned into a revival meeting instead of a sales meeting. I'm telling you, she was like a voodoo priestess. If she had told these people to climb up on the roof and jump off, they would have."

"Tell me again. What did she call this fuckin' half-ass church?"

"The Cosmic Ray Scientific Church of Prosperity, and she said she is the high priestess called Sun Raye," Bobby replied as he swallowed another bite of his pie.

"Don't go nowhere," Valdes said. "I'm calling Soltero. I want you to tell him this shit. This goddamned thing is fuckin' blowin' up in our faces."

Thirty minutes later Al Soltero walked in. Bobby again told the whole story. Soltero just quietly listened and did not interrupt. He sipped his coffee when Bobby was finished and mulled what he had just heard.

"Did the distributors buy any merchandise?" Al asked.

"Oh, yeah. Biz was never better. We sold out of everything. I could have sold snow-cones and told them it was sunscreen," Bobby responded. "And the next night we had more people attending than we've ever had – the same people, but they brought new marks with them. People had to stand. She preached about the causes of prosperity and had people take an affirmation of their faith. She made them chant, "I am everyone. I am everything. I am God. I will control my universe with the output of my inner thinking." They said it over and over until it creeped me out. It was like zombie mind control."

"This matter bears watching, but I don't think CANDO is imploding. I think there is a high likelihood it may be starting to explode with growth. I want to be kept apprised of its activities on a more frequent basis. This new fervor and zeal may be opening up new opportunities for them as well as us, and you as well. Do what you can to become closer to Ms. Koury-O'Dare … I mean Sun Raye. I am reasonably sure it will be worth your while."

"Sun Raye … Sounds to me she's ready for the fuckin' nut house," Valdes said.

"Maybe so, my friend," Soltero said, "but no-one ever said the world of business is a rational one. You take your opportunities as they present themselves and then make the most out of them. I have an idea jelling in my mind.

Maybe you should consider attending one of Sun Raye's lectures. It sounds like you could use the power of positive thinking."

"Speaking off opportunities," Bobby said. "If you don't need me, Mr. Soltero, I need to get to the gym and give my muscles the opportunity to go to a higher plane."

"I know. So you can be Mr. fuckin' America," Valdes said derisively. "Good luck, meathead."

As he drove to the gym Bobby started thinking:

I don't get no respect from those big shots. They think I'm just all muscle and no brain. I bet if I was running CANDO, they'd see what a good businessman I can be – sure as hell better than that whacked-out religious bitch who is running it now. It wouldn't take a whole lot of persuasion to get me to put her out of everybody's way permanently. I'd be doing everyone a favor. I just need to do it in a way that Mr. Soltero doesn't find out. Maybe I can arrange an accident. Then my wife would be in charge, and she knows to do what I tell her to. I'll beat the shit out of her otherwise, just like I'll beat the shit out of anyone else who gets in my way.

No hurry, though. My time will come and when it does, I'll put the bitch six feet under. That's what Pablo Escobar would have done. Nobody ever got to the top being Mr. nice guy.

He held his fingers like a pistol and pretended to pull the trigger. He laughed and said out loud. "Your ass is grass, Sun Raye, and I'm the power lawn mower."

Bobby started singing, *No more Mr. Nice Guy, No more Mr. Clean.* He felt a rush, blasted his horn at a slow tourist on a scooter and flipped the man a bird.

CHAPTER 14

Over the next few months Sun Raye became more and more preoccupied with her newfound following as the high priestess of the Cosmic Ray Scientific Church of Prosperity. Frequently she delegated humdrum CANDO business to other people in the organization. She began to rely on Mary and Mildred more and more to conduct the mundane day-to-day operational matters. Mary and Mildred in turn relied on Billy and Bobby. Billy and Bobby relied on Miguel Valdes who relied on Adolfo Soltero and the experts Soltero recommended. To ingratiate themselves to their mother as well as humor her, Mary started to call herself Sea Raye and Mildred renamed herself Blue Raye. They even convinced their husbands to play along. The Perez twins refused to take "sissy" first names so they simply became Bobby Raye and Billy Raye.

"I'll play along with your crazy mother on one condition," Bobby said to his wife, Blue Raye. "Never call me that in public. If you ever use these fucked-up names around anyone outside of this church, I'll beat you until you can't walk. My buddies on Stock Island or at the gym would never let me live this sissy shit down. They'll think I'm some kind of fag."

Meanwhile, Sun Raye had discovered Indian numerology, enhancing her belief that numbers were symbols of certain types of cosmic powers. She began to link numbers with newfound spirituality. Sun Raye began to stencil large numbers on the walls of Kingdom Hall's meeting room and was quick to explain to anyone who mentioned it the significance of these numbers.

"'0' is the number which encircles some part of the infinite universe," she told Billy Raye one day after stenciling it on the wall. "Notice, the inner part of it is separated from the outer space just as a human being always feels he is separate, making the outer universe different from him. Because of this Maaya or cosmic delusion, man confines his soul to his present body and thinks that he and his body are one and the same. Thus man has forgotten the truth that he himself is the all-pervading God."

Billy Raye just stood there and nodded. He later admitted to his wife Sea Raye that he didn't have a "goddamned clue as to what in the shit she was talking about" and "I don't think she did either."

Sun Raye had become even more hung-up on the number '1' than she used to be when she was younger and meditated about its implications for her personally. As she demonstrated for her daughters, when any series of points in a single direction were connected they became a number '1'. Therefore '1' represented her single-mindedness in achieving objectives as well as her creativity and ability to succeed when starting new ventures. She said its column-like appearance represented her independence and her leadership qualities, and besides that, she said the number "1' was ruled by the Sun, confirming why God wanted her to go by the name Sun Raye.

She explained to Blue Raye and Sea Raye that because they were twins married to twins they were both ruled by the number '2'.

"Notice my darlings, '2' is round shaped at the top and is nothing more than an open 'o', telling you that there is no complete cosmic delusion at the mental level. Since there is a scope to receive and release new ideas and concepts, '2' represents flexibility and diplomacy. The horizontal line on the bottom proves you are both firmly attached to the ground, which means if your inventive ideas are properly used, you can achieve the highest success in the material world."

Blue Raye and Sea Raye were both stunned by their mother's new-found familiarity with Indian numerology. Bobby and Billy just thought she was nuts.

~ ~ ~

Bobby was finishing a slice of key lime pie and drinking coffee at Casa Camilio Sur so he could head to the gym when Al Soltero came in. Al greeted the young man warmly and ordered himself a cup of coffee.

"And how are things with my favorite young couples?" he asked.

"Oh fine," Bobby said despite his mouth being full of pie as he burped and wiped a dab off his lips and onto his sleeve.

"And how are things at CANDO?"

Bobby laughed and said, "You mean the Star Wars Church of Cosmic Bullshit."

He laughed at this line and pretended to shoot a fly with an imaginary laser gun.

"Believe it or not, never better. Goddamned membership is going through the roof and these people can't buy enough of everything. I can't believe how many nuts there are out there who just hang on every word Sun Raye has to say like she was Elvis Presley or somethin'. They sure never thought she was so hot when she was plain old Madelyn from Key West. I ain't never seen nothing like it in my whole life."

Soltero said nothing. He just listened. Finally he asked, "Exactly what does she talk about at these meetings?"

"A lot of happy horse-shit I can't usually follow. Off-the-wall shit. Things like how you can be transformed if you renew your mind and how this transformation will make you able to test and approve of what God's will is. And then stuff like the sky is not your limit because you have no limitations. She talks this weird shit about ideas vibrating from your mind and going out your mouth and how this shows the power of God in you. Wacky stuff like that. It sounds like a bunch of crap to me but people seem to eat it up and keep coming back for more. They can't seem to get enough. She has a meeting seven days a week. And when she tells them to give her money, they give money. They act like they're zombies in a goddamned trance.

"I'll tell you something, Mr. Soltero, if you promise not to tell the boys – they wouldn't let me live it down. Madelyn has even renamed her girls and us. My wife is called Sea Raye and Mildred is called Blue Raye. Have you ever heard such shit?"

"And you said she has assigned you an alias as well?" Soltero asked.

"Yeah! Get this!" Bobby said as he filled his mouth again with pie. "I'm Bobby Raye and Billy is now Billy

Raye. Just call me the Ray man, space cadet. At least I ain't Ray Charles." He laughed again. "It would take a blind man not to see through that one." He began to chant, "You can call me Ray; you can call me Sugar Ray; you can call me Martha Ray or a sting-ray; you can call me any goddamned kind of ray as long as you remember to call me for every meal."

"Don't be so quick to jeer, my vociferous and expressive Paleozoic friend. Many fortunes have been made from evangelism. God chooses to speak through mysterious mediums. People like Billy Graham, Rex Humbard, Oral Roberts, Robert Schuller, and Jimmy Swaggart are a few of those who became extremely famous and wealthy spreading the gospel to the masses. It is a most lucrative profession in the hands of the right person."

Bobby wasn't sure who these people were or what Mr. Soltero had just called him, but he felt Soltero had probably paid him a compliment. Soltero after all was an educated man who had a way with words. He took the comment as a sign that Soltero was pleased with him.

Adolfo continued, "Do you remember our in-house financial counsel, Rodney Chamberlain and Chip Talbos?"

"Oh, sure! Fast Fingers and Charlie-horse," Bobby said.

Soltero gave him a withering stare before continuing. "Rodney and Chip. As I was saying, I think CANDO is at a juncture where it could use Rodney and Chip's services once again."

"Whut for?"

"I have been thinking for some time that a diversification program into financial services could add a new dimension and level of profitability to CANDO's business. The ability Sun Raye has shown recently to influence people and strongly tie them to her organization gives her an opportunity to be more than just a sunscreen distributor. Broadening her impact on her captive audience also creates rewarding possibilities for us as well. Are you familiar with AARP?" Soltero said.

"Yeah, it's like AAA for old people," Bobby said.

"I will use it as an example to illustrate my point. AARP is an organization that provides support and opportunities in many areas for those over 55," Al continued. "Because their members see them as *the* lobbying voice for their age group, they have developed an extremely loyal almost cult-like following. Many people rarely question their integrity or motives. Several years ago AARP decided to leverage this influence and become a source of investment products to their members as well."

Bobby shrugged so-what.

"The products AARP offers its membership are not necessarily innovative or even overly cost efficient, but their members buy them because of the loyalty they feel to an organization that supports seniors. It goes without saying that these offerings are very profitable for AARP. With our help I think Madelyn...Sun Raye...can use her congregation to raise investment capital in a similar manner. All I want you to do is get your wives to convince her to see Chip and Rodney again. We'll handle matters from there. OK? I will tutor you on what to say."

"I don't know nothin' about investment products, but you can count on me, boss," Bobby said and gulped down his last bite of pie and slurped the rest of his coffee.

"I knew I could," Al said and left the restaurant.

CHAPTER 15

Bobby Raye picked up his brother to join him on a trip to Gordon Food Services to pick up some supplies for Casa Camilio Sur. He could have easily managed this errand himself, but it gave him a chance to talk to his brother alone.

On the way, he explained to Billy that Mr. Soltero wanted their help in convincing their mother-in-law to have a meeting with Soltero's financial and investment consultants.

"I'm not sure what Mr. Soltero has in mind, and he told me not worry about the details. Just make the appointment and his people will handle matters from that point," he said. "He acted like this is important."

They both agreed that getting Sun Raye's attention on anything that did not pertain to religion was getting tougher and tougher. Billy came up with the idea of telling her he had had a recurring vision in his sleep in which he kept seeing a blinding sun in his mind with the numbers "1", "10", "19" and "28" going by in a continuous procession. He would tell her the dream was trying to tell him of a coming opportunity.

Bobby was amazed at his brother's fertile imagination. "Kind of like seeing sheep? How'd you come up with that shit?" he asked. "Do you know you got the numbers right?"

"Trust me. Hell, all you got to do is go on the Internet and read, dumb-ass. You wouldn't know, but there is stuff on the friggin' Internet besides the porn sites you look at,"

Billy said. "You just let me take care of this, and don't say a damned word to our wives. I don't want them giving either of us away."

"I think Mr. Soltero expects prompt action," Bobby said.

"What he expects even more is 'mission accomplished'," Billy replied.

The next evening before Sun Raye's regularly scheduled meeting at Kingdom Hall, Billy pretended to be preoccupied. Sun Raye and Sea Raye both unsuccessfully tried to talk to him about what his problem was. The next evening he went through the same charade but still refused to discuss matters with them. Finally on the third night he allowed them to drag out of him his elaborate fantasy of dreaming about numbers each night and his conclusion that they were trying to tell him of a coming opportunity. The hook was set. All he had to do now was reel in the fish.

Sun Raye probed him about which numbers he kept seeing on a recurring basis. Billy replied, "They were '1', '10', '19', and '28'."

Sun Raye's face brightened. "My God," she exclaimed. "These are all numbers ruled by the sun."

The following evening he reported that now there was now another number in the latest sequence. Now he was seeing larger "1's" in addition to the others.

About a week later Billy casually mentioned to Sun Raye that Mr. Valdes thought it would be in CANDO's best interest to meet with the financial consultants who had advised them about taking CANDO public and that this could possibly be the opportunity he had been dreaming about. Sun Raye was only mildly interested but asked him to refresh her memory on their names.

The following day when Sun Raye saw Billy her attitude had changed dramatically. Sun Raye had assigned a number to each letter in their names and added the numbers. She continued adding the arithmetic totals until she had finally reduced each name to one number. Rodney's number was "1." Chip's was "1" as well, the exact recurring numbers Billy had seen in his dream. Now she insisted on meeting the investment consultants. Billy had been right. She was finally convinced she needed to meet with these men as soon as possible and listen to their latest proposal.

Billy told Bobby to tell Mr. Soltero "mission accomplished."

CHAPTER 16

Sun Raye still only had a vague idea why she was meeting with Chip and Rodney, but she could feel the numbers' vibratory resonance and knew this was something her psyche was telling her she needed to do. Billy's ruse had worked.

Chip and Rodney arrived at Kingdom Hall in their new Mercedes. They were once again wearing expensive Brooks Brother suits, and each carried an expensive monogrammed leather briefcase. Sun Raye could see the expensive silk suspenders under Rodney's suit-coat. With their oiled straight-back hair and gleaming teeth they looked like they had stepped out of a GQ ad.

After a brief prayer, Chip started the presentation with a recap of their previous business with CANDO and the success of CANDO's stock in the after-market. The charts he showed Sun Raye were impressive, even if she didn't understand most of the information they were imparting. All she knew was lines going up were good; lines going down were bad. He carefully said nothing about the market manipulation partially responsible for the stock's good performance or the accelerated depreciation techniques that had artificially enhanced the company's earnings statements over the short term. A mute Sun Raye nodded her approval docilely on cue.

Rodney took over the presentation and gave her a primer on the sophistication of the modern financial services industry and its importance in today's complex world. She still had no clue as to where the conversation was headed, but she nodded again.

Chip took the conversation back over at that point. "Ms. Raye," he began, "sometimes it is possible to take over the shell of an existing company and spare the expense and scrutiny of establishing a new company. We have been able to uncover just such a company that will serve the purposes of CANDO very well. The company is called First Caribbean Sun Life Assurance Company. It is a bankrupt Grand Cayman company. The stock is trading at one penny a share, and there are 20 million shares outstanding. Therefore we can control 100% of the stock for a $200,000 investment. The initial investment will be recouped many times after we enhance the stock's value and then sell it back to the public. I'm sure you realize $200,000 is far less than one would spend if one tried to start a company from scratch. We have a source of private placement venture capital that will provide the $200,000 for 30% of the venture. You will not have to come out-of-pocket for our services. We will take 20% of the stock as compensation for organizing the venture. You will have nothing at risk."

He waited for his words to sink in. All Sun Raye heard was "first" and "sun". To her this was surely another omen. She thought her karma must have led her to this destiny. She decided maybe this reward had also been predetermined by the karma accrued from her past lives. Billy had conceivably been right about a looming opportunity. Sun Raye was so preoccupied with these thoughts she didn't think to ask the purpose for buying First Caribbean Sun Life.

This issue was addressed when Rodney spoke up. "Ms. Raye, we propose to you that First Caribbean Sun be used as the nucleus to offer a series of tax-advantaged religious mutual funds.

"State and federal securities laws should not apply to investors who belong to the Cosmic Ray Scientific Church of Prosperity since their investments will be gifts to the church and dividends should also be tax-sheltered.

"The funds will be off-shore and therefore less regulated and not closely scrutinized by the SEC. The initial fund will be offered to members of the Cosmic Ray Scientific Church as well as CANDO distributors. The securities in the portfolio will be selected from a list of companies that not only support the beliefs of these venerable institutions but do not engage in practices abhorrent to them.

"We strongly suggest that the First Caribbean stock should not be owned by you but by a blind corporation we will establish. This will prevent the appearance of a conflict of interest, thereby making it feasible for the fund to be able to own CANDO stock in its portfolio. The fund will be structured as a balanced fund leaving the possibility that it might own CANDO debentures if the company were to ever float bonds.

"This fund will be the forerunner of a family of religious funds designed and sold to socially conscious members of various religions. I can envision a Catholic fund, a Lutheran fund and a Jewish fund for starters. 21st Century Securities will provide the seasoned investment professionals the company will need as portfolio managers.

"Berrios & Aguinaga will do the accounting and audit work. Your contacts and influence will be invaluable to the marketing efforts. Do not think of yourself as a mere salesman but as a fiduciary who will not only be providing your followers with a valuable investment service but will be solving their moral dilemmas at the same time. After all Luke 6:38 says, 'Give and it shall be given unto you.'

"It is merely a bonus that everyone involved will profit handsomely as well. These mutual funds will become a cash-cow that will provide you with the capital necessary to continue your holy mission for mankind by growing your primary business."

Sun Raye was overwhelmed. She told the family that she would retreat again to her favorite small unoccupied key and pray for guidance. Billy and Bobby decided matters had gone too far to be left to chance. They spiked one of Sun Raye's bottles of water with LSD.

Thanks to a breeze the weather was hot but still pleasant as Sun Raye kayaked to the out-key. It was about a mile and a half trip – long enough to feel like she was getting away but close enough for her to easily paddle her boat without exhausting herself. She took a supply of granola bars to munch on and a small cooler of bottled water. The proposal felt right. The astrological numbers were seeming to fall perfectly into place, but it had started to bother her that both Chip and Rodney were "1's". Was she setting herself up for a possible future threat from rival "1's"? Was she letting a pair of well-dressed foxes in her hen-house? Painful reminder of when Valdes had muscled his way into her sunscreen operation returned.

After paddling to the island Sun Raye was ravenous.

She sat on the beach and ate a granola bar and drank a bottle of water. She watched a dolphin jump. Bait fish came up into the shallow water. Gulls flew overhead. The clouds seemed especially fluffy and expressive. She felt very close to nature. She briefly wondered if she was cut out for the life she had chosen. Maybe she should have been a nature tour-guide instead. As she watched a crab she thought of one of Glenn Turner's old moral lessons:

A winner is sensitive to the atmosphere around him. A loser is sensitive only to his own feelings.

She hadn't thought about Glenn's teachings for awhile. Was she being too suspicious and critical of Rodney and Chip's proposal? She tried to think of a Turner adage that would be applicable. One of his best known statements jumped into her mind.

No statue was every erected to a critic, but of the people they have criticized, many statues have gone up.

She wondered if being an investment manager was her destiny. A jet from the naval air station suddenly flew overhead. The plane left a column of white behind it that reminded her of a "1". She unwrapped another granola bar and opened another bottle of water to wash it down. *Funny*, she thought as she opened it. *The seal is broken. I must have opened it earlier and forgotten about it.* She took a few swigs and then finished the bottle. Within a few minutes her anxiety began to lessen as the LSD took hold.

Time seemed to be frozen. She found herself drifting into another world and thought she was on a staircase at the bottom of the ocean. At the top of the staircase, going into the clouds, she could see a gleaming light that she thought must be a bright star or maybe a huge jewel of exceptional brilliance. She felt she was two people in the same body. One was insane. The one with the insane mind was trying to pull the other over to its side; the sane mind was resisting. Then things became even more confusing and frightening. Now it seemed as if she had three minds, two of which were insane. Her sane self had a front row seat so it could watch her other two insane minds. She looked at a sea gull. Its face became distorted, and its eyes peered at her cruelly. They seemed to penetrate her soul and read her thoughts. It squawked and sounded a hundred times louder than normal. She thought the bird must be the devil.

Sun Raye felt herself ascending the stairs and when she reached the top she saw a gleaming, blinding light more brilliant than any light she had ever seen. It had no shape or form, but she felt like she was looking at God himself. She had never felt so pure in her entire life. All trash and impurities suddenly washed out of her heart, mind and soul. She felt as if she had been reborn, and a great peace and contentment flowed through her body as all sounds ceased, and she began to float in a huge still void where she was overcome by an overpowering feeling of peace and contentment.

At the peak of the experience God told Sun Raye a great scene was about to unfold and she would be a part of it. She felt a massive earthquake building up in her. Suddenly there was a tremendous force, and she saw her family in a rainbow of glorious beauty of light, color and music and felt the oneness of fellowship telling her of the importance of belonging. They exuded love. An organ began to play. It suddenly vanished and became Jerry

Butler and the Impressions who began to sing "Amen" in harmony.

Sun Raye's two-piece bathing suit slithered off her body and swam away like two eels. The pieces slithered up the side of the kayak and disappeared. A granola bar mystically appeared in her hand and turned into a sacrificial communion wafer. She sat on the beach nude, eating it, talking with God. He was surrounded by his twelve disciples. They introduced themselves as Aimee Semple McPherson, Jim Bakker, Lonnie Frisbee, Jimmy Swaggart, Peter Popoff, Creflo Dollar, Morris Cerullo, Paul Crouch, Robert Tilton, Richard Roberts, Billy James Hargis and Garner Ted Armstrong. Then as she sat naked on the beach that had now turned to quicksand, they began to debate theology and money-making. At the conclusion of their discussion, God clapped his hands, and the disciples sank into the quicksand, leaving them alone.

After the euphoric feelings began to subside, Sun Raye, still not suspecting that her water had been spiked with LSD, was convinced God and his disciples had been talking to her and telling her to proceed with the mutual fund project. All-knowing, all-powerful God had spoken. He had blessed her new venture. He was not to be denied.

CHAPTER 17

T he effects of the LSD continued to linger as Sun Raye donned her bathing suit again and paddled her kayak back to Little Torch Key. She continued to feel intoxicated with a deep sense of awe as well as with an unexplainable ecstatic joy. The euphoric feeling included elements of profound peace and steadfastness that seemed to spring from the depth of her being. She harbored no suspicions that LSD was the actual root of her awakening. She primarily felt an unexplainable need to be alone for open and wordless prayer and meditation. She stopped paddling as she approached Little Torch Key, sat for a few minutes, munching another granola bar, and watching as the sun fell lower in the sky in preparation for another stunning Keys sunset.

Sun Raye decided as she munched her granola bar that she would have a séance with her family to confirm God's message. If God confirmed his directive, the undertaking was a go.

Blue Raye and Sea Raye were relieved to see their sunburned mother back home safe and sound. They wondered why she seemed to be sunburned all over her body but decided it was best not to ask. Sun Raye babbled about what she remembered of her mystical day. She also chattered about her plans to conduct a séance to communicate again with God and clarify his purpose. She insisted on both daughters and their husbands sharing the upcoming encounter. Blue Raye and Sea Raye decided to humor her, hoping the sun had just gotten to her and she would forget about this nonsense by morning.

The following morning as Bobby Raye sat in his gym shorts and t-shirt, eating key lime pie and drinking coffee at Casa Camilio Sur, he mentioned the upcoming séance to Miguel Valdes. Valdes' response was to be expected.

"You say that oddball fuckin' broad is doing what? Jesus H. Christ! Sit tight while I call Al."

When Soltero arrived Bobby repeated what he had told Valdes, purposely eliminating any mention of the LSD he and Billy had used to spike Sun Raye's water bottle, since he wasn't sure how Soltero would react.

"Interesting. And she says she will abide by the mandate she receives from God during the séance?" Soltero asked.

"That's what she says," Bobby repeated. "She says God will be her celestial guide. Can you imagine that shit?"

"If this séance is that important to her, we'll have to make sure she gets the right message," Al said. "I want both you and Billy to be sure to participate in the upcoming event. I believe there's a good possibility God will speak to her."

Bobby looked quizzically at Soltero, shrugged and ate another big bite of pie.

Sun Raye cleared her calendar and devoted her whole day to readying herself for the séance. She needed a round table to create the symbolic circle for the ritual. There was a round folding table at Kingdom Hall which was just the size she needed. She put a tablecloth on it and then set the table. Sun Raye baked a loaf of homemade Cuban bread and cooked a pot of conch chowder to use as an offering to

God. She placed three candles on the table to represent the father, the son, and the Holy Ghost and then she set up some lamps on nearby tables so she could turn off the main lights in the room to create the right atmosphere. Now everything was set to go.

~ ~ ~

Both of Sun Raye's daughters and their husbands were at Kingdom Hall precisely at 7 p.m. not knowing what to expect. They could smell the conch chowder when they entered the dimly lit room. The three candles burned brightly. Sun Raye was nude.

"Oh, I didn't know we were going to have dinner," Bobby said. "That smells delish'. And fresh Cuban bread too? You want me to get everybody a brewski out of the kitchen? You forgot the butter. I'll get some while I'm in there. Hell, if I'd known we were going to be eating, I'd have brought some key lime pie from the restaurant."

"My son, this food is not for you," Sun Raye said. "It is an offering to bless our maker."

"So I'll bless our maker. Good bread, good meat, good God, let's eat," said Bobby.

Sun Raye gave him a cutting look, summoned them to the table and when everyone was seated and asked them to hold hands.

"Our beloved God almighty, supreme ruler of heaven and earth, we bring you gifts from life. Commune with us, O holy one, and move among us."

Bobby nudged Billy under the table. His wife, Blue Raye, gave him a dirty look and pinched him on the leg causing Bobby to hit the table leg. It rocked slightly. Some of the conch chowder slopped out of the bowl.

"Is that you, O exalted one?" Sun Raye asked.

Bobby squirmed uncomfortably on a wedgie and accidentally bumped the table leg again, spilling more of the soup.

"Most powerful God, we are here to ask you to confirm your divine message to me concerning the investment proposal that has been presented to CANDO. We pray for you to send us a sign that this is your wish," Sun Raye said.

Miguel Valdes lurked silently out a side window. *Pretty good tits and ass* he thought. No one in the room knew that Al Soltero had sent him over to Kingdom Hall to insure the séance's outcome. They had not told either Bobby or Billy, trusting neither of them to not inadvertently give the plan away. Al also wanted them to be genuinely surprised as events began to unfold. Valdes found an unlocked window in the meeting room and raised it slightly. It was far enough away from the séance table not to be noticed. A sudden breeze came in through the partially opened window and made the candles flicker. Miguel sneezed.

Sun Raye perked up and said, "Gesunheit, Lord! Yes, my precious lord, I feel and hear your presence. Make your divine wishes known."

After this second request for a divine sign of God's will, the Colombian released a dove Soltero had obtained for the purpose into the room. The terrified bird began to fly randomly through the room, bumping into a light fixture and causing it to sway. Bobby was caught off guard and jumped up with his pistol. He shot the bird, which came tumbling down into the conch chowder in a mass of blood and feathers. Hot soup went everywhere, soaking the participants and burning Blue Raye's hand. She jumped up, knocking over the table, sending the rest of the soup and the dead bird onto her mother's naked lap.

Sun Raye looked in horror and screamed, "Bobby Raye, God sent his symbolic message and you shot the goddamned thing!"

Both Blue Raye and Sea Raye looked at each other, shocked at their mother's epithet.

A feral cat had gotten in through the open window and was patrolling the pantry looking for rats. When it saw the dead bird land on Sun Raye's lap, it spotted a much better meal. The cat, which was now panicked by the gunshot, leaped onto Sun Raye's lap, grabbed the dead bird in its mouth, and sprinted for the open window. As it leapt to exit the building, it hit Soltero's shell-shocked henchman who was peering in from the darkness, knocking him into the bougainvillea adjacent to the building.

As Valdes tried to disentangle himself from the thorns, he mumbled, "Fuckin' Soltero's not going to like this one little bit." He peered back in the window and muttered, "Mother of God!"

Sun Raye now lay on the floor, nude and stunned the soup, looking like vomit all over her. "God has spoken. This is a sign he does not want us to go forward. God's will be done. Praise Allah. Thank you for making your will be known."

She jumped up and began to pray, gobs of potato, conch and tomato running down her front.

Billy screamed, "Bobby, you stupid trigger-happy son-of-a-bitch!"

Valdes limped off into the night bleeding and cursing.

Valdes walked back into Casa Camilio Sur still bleeding from bougainvillea scratches. Soltero was having a leisurely meal with a good bottle of pinot noir. He looked surprised by Valdes' disheveled appearance.

"Don't even fuckin' ask," Valdes growled. "I'm going to kill that stupid pendejo Bobby Perez the next time I see him."

Valdes went into the restroom to clean up and put Band-Aids on his wounds. When he came out looking like the loser at a cockfight, he waved a waiter over.

"Give me a fuckin' double rum – on the goddamned rocks," he said rudely. "Now."

"What happened?" Soltero asked nonchalantly.

"I took the bird over there just like you wanted, and when the dumb naked twat asked for a sign from fuckin' heaven, I released it into the room. Can you believe it? A dove – a goddamned universal peace symbol – and that goddamned brain-dead Bobby Perez shot the son-of-a-bitch. Shot it like it was a clay pidgin."

He then described how the bird had fallen in the soup and how the feral cat had then pounced on dead bird.

"So what happened to *you*?" Soltero asked.

"The goddamned cat knocked me into a bougainvillea. That's what happened. Next time you can release your own goddamned birds. The dumb bitch took the dead bird as a sign that God would not endorse the project. I swear by the Virgin Mary, Bobby Perez is going to be a dead man with key lime pie up his ass."

Adolfo Soltero sat silently and drank his wine as Valdes chugalugged his rum-on-the-rocks and ordered another.

Finally Soltero said, "I've got a way out of this dilemma. Didn't Madelyn work for awhile as Reverend LeRoy Cho-Arturo's receptionist? Well, LeRoy is going to help us right this misunderstanding. Tell him to call me in the morning. I've got a plan."

The following morning after talking to Soltero, Reverend LeRoy made a visit to Kingdom Hall. He told Sun Raye that he had had a vision in his sleep the night before that told him she needed his guidance.

Sun Raye explained the events of the previous evening, telling LeRoy that she had asked for God to send her a heavenly sign and he had sent the dove. She also said that he had sent her a second sign in the form of the cat telling her he was not blessing the mutual fund project.

"The cat predicted the failure of the project when it gobbled the dove," she said.

LeRoy pretended to think for a moment and said, "Raye, sweet thing, you're right. God did send you two symbols, but you misinterpreted them. You got things backwards. The dove does not signify your upcoming venture; the cat did. The dove stood for your detractors, disbelievers and competitors. The cat signifies you, and since the cat ate your competitors, God was trying to tell you that your venture is a go after all. Not just a go, but he's trying to tell you that you will eat up your competition and spit it out. He sent you the strongest possible sign that you need move ahead as fast and furiously as you possibly can. He is telling you that you will succeed and devour your competition. Go for it, mama. God is on your side. This is an opportunity of a lifetime. How many people can say they have God's blessing from the start. This puts you in the same league with Moses. I think we should offer God a thank-you prayer, right now."

He took Sun Raye's hand and before she could object started to pray.

"Oh gracious and generous God, I surrender my financial affairs and concerns about money to your Divine care and love. I ask that you remove my worries, anxieties and fears about money, and replace them with faith. With your help more money will flow into my life. I release all my negative thoughts about money knowing that prosperity is my true destiny. I will manage my finances wisely by seeking help where needed. Bring me a greater understanding of my purpose in life and help me act on that purpose with divine courage and strength, knowing that prosperity will follow. Thank you, God in the name of the trinity. Amen."

After the prayer Sun Raye thought about Reverend LeRoy's comments at length. Later in the day she called Chip and Rodney and told them she had decided their proposal had merit. CANDO was about to be in the religious mutual fund business.

Reverend LeRoy Cho-Arturo reported back to Adolfo Soltero that the mission had once more been accomplished.

CHAPTER 18

It was a perfect day for flying, but Adolfo Soltero took little notice. As he sat in his first class seat, he was preoccupied with his upcoming meeting in Colombia. He wasn't concerned that he was in trouble because he felt matters were under control in the Keys, but he knew he had to put the best spin he could on his current assignment there especially since he only occasionally got the opportunity to communicate with the top echelon of the cartel's power structure, and he understood the importance of maximizing the effectiveness of these infrequent communications when they occurred. Once this meeting was concluded he would again be forced to communicate through channels, and he knew from past experience that other ambitious cartel intermediaries would put their own twist on his reports, a twist that would primarily benefit them.

Soltero's plane flew over Isla Grande as it approached Cartagena. He saw the enormous statue of the Virgin Mary standing on its platform in the middle of Cartagena Bay, welcoming home sailors and fishermen. When the plane landed in Cartagena, he was whisked away in a chauffeur-driven, bulletproof Mercedes to his destination in El Centro.

Soltero relaxed somewhat as he watched life on the street. It always felt good to be home. They passed through Plaza de Bolivar. He saw familiar sights — a newspaper boy, a shoeshine man, a man selling lime water, and a woman with a sign around her neck advertising ten-cent phone calls on her mobile phone. He saw a coconut confectioner and the palenguera, who was selling watermelon and bananas from an enamel pot on her head. They rode through the Plaza de los Coches, the site of the old slave market. Here a woman in a white beret was selling watermelon shakes and the street was jammed with moto-taxis. Yes, the languid, legendary walled colonial city made familiar to most Americans by the movie "Romancing The Stone" seemed to never change in his absence. It was the same steamy, tropical city by the sea that it had always been.

For over twenty years Cartagena had been a haven for Colombia's middle and upper classes. The middle class came on holiday. The upper classes had bought and restored the crumbling mansions that abounded in the city. Cartagenians prided themselves that they had managed to stay insulated from the drug wars that had plagued the country. Colombia's long-running civil war and waves of narco-terrorism had never erupted on Cartagena's streets. When a person visited, political strife and violence felt very far away. Soltero smiled as he thought that upper-crust Cartagenians would be horrified if they knew a major figure in the cartel was quietly residing in their midst.

At last the driver pulled up to the wooden gate of Casa Carlos. Its owner, Pablo Emilio Jorge Carlos de Gaviria had bought and restored it in the early nineties. It was an extravagant nineteenth-century mansion whose arched windows were copied directly from the Alhambra. It was built around a courtyard and swimming pool with doors leading to a multitude of sitting rooms and bedrooms. A fountain trickled restfully. As with most houses in Cartagena, Casa Carlos was built all the way out to the curb. The street in front of it was only wide enough for a car and a half.

The wooden gate which was decorated with brass buttons had a smaller door cut into it. A security cage of wooden spindles allowed the guard inside to identify visitors, and Soltero was quickly admitted.

An armed servant escorted Soltero through the courtyard into a corner room where Carlos was admiring the newest addition to his antique weapons and torture-device collection. Carlos' wife Teresita came out of another display room to greet Soltero. Teresita had Colombia's largest collection of Napoleon-era ladies fans. She had an assistant who helped her label, catalogue, and clean her collection. The collection had begun initially with fans given to her by a former suitor who had been one of Carlos's smuggling competitors. When Carlos became enamored with Teresita, he arranged for the suitor to be eliminated. When they were married, he allowed her to keep and add to her collection.

"You are just in time for lunch," Señor Carlos said, after they had exchanged their greetings. "I have arranged lunch to be served on our rooftop terrace so we can enjoy a view of the sea as we talk."

He led Soltero to the rooftop terrace. Despite the cruel midday sun, the ocean breezes made the terrace very comfortable. The table was covered with a canvas awning. Armed guards were posted at strategic points around the roof.

Carlos, as always, was a gracious host. The meal began with a fresh avocado salad with sautéed fresh corn, chopped green and red peppers, with sautéed scallions on top. Next Soltero was treated to hearts of palm baked in white wine and topped with Parmesan cheese. Finally he was served an herb encrusted yellowtail snapper filet over rice, topped with a lemon, butter, and caper sauce. Each course was served with a different wine. Neither man attempted to talk business during the meal, as this would be considered bad manners. They confined their conversation to inconsequential small talk. The meal concluded with an assortment of freshly cut fruit. Only when the coffee was served did Carlos open the conversation to more serious matters.

"And how is my good friend Miguel Valdes's new restaurant going?" Carlos asked.

"Casa Camilio Sur is doing quite well," Soltero answered, "and because of a member of Miguel's network, we have been introduced to a venture with much potential to further our primary interests."

"Please tell me more."

Soltero refreshed Carlos's memory about CANDO.

"We have infiltrated the CANDO organization on every level. We even have two of our young associates married to the CEO's daughters," Soltero continued. "With the help of your subsidiary Tango Products we control their manufacturing which we are able to use for our purposes. Tango people now represent a meaningful group of their distributors. We manufacture a special line of sunscreen that is only shipped to our select group.

"With the help of our business consultants, the

CANDO has gone public and trades on NASDAQ. Our auditor, Berrios & Aguinaga, is producing profit reports that are enhancing the stock values creating internal trading opportunities for our brokerage network. It has also given our securities sales force an easily manipulated financial product to sell to the public."

Carlos nodded his understanding and approval. Soltero continued his presentation.

"Since my last report we have completed the purchase of Federal Discount Brokers and renamed it 21st Century Securities Group. Federal Discount has 35 domestic offices and 26 offices abroad. It employs 1400 registered representatives as its sales force and has over half a million retail accounts.

"We spent several weeks training the sales force to do business our way. Most have had no prior experience in the securities industry.

"For the first two weeks each month we encourage them to spend their time cold calling. On the third week, we inform them that a recommendation will soon be forthcoming from our research department, but we give them no specific information about the security. The salesmen are then instructed to re-contact the leads they have generated in the previous two weeks and inform them that a recommendation from research is imminent. Their goal at this point is to try to determine how much money the customer would be willing to invest in a 21st Century recommended security.

"At the beginning of the fourth week of each month the branch manager conducts a sales meeting with branch personnel to disclose the name of the recommended security. The sales force is given a script which they are required to use verbatim. They then spend the remainder of that month selling only that recommended security to their prospects and clients. Different branches are given different recommendations. It has worked very well thus far," Soltero said.

"And what if they wish to sell something else?" asked Carlos.

"That has been easy to control," continued Soltero. "We pay them a 10% commission if they sell the recommended item and less than one percent if they sell anything else."

"You mentioned that recommendations differ from one branch to another," said Carlos. "Isn't this a potential problem?"

"No. A salesman is prohibited from talking to any company employee who is not in his branch. Disobedience means dismissal."

Carlos nodded his approval.

"Our first underwriting opportunity was CANDO Corporation," Soltero continued. "We sold 1,100,000 units, each consisting of three shares of class A stock and one warrant for three dollars each. We also sold 2,000,000 shares of a class B common stock for $.50 each to insiders, who primarily consisted of ourselves. The units could not be split for sixty days except by 21st Century Securities. We were oversubscribed and exercised our option to expand the offering to 1,700,000 units. This brought in revenues of $5,100,000.

"Shortly before the end of the sixty day quiet period we repurchased 1,300,000 units at $3.50 per unit. We immediately split the units into their components and priced each of the three shares at $2.50 per share and the warrant for $1.00 for a total of $8.00. This stock was only sold by branches that did not participate in the original offering. This brought in an additional $4,250,000."

Carlos was very impressed.

"This is a business model we should be able to repeat many times over. Sellers willingly roll their profits into one of our new underwritings. With 35 domestic offices and 26 international offices we will be able to continue to exploit CANDO and other offerings for some time to come," Soltero said. "We were also able to sell our class B CANDO stock at the higher price, giving us more cash to invest in legitimate enterprises. While we are evaluating opportunities we are holding the cash in a nominee account on the Isle of Man."

"Very innovative," said Carlos. "I commend you."

"With your permission, I will change the topic slightly," Soltero said. "Our investment counsel convinced CANDO to spin off the manufacturing division, WILDO, for which, if you will recall, we have long done the private labeling. Since we control 50% of CANDO stock, this immediately gave us 50% of WILDO. 21st Century bought substantially the entire remaining portion of the float in the open market, and the board of directors voted to take the company private. We installed hand-picked people in key positions and were subsequently able to artificially increase our sales to our affiliates dramatically."

"What do you call dramatically?"

"Several thousand percent thus far," Soltero said. "And since it was now a private company, our flexibility increased substantially since its books were no longer subject to SEC mandated reporting requirements and public scrutiny. As these invoices are paid, it cleanses monies that otherwise up to that time have been a challenge. With WILDO's sales and profits rising exponentially, the board has been able to declare very generous dividends on the stock, giving us capital to reemploy in a variety of new legal ventures."

"Very impressive, my friend. You have done your job well."

"Thank you," said Soltero. "May I continue? Recently we were presented with what Miguel Valdes interpreted as a challenge but what I see as an opportunity. The CEO of CANDO has started a church which she calls the Cosmic Ray Scientific Church of Prosperity. The teachings of the church are based on promoting capitalism. The nucleus of the membership is CANDO's distributors.

"Miguel was reluctant to embrace this latest venture, but I thought of a way it can be used to our advantage. We have convinced CANDO to buy a shell company we found in Grand Cayman for a nominal price. Our people control a meaningful amount of the stock. Our business consultants are aiding and advising CANDO with setting up a family of off-shore religious mutual funds which will then be run by portfolio managers answering to us. We will charge a management fee for our services to the fund.

"The initial fund entitled Chosen Ones Growth Fund will be designed for and marketed to CANDO distributors and members of the Cosmic Ray Church. We will make a 5% commission on each sale and then trailing commissions. This will help strengthen their bonds to the organization. A major position in the fund will be CANDO stock. We can use the fund's trading activity to further enhance the stock and in the process enhance the value of our investment.

"There is also a possibility that we can place CANDO fixed income instruments with the fund or purchase them ourselves. I foresee that the purchase of various instruments by people in our organization will help legitimize funds from our other ventures. There are a myriad of possibilities."

"This sounds like, as you said, an endeavor that might have a 'myriad of possibilities'," said Carlos, after giving Soltero's report some thought. "I will look forward to future updates. Thank you for coming this long distance. It is always good to see you."

As Adolfo Soltero returned to the airport, he thought his trip had gone well. *I'm just glad he didn't quiz me about Sun Raye's mental stability*, he thought. *But I think I can control that.*

THE PRESENT

CHAPTER 19

As Will Black cleaned and waxed his boat early Saturday morning and gazed at the incredibly blue sky, he thought about how fortunate he and his wife, Betsy, were to live in Florida, especially the Florida Keys. He looked over the edge of the boat into the canal behind his home just as a nurse shark swam by. Residents of the canal knew this shark and had named it Sheila. She swam by about this same time most days. A land crab popped out of his hole and rushed back in as an iguana darted by. A pelican sat swaying high in an Australian pine surveying its surroundings; as it presided over Act One of nature's daily scene. The tide seemed higher than usual this morning. *Must be the phase of the moon* Will thought.

Will was the branch manager for the Key West office of Reynolds Smathers and Thompson Securities; his wife, Betsy, was the local area president for WB Bank. Even though they were now seasoned Floridians, Will was originally from the Mississippi Delta; Betsy was a native of Mobile, Alabama. Will and Betsy met in Mobile when both were working in the financial district. They had moved to Vero Beach, Florida when Will was offered a transfer there. Their daughter Lexie was born in Vero. After a number of years in Vero Beach and after Lexie had applied to and had been accepted by the University of Miami, Betsy was offered the presidency of WB in Monroe County at the same time that RST wished to open a branch office there. It seemed a no-brainer for the Blacks to move to the lower Keys, and just as it had turned out when they moved to Vero, it was a marvelous decision.

As he cleaned the Grady-White, Will was playing a CD on the boat stereo. The theme of every song on the disc was about the sun. At that moment Osibisa, a British Afro-pop band comprised mostly of expatriate musicians from the Caribbean, was singing their American hit "Sunshine Day". Will loved the song's catchy beat and hypnotic repetitive lyrics.

> *Everybody do what you're doing*
> *Smile will bring a sunshine day*

Will could appreciate why so many Keys residents only returned to the mainland as a last resort and more often than not chose to do a "staycation" when they had free time. He laughed to himself. He thought about Howard Livingston's song on the topic, "Staycation". *Hell,* he thought, laughing to himself, *the world might take itself a lot less seriously if it did a 'nakation' like the Keys did during Fantasy Fest.* He looked at himself almost nude in only a bathing suit, barefooted with no shirt and thought, *I almost qualify right now.*

About that time he heard pea-rock crunching, and saw Jason Pearson's truck turn in his driveway. Jason was Big Pine Key's assistant fire chief who worked as a contractor on the side. He had done many projects for Will and Betsy since the couple had moved to the Keys but more than that, he was a very good friend.

Jason walked back to the dock drinking a Mountain Dew.

"Looking good," he said. "The fiberglass was starting to look chalky."

"Yes, it was. Got to do this once a year or so. Our friends from Vero Beach, Guy and Penny, are coming down to visit next weekend so I want to make sure the boat looks its best," Will replied. "What's up with you?"

"You probably wouldn't believe me if I told you," Jason said. "We got a really strange call yesterday."

"Try me."

"We were called to go pick up a dead body," Jason continued. "A commercial fisherman spotted it four and a half miles off shore floating naked except for a sock on his left foot, so he called for help. We thought it was just a routine call. Boy, were we wrong.

"It turned out to be a guy from North Carolina who had died of Lou Gehrig's disease. He and his family used to come to the Keys to fish every year. His family decided it would be appropriate to bury him at sea. So the day after he died they put his body on dry ice and brought it to Islamorada. They rented a boat, said their last goodbyes, and released him to the sea. After the body was released, they went fishing in honor of the deceased and then returned to North Carolina. It was the next day when a commercial fisherman spotted the body floating and called us."

"Isn't that against the law?" Will asked.

"Officials are still trying to decide that," Jason said. "It is legal to bury a body at sea if you follow certain rules. You're supposed to be at least three miles out...which they were ... but you're supposed to make sure the body sinks to the bottom rapidly and permanently. This bunch of morons wrapped the body in a plastic tarp and then weighed it down with coral rock and sea shells."

"You're right. That was an unusual call, but I guess the big question is, 'Did they catch any fish?' By the way, we have finally figured out why you and Kevin are involved in such a wide variety of rescue, fire department, and EMT activities. You're adrenaline junkies!"

Jason smiled and knowingly nodded in agreement.

"So, are you here to install those new doors upstairs?" Will asked.

"Wish I could," Jason said, "but they're too heavy for me to hoist up there by myself. I'll have to wait until I have some help."

"What about your fire department buddies?"

"That is a bit of a problem at present," Jason said. "Nobody wants side work. They're all selling sunscreen distributorships."

"Whoa!" Will said.

"Yeah, some company named CANDO. They bought the Jehovah's Witnesses building across U.S. 1. Everyone is convinced they will get rich selling for them. When they sign up one of my men, they tell him all he needs to do is sign up ten of his buddies and he will become wealthy. He will receive an override off each of the ten people. Then if each of their ten buddies sign up 10 people, he'll be getting an override off of 100 more people. Then if each of the 100 people sign up 10 apiece, he'll be getting an override off 1000 people. And finally if each of the 1000 recruits 10 people, he'll be making money on 10,000 people."

"If," Will said. "That's a big 'if'. If frogs could fly, they wouldn't bump their butts along the ground."

"Yes, if," Jason said. "And all each of them personally has to do is recruit 10 people. They think it's an easy lay-up."

"I think we both know making money isn't that easy," Will said. "You know that, and I know that. If you'll remember, Club Tropic was supposed to be a lay-up too," Will said. "I assume one has to pay to become a CANDO distributor."

"Oh, yeah! 900 bucks, and that doesn't include all the ongoing supplies and materials that they sell to a distributor," Jason said. "And once they become distributors my guys don't have time to work for me on their days off. Between all the meetings they go to, plus the time they spend trying to peddle distributorships, add to that the time they spend trying to sell sunscreen, they barely have time left to work at the fire department. They sure as hell don't seem to want to devote the time to help me do sweaty projects like put your doors in. And then I have to go around making apologies to people like you who I've made commitments to. CANDO is beginning to be a problem. It's even interfering with fire house business. I've had a couple of people recently who didn't answer to the calls of the dispatcher, only for me to find out later they were out doing CANDO crap. I'll be glad when this fad blows over."

About that time Betsy came downstairs and saw Jason. She whistled when she saw her husband Will's skimpy attire.

"Hi, Jason. I wish I had known you were coming," she said. "I would have moved stuff away from those doors so you could install them."

"I'm sorry, Betsy. The reason I didn't call is I can't install the doors today," Jason said.

Betsy looked disappointed.

"He doesn't have any help," Will explained. "All his helpers are busy for the time being."

"Oh?"

"All my regulars from the fire department have gotten involved in a multi-level marketing program," Jason said.

"Selling sunscreen?" Betsy asked.

"How did you know?" Jason asked.

"A company named CANDO, I bet," Betsy said.

"Where'd you hear about it?" Jason asked.

"From Key West Police Chief Walter Wanderley," Betsy said. "He's having a problem with his department also. He was in my office earlier this week telling me about it. A lot of his younger employees have bought into this program. In fact at the festival they had on Duval Street last weekend, he had a hard time finding off-duty people to work security for it. He also told me when he attended the festival himself, he found some of his secretaries had set up a booth to sell sunscreen. Walter said that some of his people seem to care more about CANDO than their regular jobs."

"Sounds familiar," said Jason. "They seem to have their tentacles in fire department employees the same way."

"Something else Walter told me," said Betsy, "was people seem to be using CANDO to recruit members for some religious sect."

"They're in the religion business too?" Will said. "What denomination?"

"Nothing Walter had ever heard of," Betsy said. "Some really strange name he couldn't remember."

"Sunscreen holy water! I guess you don't drink it; you rub it on and you become one of God's chosen people," joked Will. "After all, the sho-nuff heavy-duty sinner needs maximum protection in case he gets sent to the wrong place when he dies, but I know firemen who are light-weight sinners don't need that. We all know they're angels of mercy who are already used to extreme heat."

"You mean like a big-time sinner needs UV-40 protection while a garden-variety sinner needs only UV-15?" joked Betsy.

"Something like that," Will said. "High-powered sinners are the good lord's skin cancer targets. That's one way of getting even."

"You two are being too cute. Seriously, that's all we need is a devil-worshiping sunscreen cult," Jason said.

"Why not?" Will said. "We have everything else in the Keys."

"Smarty-pant husbands are especially prevalent," Betsy said.

"What pants? I was preparing to have a 'nakation'."

Jason and Betsy just looked quizzically at each other and thought, *What's he talking about now? Maybe he's the one who has been out in the sun too long.*

CHAPTER 20

"I'm looking forward to this weekend," Betsy said to Will as she brewed coffee. "I'm glad Guy and Penny can come down for a long Memorial Day weekend.

"I am too," Will said as he read the morning paper. "They're always fun. Plus we'll get a chance to catch up on all the gossip about Vero Beach."

Guy and Penny Walsh were old friends of the Blacks. They had become good friends when the Blacks lived in Vero Beach through their daughters who had been in the same class together at St. Edwards School. Like Will, Guy was a securities broker in Vero. Rather than being affiliated with a national "wire house" however, he owned his own independent financial planning firm. His wife Penny also worked in the family business. Despite technically being competitors, the Blacks and the Walshes had formed a friendship that had survived even though Will and Betsy now lived in the Keys.

"Why don't we take the Walshes out to Marvin Key one day and downtown the other," Betsy said. "I'm not sure they've ever been out to Marvin."

"That works for me if the weather is good," Will said. "Picnic Island will be jammed and the sand at Marvin has got to be the most pristine in the lower Keys. On a nice day it's worth the extra ride. Listen up. Here's another great Keys story in the morning paper's 'Crime Watch'."

Psychological Exam Ordered

"A man arrested for allegedly breaking into a woman's house on Caroline Street to tickle her feet has been ordered to undergo a psychological examination.

"James D. Buff, 50, pleaded innocent Friday to battery, criminal trespassing and resisting law enforcement.

"He was arrested Sunday near the home of Velma Poer, 76, of Key West.

"Poer told investigators she awoke to find Buff tickling her feet. Buff ran outside and Poer called a neighbor, who found Buff standing behind the house demanding a drink of water, authorities said."

"The poor woman," Betsy said.

"It's a good thing he wasn't in the buff," Will shot back.

"I guess the 'D' in his middle name stands for demented," said Betsy.

"I think it just means dumb," rejoined Will.

Guy and Penny arrived late. Guy had gone into his office and worked a partial day before they hit the road.

"How was the drive?" Will asked.

"OK until I almost got to your house," Guy said. "There was some kind of revival type meeting going on the Jehovah's Witnesses building on US1."

"Jehovah's Witnesses doesn't own that building anymore," Betsy said. "They sold it to another church which calls itself the Cosmic Ray Scientific Church of Prosperity."

"Some kind of holy-roly sect?" Guy asked.

"I'm not sure what their shtick is," Betsy said.

"Why don't we talk about it over dinner? Square Grouper, OK?" Will asked.

"Let's hit it. I'm starved from being on the road," Penny said.

As usual, the Square Grouper was packed, mostly with locals. The Blacks and the Walshes decided to have a drink at the bar while they waited for a table.

"So bring us up to date," Will said. "What's going on in Vero Beach?"

Guy and Penny updated them. After a few minutes Guy and Will got around to talking shop. As usual they were both candid about bad things as well as good things that were happening.

"Have you heard of a new religious mutual fund being sold called Chosen Ones Growth Fund?" Guy asked.

Will admitted he was not familiar with it.

"I've lost some money to it recently," Guy said. "I assume you remember Ralph Ness."

"Oh, sure," Will replied. "He was the guy who came to Vero from Tampa. Married money and had never had a job in his life. He lost a good portion of his portfolio letting Dave Tressler sell naked options. Didn't his wife, Jinx, get a job as receptionist at St. Edwards so they could get the tuition break to keep their kids in school there? Seems like he had to get a job clerking at the mall. I remember he hated the securities industry and especially Tressler. Swore he'd never buy a stock again. He gave me the 'can't get hurt with dirt' lecture one day."

"That's him," Guy said, "but he's singing a different tune nowadays. He may not be buying stocks, but he's sure as hell selling them. Jinx doesn't work at the school anymore. She's now involved in a multi-level marketing program, and he's got his series 6 to sell mutual funds."

"Ralph! You've got to be kidding," Will said. "I didn't think he could sell snow-cones in the middle of the Sahara."

"Yep, and he knows just enough to be dangerous. Ralph's hot-to-trot about this religious mutual fund he's selling entitled Chosen Ones Growth Fund. He's taken the few good quarters this fund has reported and is extrapolating the returns out to be a long term projection. He's telling people they will double their money every three years. We both know the market is not going to give consistent returns like that over the long haul."

"That's for sure."

"I looked at this religious fund he's peddling. It does have an above average short-term track record, but it's because of a concentrated position in a high-flying NASDAQ stock named CANDO. It trades over 60 times earnings," Guy said. "If that stock ever starts to tank, the fund will dig a hole it'll never dig back out of. Anyway, as I was saying, I've lost a few accounts to him recently."

"It's not coincidental that you bring up the name CANDO – this firm has also hit the Keys," said Will.

"In fact, our friends here are telling us that many of their employees have become CANDO distributors in hopes of riding this multi-level marketing firm to great wealth," added Betsy.

"Fools and their money..." Guy contributed.

"Are my best friends," Will said.

"I can top that," Betsy said laughing. "The average

man has more money than sense; the trouble is he doesn't know it."

Penny added, "I guess what I don't understand is how a fool and his money ever get together in the first place."

"Oh, just because a person has an empty head doesn't mean he has an empty pocket, but he eventually will," Betsy said.

"Enough already, you kooks," Penny said. "Let me offer a toast to a good friendship. It's really great to see you two nuts again. Vero misses you."

Will and Betsy changed the subject and over dinner told their friends about the Minimal Regatta at Schooner Wharf, and the group decided it would be fun to attend.

The Minimal Regatta had evolved into an annual tradition in Key West. The captains of the more than forty home-made makeshift boats were certainly not licensed by the Coast Guard and their seamanship was often questionable. These vessels bobbed and blundered in the harbor and bore little resemblance to any graceful schooner, sleek yacht, or functional fishing boat most people were familiar with.

The Minimal Regatta was the brainchild of "Red Dog", the carpenter at the Schooner Wharf Bar. The only building materials allowed were one sheet of plywood, two 2 x 4's, a roll of duct tape, and one pound of fasteners. No caulking or adhesives could be used, and painting was optional. The objective was simply to cross the finish line on the 200 yard course. Prizes were awarded to winners, and much beer and rum would be consumed before the day and night's festivities were completed.

Will and Betsy parked in their usual parking lot

adjacent to the Conch Republic Seafood Company on Greene Street. After some bantering with their favorite parking attendant, Thomas, they walked the half-block over to the Schooner Wharf Bar.

Michael McCloud was singing one of his original songs, "Schooner Wharf Bar Dog", when they walked in. He nodded recognition when he saw Will and Betsy.

Schooner Wharf Bar is a rustic dog-friendly local's hangout on Key West's harbor, but it has also been adopted by some visiting celebrities such as Kenny Chesney, Beach Boy Al Jardine, and treasure hunter Mel Fisher. Charles Kuralt once called it "the center of the universe." It is mostly an outdoor venue and has a second floor deck overlooking the Key West Bight. Locals think it is one of the last great Key West dives that has not been gentrified.

Despite the full house, Will and Betsy found a table on the ground level. A waitress quickly took their order for drinks and lunch.

At one o'clock the race began. Spectators crowded the dock. Entries were either of a kayak design or an open one that provided more opportunity for creativity and ingenuity. The boats had exotic names like *Suck It Up, Cock Buster, Batman, The Illegal Immigrant, Butt-Wipe, and Sam Pam.* One boat was called *Gas Busters* and advertised "Who you gonna call?" on the bow and "Bite Me" on the stern. Captains and race teams dressed in a variety of costumes. One team dressed like the wizard of Oz; the boat was a ruby slipper named *Wizard of Odd* and its captain was Dorothy in drag using rainbow paddles. Another boat was made to look like a pink bathtub and called itself *Rubba Dub Dub*.

It wasn't long after the race began before some of the exotic craft began to flounder. *The Penetrator* was the first to be pierced, flip and sink. *Liquid Viagra's* captain was the next who couldn't keep it up. Very soon after, *The Breakfast Club* lost its breakfast. The *Shad Rack* sunk with a clunk, and *Foo-Kin Tsunami* hit a tidal wave. *The Morning Wood* had the sinking feeling that there's no morning after. There were more casualties than Pearl Harbor.

The surviving boats continued to race toward Conch Republic Seafood Company and the course turn near Sebago Catamarans. Leading the race was Sushi, a local drag queen, who was wearing all of her paraphernalia complete with a diamond tiara. She was no demure lady and paddled like a woman possessed. Captain Morgan and his Morganettes presided over the crowd of wildly cheering spectators.

Headed back for Schooner Wharf, Will and Betsy noticed a new addition to the pack coming out of the turn. It was a factory-built dinghy paddled by a severely sunburned, scantily-clothed and bald young woman. The race organizers tried to get her attention, but she was oblivious and paddled erratically into the middle of the makeshift fleet. Sushi redoubled her efforts to keep the lead.

The bald woman's boat blundered into *Johnny B Goode* which wiped out *Little Fart* causing it to give *Butt-Wipe* a hemorrhoid. She then prevented *The Illegal Immigrant* from making it past the border. *Three Sheets To The Wind* had the presence of mind to avoid *D-Day* and continue the race. Dorothy from Kansas continued her pursuit for the prize at the end of the rainbow, but Sushi was not to be denied as she dueled for the lead with *Sea Whore* which slowed her down by ramming her.

The last prevailing boats approached the finish line in a dead heat. The frustrated captain of *Flying Kielbasa* yelled, "Get the crazy bitch!" and *Cock Buster* reached out for the interloper. This panicked her, and she began to swat rival captains with her paddle. Even more contestants went in the drink. By the time the mob reached the finish line, it was impossible to tell who the winner was. The ever competitive Sushi raised her arms and claimed victory.

The bald woman capsized her boat near Schooner Wharf. Several people jumped over to rescue her. As the crowd rushed around, a man stepped on the tail of a black lab which bolted. Its leash wrapped around Guy's leg causing him to fall off the wharf, taking Captain Morgan with him. Guy fell straight into Sushi's outstretched arms. Captain Morgan wasn't so fortunate and went in the drink. *Ella Fant's* captain reached for him but was only able to grab his pirate hat.

Sushi, still the showman, yelled, "Oh, is this my prize? Yummy!" and bussed Guy on the cheek. Guy involuntarily jerked, and her boat flipped. He and Sushi both went into the water with a giant splash. All that could be seen of Sushi's boat above the water was the growling cougar painted on the bow. A flailing Guy grabbed for Sushi but instead came up with her sopping wet wig. Sushi's falsies came out of her gown and floated to the surface. The whole scene was captured by a photographer.

In the meantime, rescuers had gotten the bald woman

onto the wharf. She was wet and sunburned but otherwise unharmed. She babbled incoherently about islands and religions and Spanish hoodlums. About the only thing she said anyone could make out was some meaningless babble about shaving her scalp because her hair was being used as a guide for brainwashing rays to go into her head. She was taken to Lower Keys Medical Center for observation.

CHAPTER 21

Key West Chief of Police Walter Wanderley plopped down in Betsy Black's office.

"Margaret," he bellowed at Betsy's secretary, "Coffee, a whole pot, black, and make it intravenous."

"I take it things are not going well," Betsy said.

"Oh, I guess it's just another day in the fruit orchard to some," Walter said, "but its harvest time for me."

"May I listen? May I listen?" Margaret said enthusiastically as she pretended to pant like a dog. "I'm not doing anything that can't wait."

"You never are," Betsy said back lightly.

"Is it a full moon, or does it just seem that way?" Walter continued. "Do you know Bob Eberle on the Mosquito Control Board?"

"I know who he is," Betsy said. "Owns a marina, doesn't he?"

Walter nodded and continued. "Well, Sunday we had a charity golf match for the Sea Camp at the golf course on Stock Island. His wife thought he had been having an adulterous alliance with one of his employees after the Minimal Regatta. They came in separate cars on Sunday because he said he had to do some paperwork at the marina. They were going to have lunch at the Rusty Anchor before the match. When he was late for lunch, she suspected he was having another affair. She seethed all the way through lunch but didn't say anything. She finally blew her top, however, when she saw him whisper to the woman at the fundraiser. She punched him in the head and gave him a two inch gash with her engagement ring. Then she jumped on her golf cart and tried to run him down. She gave him one hell of a bruise on his shin and wrenched his knee. We had to throw her in jail and book her for a felony count of battery with a deadly weapon. Their two children saw thing."

"You think she was just paranoid?" Margaret asked.

"I don't know, but this guy does have a reputation for philandering," Walter said. "And I guess you heard about the disaster at the Minimal Regatta."

"Heard about it! Will and I were there," Betsy said. "In fact one of the people who went for an unintended swim in the Bight was our guest from Vero Beach. He was the one who ended up in the drag queen's arms. Did y'all ever figure out who the mystery woman was?"

"She had no I.D. and refused to talk. Her fingerprints were not on any of the data bases that are available to us. A real Jane Doe. I'm going to guess she was a bum not a tourist. When we got her to the hospital, she died of a heart attack. The body tested positive for cocaethylene. That's a drug that builds up in the liver from people who mix alcohol and cocaine. Cocaethylene is unique because it is the first known example of the body forming a third drug following the simultaneous ingestion of two other drugs. People ingest both coke and booze because the two produce more euphoria and a longer duration of action together than cocaine alone."

"What do you mean by longer duration?" Betsy asked.

"Half the powder cocaine users questioned in a recent

medical survey said that their last heavy drinking episode continued for more than 12 hours. In other words, using the two drugs can stretch the good times without the reveler getting totally drunk. By the way, heart problems and heart attacks are not uncommon with younger users. Because so little is known about the drug, few experts can agree on the nature of the threat to users, or indeed society as a whole. But I can tell you from firsthand experience that coke and alcohol together have been a real problem for law enforcement. Half the young people we arrest for violence are on drugs and over half the drug users are on cocaine. It's a miracle no one at the regatta was hurt because of her stunt."

"You're right. Thank God we've never had drug problems with our daughter," Betsy said, "but that crazy woman is sure going to give locals something to talk about for a long time. I guarantee our friends from Vero won't forget the regatta for a long time either."

CHAPTER 22

Ramrod Key is a small island nestled between Summerland Key and Middle Torch Key. It was named for the ship Ramrod which wrecked near there in the early 19th century. Most tourists on a wild tear to get to Key West probably don't even notice this key on their way through. It is sparsely populated and has a few businesses like Bayshore Nursery, mostly patronized by locals. Five Brothers Two grocery store no doubt makes the best Cuban mix sandwiches outside of Key West, just as its other store, 5 Brothers, on Southard Street makes the best Cuban mixes in Key West. Looe Key Tiki Bar has a bar-full of locals from about eleven a. m. seven days a week. The Looe Key dive shop runs head-boats daily. Ramrod's greatest claim to fame, however, is probably the Boondocks Grille and Draft House, one of the largest tiki bars in Keys. Not only is the Boondocks one of the largest tiki huts, but it also contains the Keys' only miniature golf course. On nights when the wind was blowing from the north, Will and Betsy could hear the bar's thumping band noises at their house a mile and a half away.

Will and Betsy had been invited to a charity fund-raiser at the Boondocks. WB Bank was a major sponsor for the event. As they walked in, they greeted various people they knew. They could hear a band playing in the background. When they approached the elevated tiki hut, they heard a familiar voice bellowing a familiar ovation.

"I'm doing outstandingly well, thank you. If I were

doing any better I'm not sure I'd be able to take it."

"I know who that is," Betsy said, gritting her teeth slightly.

"I do too," said Will said. "Do you think we can avoid him?"

"What you need is a coldbeer," they heard the familiar voice say. "You can put it on my tab."

"His tab, my ass," Betsy murmured. "He wouldn't know his tab from the hole in his head. As usual, the bank's paying for this event."

Suddenly the speaker noticed Will and Betsy and made a beeline over to them.

"Hello, boss lady," he said loudly enough for the whole room to hear. "The coldbeer was running out, but I made them save a special brew just for you."

"Hello, Carson," Betsy said, trying to be gracious. "What are you doing here?"

Some people had chosen to wear costumes to the event. Carson had on a yellow sheet and a white hood. On his front was a sign that said PREPARATION H OINTMENT.

Carson Crown was a loan officer at WB Bank. Betsy had inherited him when she was transferred to Key West. She had to constantly ride herd on him to keep him from doing harebrained things, encourage him to meet his goals, continuously give him hints about keeping his priorities straight, frequently tease him about his short office hours, and remind him to attend meetings. In fact, Betsy had to badger him about virtually everything.

Despite her ongoing supervisory nagging, Carson never took her evaluation personally. It bounced off him like the proverbial water off a duck's back. He was Betsy's "Odie." She was his "Garfield." Carson or "CC", as he liked to be called, always had a smile, always had a glad-hand out, always meant well, and often managed to screw something up. Betsy would never forget the first time she had met Carson. She had not even officially started her the job yet. Carson had taken the stock from a liquor store as the payoff on a loan. The bank lobby had been stacked with cases full of bottles of booze. As word got out, it seemed like every wino in town descended on the bank. When she went to regional meetings other area managers still teased her about the incident.

"I'm here to support my wife, Cass. Cass recently became a CANDO distributor, and they're a major sponsor for this shindig. Are you guys into CANDO too?"

"CANDO is one of several sponsors. The bank is a major underwriter as well," Betsy said.

"I didn't know that," Carson said.

"You obviously missed that meeting," Betsy said sarcastically.

Carson shrugged and said, "Well I guess you can't be everywhere. I may have been at Rotary. You know a super-banker has to stay out there flying the flag. I'm not going to make a living selling banking services to fellow bankers."

"I also had Margaret send out an e-mail about our involvement in this event," said Betsy.

He smiled, showing a gap between his front teeth, "I guess I missed that too."

He quickly grabbed his wife's arm before the conversation could continue.

"Cass, there's someone I want you to meet," he said.

Carson's wife joined them. Like Carson, she was a big person. Big boned, big hands and feet, and like him, chunky. She smiled meekly but sincerely and held out her hand.

"Boss lady, I'd like you to meet Mrs. CC, my wife, my better half and the mother of little CC," Carson said. "Mrs. CC, I'd like you to meet Betsy Black, the president of our bank I've told you so much about. Boss lady, I'm real proud of this special little lady. She's going to make me a rich man before little CC, our son Calvin, goes to college. All she's got to do is recruit ten distributors like herself, and the Crowns will be wearing a crown. They'll be on easy street. Shoot, she might even make more money than I do. She's already signed up her mother to be her first distributor. Her aunt Katherine will be next."

"Well, that sounds like a good start. I certainly hope it works out," Betsy said. Cass looked embarrassed and turned red.

"And wait until you see me bring CANDO's banking relationship into the bank. They can't wait to do business with a super-banker. I'll blow all my goals away," Carson said and pretended to hit an imaginary ball with an imaginary bat. Grand slam. Home run," he announced.

"Make sure you don't hit the ball through a window," Betsy said.

Carson gave her a slightly puzzled look, but then his face lit up again as he saw someone across the room. "Gator," he bellowed and flapped his arms in a chopping motion to signify the Gator cheer. With no further hesitation or thoughts about continuing their talk, he left, his glad-hand out to greet his next target.

The next thing they heard was Carson on the bandstand in his Preparation H Ointment costume singing "Ring Of Fire".

"What an asshole," Betsy whispered to Will.

Cass overhead her but just stood there and looked embarrassed or at a loss for words.

"We're sponsoring the band," Cass said, not knowing what else to say. "The lead singer is a member of our organization.

They listened to the band play one of their Christian rock songs, "Faithful Father".

The band had been formed locally several years back. At first they played mostly for Club Tropic establishments in the Keys and developed a reputation as a hard-rocking, substance-abusing group. After the band's leader almost overdosed on cocaine at a strip club on Truman Avenue in Key West, he began to attend services at the Green Rainbow Ashram in Key West where he met Madelyn Koury-O'Dare. The band then began to occasionally play Christian rock for CANDO functions. They worked off some of their drug debts by selling the rights to one of their songs to Club Tropic. After Club Tropic's demise these rights ended up the property of Adolfo Soltero who had the band taken to a studio to record it. The song began to get local radio play and had broken out on the Christian rock charts. Now the band was in constant demand, and the boys were considered local celebrities.

Finally after they listened to a couple of numbers Cass said, "Would you like to meet the founder of CANDO? She's standing over there."

"We would love to," Will said.

Cass led them towards a thin middle-aged woman in a floor length dress. She wore practical strap-on sandals. Her hair was pulled back tightly from her face accentuating high cheek bones. She was well tanned and had an almost middle-eastern look. When Will and Betsy approached they noticed she wore virtually no makeup.

"Mr. and Mrs. Black, may I introduce you to the founder of CANDO, Sun Raye?" Cass said.

They shook hands and exchanged pleasantries.

"That's an unusual name," Will commented. "Very catchy."

"I adopted this name in conjunction with my ministry," Sun Raye said.

"Oh," Betsy said. "I thought you marketed skin products."

"I do," Sun Raye said, "but I'm also pastor of the Cosmic Ray Scientific Church of Prosperity, formerly Kingdom Hall on Little Torch Key."

"Oh, you're the ones who bought the Jehovah's Witness building," Will said.

"That's correct."

"You must have lots of followers," Will said. "We live near there, and there seems to be a meeting happening in the building almost every day."

"We are a growing sect. God has blessed our efforts," Sun Raye said. She then asked Will and Betsy about their profession and seemed impressed with their responses.

"May I have an appointment one day to discuss a possible banking relationship?" she asked.

Of course, what do you have in mind?" Betsy asked.

"I've been told I need a merchant banking relationship," Sun Raye answered.

"Since you know the Crowns, would you like for me to include Carson in our discussion?" Betsy asked.

"Number '1's' are accustomed to dealing with fellow number '1's'," Sun Raye said, looking Cass in the eye.

"Then by all means, call my secretary, Margaret, and make an appointment."

They exchanged business cards.

As Will and Betsy turned to leave, they heard a familiar blustering voice clearly from across the room, "Want a coldbeer? It's on my tab."

Cass excused herself and went to join her husband.

Betsy winced and hurried Will toward the parking lot before CC could collar them again.

CHAPTER 23

Police Chief Walter Wanderley sank down on a chair in Betsy's office. Margaret immediately went to fetch him a cup of coffee to go with the bag of fresh bagels he had in his hand.

"Long time, no see," Betsy said. "This must be the police department's week for working."

Walter waited until Margaret got back with the coffee.

"I'm hungry. I didn't get anything on the way to work this morning because I figured you were overdue to bring some goodies in," Margaret said.

"So what's new?" asked Betsy.

"Every once in a while an arrest leads to the solution of something totally unrelated," Walter said. Yesterday one of my men arrested a bicycle rider on Whitehead Street. He was wearing a dress that was just a little too short for him."

"So what's wrong with that? After all, this is Key West," Margaret said.

"It would have been fine if he had been wearing some underwear," said Walter. "Every time he pedaled the bike he exposed himself."

"Why is it that I'm never at the right place at the right time?" Margaret said and giggled. "Did he have anything worth showing off?"

"I'll let you be the judge of that," Walter said. "It's not my week for boys. We also got him for public intoxication and resisting arrest since he tried to outrun the patrol car on his bike."

"I'm starting to visualize this whole scene," Betsy said.

"He ran his bike into a fence and turned over," Walter continued. "When he did, all the contents of his handlebar basket fell out on the sidewalk."

He paused to take a bite of bagel and sip his coffee.

"Don't leave us in suspense," Margaret said. "So what was in the basket?"

"Women's underwear," Walter said. "We've been getting reports that someone has been breaking and entering and then stealing women's undergarments off of clotheslines along Whitehead. Looks like he's our man."

"I think you're using the term 'man' loosely," Betsy said. "One consolation, if he was stealing them off clotheslines, he wasn't a sniffer."

"That probably wasn't the only kind of line he was sniffing. You should come by more often," Margaret said, "and not just because you bring goodies. The other morsels you bring are every bit as good, and a lot less fattening."

"I hate to cut all this merriment short," said Betsy, "but I have an appointment due in here most any time.

At that moment, Carson arrived with Sun Raye.

The meeting about opening a merchant banking relationship then revealed how little Ms. Raye understood the concept. As Betsy explained what the bank would need from her organization to get credit approval, she realized Ms. Raye seemed not only confused but preoccupied.

"My accountant said that all we had to do was ask a bank to handle credit card sales and they would jump at the chance," said Sun Raye.

"Certainly that is a starting point for establishing this service," said Betsy. "However, there is pertinent information required about your company to get this service set up. We will also need financial information on CANDO so we can provide you with the limited discount charges on your sales."

"What do you mean by discount?" asked Sun Raye.

Betsy calmly began to explain the term as she discreetly broke the pencil in her hand that was under her desk.

"A discount is a percentage of the sale the bank retains from each sale to pay for processing this credit card service for your company." Betsy continued, "The smaller the discount, the greater the percentage of each sale your company will retain. To determine this discount, the bank would review current financial data on CANDO, determine the average sale size and the potential number of sales CANDO will make via credit cards versus other payment methods."

"Oh, I think I understand," said Sun Raye. "But I also want your bank to process credit cards for the church."

Betsy looked around for another pencil to break.

CHAPTER 24

Betsy listened to the radio as she drove to the former Kingdom Hall building. The Vince Guaraldi Trio was playing "Cast Your Fate To The Wind" on the radio. She was thinking it had been a long time since she had heard that song; how appropriate that this should be playing as she drove to her appointment with Sun Raye.

Betsy looked at her watch as she came across Niles Channel. She was running right on schedule. She was almost phobic about being punctual for appointments. She wondered what the inside of the building would look like. She and Will had seen it so many times from US 1, but she never thought she'd actually go in it. Betsy was looking forward to the meeting since the news she would be reporting was the successful underwriting of CANDO.

As Betsy parked her car in the almost empty parking lot, she looked around for the front door to the building. Although she had driven past this former Kingdom Hall facility many times, she had never paid much attention to the building since it was at the intersection and across the street from the turn into her residential subdivision.

A quick glance at the building revealed what she assumed to be the front door. There was no signage present so she knocked at the door. Nor was there any response so Betsy gently opened the door and walked in, calling out, "Hello. Is anyone here?"

"I'll be with you in a moment," a receptionist's voice called out in return as the phone rang. Instead of picking up the ringing phone, she hit her speaker button.

"CRSCP," the receptionist said.

Betsy saw a scaffold in the back of the large meeting room.

"Is this the YMCA?" came the voice from the other end of the line.

"No, this is Cosmic Ray Scientific Church of Prosperity," said the receptionist.

"That's not the same as the YMCA?" the voice said.

"No, we are affiliated with CANDO," the receptionist replied. "We're a cosmetics company."

Betsy heard a dull *thunk* from the back of the large room.

"Oh," the voice said uncertainly. "May I speak the person in charge about a job?"

"She is predisposed with a previous commitment," the receptionist said. "May I give her a message to call you back?"

"Only if she'll be able to call within the hour," the voice said.

"I pray she will," the receptionist said.

"Oh ... alright ... But you don't have to pray for that."

Betsy heard another *thunk*.

"It's no trouble at all," the receptionist said.

"Nah, really. Don't bother ... I'm an atheist."

There was a long pause before the receptionist said, "I'll pray for you too," and hung up. She turned to Betsy, "Now, may I help you?"

"My name is Betsy Black from WB Bank," Betsy said. "I have an appointment with Sun Raye ... and you don't have to pray for me."

"I'll be down in a moment. Let me finish this star," Sun Raye's voice called out. "Come on back. Would you like some coffee?"

"No, thanks,"

Betsy heard another *thunk*.

"Bobby, now stop that," Sun Raye said.

"I thought you didn't mind if I play 'pin the tail on the jackass'," Bobby said. "I guess you know this broad's got Zacoly disease."

"And that is?" Sun Raye replied with a sigh.

"Her face is Zacoly like her ass," Bobby said and laughed heartily at himself.

Betsy walked across the room and saw Sun Raye lying on her back atop the scaffold. She was painting stars on the room's tall ceiling. Bobby Perez was leaning back in a folding chair with his feet propped up on another folding chair. He was lazily throwing darts at a "Time" magazine portrait of Hillary Clinton which he had stapled to the bottom of the scaffold.

So that was the thunks I heard, thought Betsy. *Hillary's fan club in session.*

Sun Raye climbed down from the scaffold. She had a few smears of paint on her sunburst tie-dyed clothing. She then introduced Betsy to Bobby Perez and told Betsy he was not only her son-in-law but also an officer of the corporation. Sun Raye invited Bobby to join them for their meeting.

"Underwriting has approved a merchant banking account for CANDO," Betsy told Sun Raye. "I'm here to go over the details, explain any questions you might have, and arrange to set up the paperwork for the account."

Bobby was not only completely unsophisticated but completely bored by banking matters, but Sun Raye insisted Betsy start with the basics. Betsy struggled to explain to Bobby the credit card payment gateway and how it captured and secured credit card information and then transmitted this data through the bank's private processing network. She then explained how the bank responded to this information by authorizing or declining each transaction. Bobby lazily lined up jelly beans on the desk according to color and then lobbed them at an empty fish bowl about a foot away. Betsy went over the cost of the service and gave them an overview of the equipment that would be involved. Bobby made a teeter-totter with a ruler and tried to flip any odd jelly beans into his mouth. Betsy ignored him and pressed on. Both Sun Raye and Bobby acknowledged that they understood very little of what Betsy had said and suggested Betsy talk to Luis on another day. It was obvious to Betsy that Sun Raye wished to return to painting stars on the ceiling and Bobby mainly wished to resume throwing darts at Hillary Clinton.

This is going to be a doozy of a relationship, she thought. *Maybe I should have sent Carson. Actually it's not too late to assign Carson this account. He'd jump at the opportunity. I'll just tell them I'm still on the account overseeing Carson.*

Betsy found herself humming "Cast Your Fate To The Wind" as she drove back to the bank.

CHAPTER 25

Seasoned securities brokers are quite a resilient bunch. They are accustomed to having some of their successes and failures being controlled to a great extent by human psychology, complete with its foibles and shortcomings. They are accustomed to not being able to control markets, economic data, the direction of interest rates, the political climate, or a myriad of other critical variables. On most days, they even have limited control of their own schedules. They have simply learned to roll with the punches, and on some days taking more shots than others. This was evolving into being one of those days.

While Will sat in his office, the phone rang. It was Meg Davis calling to tell him that the proxy on her Tel-Mex stock had again arrived only two days before it was due back in. She said this did not leave her enough time to read the enclosed material and make an intelligent decision on their proposed slate of directors. She demanded that Will get the head of the RST proxy department to call Tel-Mex in Mexico City and secure a promise it wouldn't happen again.

"Meg, we're only a conduit for information. We can only send out what is sent to us. And after all, this is a foreign stock. May I suggest you might be happier with a domestic telephone stock?"

"Young man, you know I have a sentimental attachment to that stock since I inherited it from my Aunt

Louise," she responded. "Do I need to remind you that *I am the client?*"

The client where my compensation is never commensurate with my efforts, Will thought. *The client who hasn't put in an order for four years. The client who thought she should begin receiving money market interest the day she mailed him a deposit.*

"I'll see what I can do, Meg," he said with a sigh.

"See that you do that," she said and hung up.

Will looked up and saw his sales assistant, Barbara, standing in front of him. Jonathan Harris is here to see you."

"Show him in."

Harris told Will he had fallen prey to a mystery shopper scam when he cashed checks for almost $1,900.

"I clicked on an Internet ad for a company advertising for mystery shoppers," he said. "The company sent me checks last month and instructed me to deposit them. I was told to keep $200 and mail the balance through Western Union to another secret shopper in Colombia. But their check bounced and your people are telling me I'm responsible for the money. They're saying I could face criminal charges."

"Yes, you are responsible, Jonathan," Will said. "Why did you get involved with something that sounded too good to be true? You should have known there are no free lunches out there."

"I guess you're right. I feel so stupid in retrospect. Would you sell enough of one of my mutual funds to pay for it?"

"I'll take care of it."

"And you won't charge me anything?"

"I have no control over mutual fund loads."

Soon after Harris left, Barbara came back in.

"Mary Perez is here to see you," she said.

She brought Mary in.

"Do you remember me?" Mary began. "I'm Madelyn Koury-O'Dare's daughter."

"Sure, we met at the benefit," Will said. His mind flashed to CC in the Preparation H costume. "What can I do for you? I thought you went by the name Sea Raye."

"That's my spiritual name. I answer to both," Mary said. "The reason I'm here is one of our subsidiaries is a management company that sponsors and sells a mutual fund for socially responsible investors. We currently have one fund appropriately entitled Chosen Ones Growth Fund. It is the first fund of what we expect to be an entire family of socially responsible funds. My purpose in calling on you today is to familiarize you with this opportunity and to tell you how it can enhance your practice. You are one of the most respected financial advisors in Monroe County - the kind of person we want on our team. Our fund invests with a total-return discipline that is coming into its own. You will find that there are more socially responsible investors than you might think and their numbers are growing."

"Thanks for holding me in such high regard, Mary," Will said, "but I am restricted by my firm on the products I can sell. In order for me to be able sell your product, Reynolds Smathers and Thompson would have to sign a national sales agreement. Otherwise I would be guilty of what is called 'selling away.' The penalty for selling away is to be sanctioned or possibly terminated."

"So you're saying you do have to be granted the authority to sell our products."

"That is correct, and I'll be very honest with you, our home office would never sign a sales agreement unless they do a thorough due-diligence investigation, and they would probably not have much incentive to do this investigation if they thought the product would only have local appeal."

"We foresee this being a much larger market. Would moving CANDO's 401-k to you give you the incentive to go to bat for us?"

"I'm only one small person in a large organization," Will said.

"We could find other possibly non-taxable ways to sweeten the pot and make it worth your while," Mary said. "Think about it."

She got up and made her departure.

Man, oh man, Will thought. *These people are ethical investors, yet they're willing to pay me under the table. I wonder what other surprises the day will bring.*

"Will, its Meg Davis on the line again," Barbara said. "Something about she thinks her statement should have been delivered a few days ago. I told her I'd mail her a duplicate immediately, but she still wants to talk to you."

CHAPTER 26

Cass Crown was in a dither. She was excited; yet she was scared. She had given dinner parties for a few guests before, but never a business party, one that had an objective of closing sales. Her husband Carson, after all was the sales person in the family. In her eyes he was the family superstar. He often reminded her how her mother had been wrong about him. He was after all Key West's super-banker, indispensible to WB Bank. He told her how Betsy Black catered to him as her most valuable producer and used him as an example in her sales meetings. With Carson's guidance, Cass knew her party would certainly be a success, and she would be off and running in her first step to become as important to CANDO as her husband was to WB Bank.

Carson suggested they do something different than just give a run-of-the-mill house party. They would plan this soirée around the recreational vehicle Carson had bought several seasons back to go to University of Florida games. The RV was an old school bus. The stop signs were still functional, but instead of STOP, they now said GO GATORS as the lights on the signs alternately flashed blue and orange. He had painted "CC" on the rear in large letters so they would be easy to find in crowded game parking lots. Below the letters it said, "Swamp Buggy." The bus was no longer yellow but had been custom-painted orange and blue and had a huge gator mural painted on each side. The horn sounded like an alligator singing during mating season. He added a toilet in the back of the bus. The door announced "CC's Head." Cass sighed when she thought about how the money they paid each month on the credit line could be being used, but Carson loved that bus like a new puppy. Carson wasn't much on helping her with household chores, but he got out a ladder and washed that bus from stem to stern at least once a month. Maybe now it would finally begin to pay for itself, she rationalized.

Carson kept the bus parked in their driveway. It was a constant source of friction with the homeowner's association. The topic inevitably became a topic of discussion at annual homeowners' meetings. Carson's response – he quit attending the meetings. After all, he rationalized, *it's not an eyesore. It is a magnificent piece of rolling art. They're just jealous.*

Carson's first inclination was to have Cass's CANDO coming-out party at either KOA on Sugarloaf Key or Boyd's on Stock Island, but the more he thought about it, the more he wanted just to do it right there at the house. He would show those assholes from the homeowners' association. Just wait until they saw what an entertainment treasure his bus really was.

Cass decided on a menu of gumbo, collard greens, French bread, and Hoppin' John for the party. She went to a fabric store and bought lengths of fabric in bright colors to use for tablecloths. She found some really neat paper place mats at The Pepper Store on Greene Street in Key West that looked like red bandanas and found a large tissue paper and cardboard "shrimp" centerpiece at a party supply store. She decided to use empty tomato cans as vases for fresh flowers. She even ordered pepper and Tabasco themed tropical shirts from the High Seas catalogue for herself and Carson. She decided she would play zydeco and Cajun music as background music. This was going to be the recruiting party to top all recruiting parties. Everyone would want to be invited to her future functions.

The more she prepared the more excited Cass became. She had a 16-quart stockpot to use to cook the gumbo, a Nesco 4-quart cooker for the greens, and a crock-pot for the Hoppin' John. Everything except the French bread would be pre-prepared.

CC was equally into his part of the planning since this party would give him a chance to really show off his precious bus. He would back the bus into the driveway. He would cover the GO GATOR stop-sign with a paper one saying "CANDO Sunscreen." He even bought a life-size cardboard Elvis to put on the roof of the bus. The cardboard Elvis would have a sandwich sign saying "CANDO Skin Products" while Bobby J, a local Elvis impersonator would be handing out sunscreen samples. CC planned to sit in the driver's seat of the bus, turn on the stop-signs each time a guest arrived, and then hit the gator horn to welcome them. Each of these could also be activated by a remote. Carson found pepper covers for some of his Christmas tree lights which he then strung from both the bus and the trees in the yard. He even special-ordered an inflatable palm tree cooler for the Abita and Crescent City beer he had special ordered. Yes, this was going to be one helluva a party. Yes, he was doing exceedingly well.

The day before the big party Cass asked Carson to run by Fishbusterz on Stock Island on his way home from work and pick up the seafood she needed. Unfortunately for him, Betsy called a staff meeting that afternoon at four o'clock. Since Carson planned to bail early the next day, he figured he had better attend. About lunchtime he began to get nervous thinking Fishbusterz might be closed if the meeting ran longer than he expected so he decided to buy the seafood during lunch just to be on the safe side. I'll just tell them to put some ice on it, and it should be just fine, he rationalized.

That afternoon when the meeting adjourned, Carson headed for home. The ice had melted in the hot car, but when he smelled his purchase it still seemed fresh to him. It would make outstanding gumbo. He knew Cass might be suspect though, so he headed by Dion's, drained the water out of the bag, and then refilled it with ice he bought. Cass will never be the wiser, he reasoned. Yes, this is going to be one helluva party.

The next evening guests began to arrive. Carson had purposely chosen the night that election results were being reported. He moved a TV into the yard. Cass had doubts about CC's plan. She thought the plan was far too complicated. Her husband insisted that this would add a whole new dimension to the affair. Yes, he reassured her, trust the expert. They were going to have a ball. This party would be legendary.

As guests arrived that evening, Carson flashed the stop-sign and honked at each of them in turn. Elvis then greeted each guest and handed them a bottle of sunscreen. He would then tell them, "Thank you for coming. Thank you very much." Things seemed to be going well, but the more the alligator horn *sang*, the more irritated one of his neighbors became. Every time the horn would sing, their neighbor's dog, Banshee, would go nuts. After the dog peed all over his newly installed Berber carpet, the irate neighbor reported the noise to the sheriff's department.

In all about thirty guests finally arrived, including several people from the bank. Carson was pleased that Jennifer Jacquette, a teller decided to attend. Cass had identified her as a serious prospect to become a distributor. The party was in full swing when the sheriff's deputy arrived.

Chubby Carrier's zydeco recording of *Cisco Kid* was playing loudly in the yard when the deputy drove up. Carson recognized him and made the gator horn *sing* in his honor. That's when Carson knew his intuition had been right. It was going to be a helluva party, not just another exceedingly outstanding evening.

"Tom Wallace! You old son-of-a-gun," CC called out. "How are things in the world of crime busting? How 'bout them Gators!"

"I'm doing well," the deputy replied. "How are you?"

"Exceedingly well," CC said. "What brings you out our way?"

"I got a call from one of your neighbors about excessive noise," Tom said. "I see you're having a party. You're going to have to hold it down. That horn you blew at me when I drove up. Promise me – no more of that."

"Cass is having CANDO distributors over to see the

election results and talk up CANDO. I guess we got a little carried away. Sorry you had to drive all the way over here, but we are going to make the drive worth your while. Got some world class gumbo in the pot! Why doncha have a bowl as long as you're already here?" Carson said.

"I don't know. I'm on duty..." Tom said.

"Oh, Tom, you're here anyway. I'm not asking you to drink on duty. You're going to eat somewhere. This will beat the hell out of the junk food you usually eat on your shift. Everybody knows gumbo is the ambrosia of the Gods – food to die for. It's Cass's mama's secret recipe."

CC started singing off key the Jimmy Buffett song
I don't smoke I don't shoot smack
But I got a spicy monkey riding on my back
Don't eat beignets too much sugar and dough
But I will play for gumbo

"OK, OK, but just one bowl," said Tom. "Just quit singing."

"Cass, serve this fine man some of your flowing flawless fare."

The deputy ate a heaping bowl and turned to go.

"No more disturbance," he said. "You promise?"

"You have my word as a gentleman," said CC. "You have a good evening."

As soon as the deputy left, CC took a disposable plastic bowl of gumbo to his neighbor and apologized for the noise. When he returned, CC started clanging a dinner bell to let everyone know it was time to dine. The group was soon chowing down and talking politics as they watched the early election results come in. Elvis joined them. Everyone was especially interested in the Florida results.

Two political novices were running for governor. A couple of political hacks were running for the U.S House of Representatives. A widow was running for her deceased husband's Senate seat. It was anything but politics as usual. Carson had CANDO marketing material by every plate.

A fishbowl full of names and addresses sat in the middle of one table. It would to be used later in the evening to draw door prizes.

Irene Carroll excused herself about the time she finished her first bowl to go to the powder room in the back of the bus. Cass noticed she looked a little piqued when she returned. Doris Smith also soon asked to use the same restroom. She too was very quiet when she returned. Elvis downed a second bowl of gumbo followed by a big bowl of Hoppin' John.

The Fox announcer came back on the air. "We have declared winners in three more races. The Senatorial race in Utah will go to the Republican incumbent, Orrin Hatch. Not surprisingly Democratic incumbent John Kerry will be returned to his post for another six years in Massachusetts. In a surprise move voters have not chosen to return Democrat Nancy Pelosi of California to the House. With us is former President Bill Clinton to discuss the implications of Pelosi's ouster."

People jumped up and began to cheer. Valerie Vest suddenly let go with a torrent of projectile vomit that covered Bill Clinton's image. He dripped with undigested shrimp, tomato, and okra. Cass happened to glance at Elvis. His jump suit was starting to turn brown as a watery diarrhea worked its way down his legs. One by one, people began running for whatever facilities were available in either the bus or the house. Some made it; some didn't. Soon there was a line in front of every available toilet. When the line didn't move fast enough, some people lost control of their bowels as they stood waiting.

Cast-iron stomach CC, who had had two bowls of gumbo himself, began to feel queasy. *What's wrong?* He asked himself. *I never get a stomach ache.*

About that time the bus was rendered more or less useless. Up-chuck covered most of the seats. CC's Head was out of toilet paper, stopped up, and was totally disgusting. Gene Holiman had lost control of his bowels on the toilet while at the same time vomiting down the underwear that was rolled up around his ankles.

Cass was horrified as she watched Bess Trooper. Bess was an older lady who was known for her prim and proper ways. Cass had always thought Bess was the most ladylike person she knew. She was horrified to see Bess grab the fishbowl with the door-prize names. Bess put the bowl up to her mouth and began to barf. The tickets were soon immersed in a bilious green bile.

She was even more shocked to see a woman she had never met sit on the decorative crab trap in their yard and let a volley of diarrhea fly. She saw their former friends squatting in the vacant lot next to the Crown home as others began to throw up in the canal.

In the background Cass vaguely heard the Fox announcer say, "The state of Florida gubernatorial race is still too close to call."

"CARSON," she called out desperately.

About that time Cass heard a strained voice, "YOU

SON-OF-A-BITCH!"

As Cass turned she saw a sunscreen bottle flying through the air. It caught Carson between the eyes breaking his glasses. When the bottle hit him, Carson lost control of his already weakened system and launched both bowls of gumbo he had eaten in a giant puke projectile, hitting Cass between her cleavage. Until then Cass had been one of the few people who had not been sick. She had been so busy serving that she had not had time to eat any of the gumbo, choosing to lightly munch on a piece of French bread. She was frozen in place as CC's gumbo ran down her sundress and out the bottom forming a puddle on her new shoes.

Cass turned to see a big black lab bounding towards what was left of the serving table. She instantly recognized the dog as Banshee, the dog belonging to the neighbor who had called in the complaint an hour earlier. The owner was limping bow-legged behind his dog, shaking his fist, yelling, "Get him, Banshee." He stopped suddenly, bent over, and a new eruption surged forth. The dog leaped on the serving table sending food and pots everywhere. The hot Nesco cooker dumped collard greens on Elvis's lap, causing him to jump up, trip on Jennifer Jacquette, and crap on himself again. The gumbo dumped on the table. Banshee voraciously lapped it up.

When Banchee failed to attack CC, the Crown's irate neighbor grabbed CC and started to choke him. The remote in CC's pocket set off the gator-horn again and it began to sing loudly. The neighbor only let go when Cass threw what was left of the Hoppin' John at him. CC scrambled away and hid behind the bus. The remote in

Carson's pocket set off the gator horn again and it began to *sing*. Behind them on the CD player she heard Buckwheat Zydeco singing "Feets Don't Fail Me Now".

Cass heard a siren. When she looked she saw the EMT truck. Jason Pearson was running towards her. He stopped dead in his tracks and looked around. The yard looked like a war zone. Sick people were everywhere. Jason slid down in the slime. The paramedics almost didn't know where to start. An ambulance arrived and started to load the casualties.

After the guests were gone, CC and Cass walked around their house. The stench was overpowering. Brown smears ran up and down most walls. Every bathroom was out of order. The bus was a disaster. The yard was torn up. CC's party flag was covered with vomit. She even found puke in her waist-high decorator bamboo vases. Some people had just abandoned soiled underwear on the lawn. Cass started to cry. CC comforted his wife and offered to take her to a hotel for the night. He pledged he would get a maid service over to clean first thing in the morning. Yes, it had been one helluva party! And Carson's prediction had been right on target. Everyone would talk about this function for a long, long time.

CHAPTER 27

Will was so involved reading a new report that had just hit his desk entitled "The Coming US Industrial Replacement Cycle: Planes, Trucks, and Automobiles" that he did not hear the tap on his door. He looked up to see Jock Jacquette standing there.

"You look so engrossed that you wouldn't have heard a fire alarm go off," Jock said.

"You're right," Will replied. "As an accountant you'd probably find this report equally interesting. It's about how capital spending has been running below depreciation, making old equipment pervasive in many areas and where the resulting case for replacement looks most compelling."

"I have some clients who'd probably like to read that report," Jock said.

"I'll run you a copy. So what do I owe the pleasure of this visit?" Will asked.

"I want to liquidate my mutual funds," Jock said.

"May I ask why?" Will asked. "Has the performance not been up to your expectations? Have your investment objectives changed? Have I done something I shouldn't have?"

"No," said Jock. "I just feel there are other opportunities out there that might fit my needs better."

"Jock," said Will. "I urge you to think this over. The American Funds you own are some of the premier funds we sell, and they complement each other well. AMCAP's main focus is investing in companies that have a proven track record of growing sales per share, earnings per share, or cash flow per share. The Growth Fund of America has even a broader investment discipline. It can buy any company that the portfolio counselors and analysts believe will have price appreciation."

"I know they are great funds, but I want to move in a different direction."

"Jock, these funds have accomplished their goals. My latest material shows Growth Fund of American has produced a return for the life of the fund of 13.62% per year and AMCAP's record is 11.2%. On top of that their expense ratios are also some of the lowest in the industry."

"But I feel I need to be more aggressive. I'm not getting any younger," Jock said.

"Jock, keep this in mind. You paid a sales load to buy the American funds. You will have to pay another sales load to buy a different fund. Between the two loads you will have paid approximately 10% of your investment capital."

"I know, I can easily make that up with the right fund."

"Did you have a specific fund in mind?"

"Yes, I do." Jock said. "I want to buy into Chosen Ones Growth Fund. Can I do that through you?"

"I'm afraid you can't," Will said. "Our firm has not done due-diligence of that fund. I guess you know it is a recent start-up."

"I know. That's one thing that makes it exciting," Jock said.

"Where did you hear about this fund?"

"My wife Jennifer is a CANDO distributor. She was sponsored by Cass Crown. The fund made a presentation and gave her some literature about it at one of their meetings. It really sounds exciting. It had an 82% return over the last twelve months, and we both know that was way above the market. All I need is a few years like that, and I'll be in high cotton. You really ought to look at it for yourself. I was hoping I could get it through you, but I guess I'll have to buy it directly from them," said Jock. "When will my money be available?"

"What do you know about the fund? Did you get a prospectus?"

"No, but nobody ever reads those things anyway. Just legal mumbo-jumbo. All I know is the fund is making money hand over fist, and I want it to make money for me."

"Do you understand the risk factors?" Will asked. "What goes up can also come down."

"I was warned you would try to throw mud on their proposal. These guys are investment professionals who have an inside track to good ideas not on most people's radar screens. You had to be there and hear them. They looked like professionals and talked like professionals. This is not small time Keys thinking. These boys have connections and are tied in to where things are happening. Do I know what makes the engine in my car run? HELL NO! I just know when I get in my car and crank the engine, it gets me where I want to go." Jock insisted.

"Jock, sounds like your mind is made up, and I want to go on record as being opposed to this, but I can't stop you. After all, it is your money. Do you want me to leave the rest of your accounts as is?"

"Yes, for the time being. For once I'm going to be right. I'm going to buy this fund before it gets discovered by the masses. Who knows? I may be on the ground floor of the next Fidelity Magellan. You'll see," said Jock. "Like I said, I only need a few of those good years."

Later that day Will received a phone call from Bobby Perez.

"I'm Mildred Perez's husband," Bobby said.

"Mildred?"

"You probably know her as Blue Raye ... Sun Raye's daughter," Bobby said. "Jock Jacquette just left our office. I bought Chosen Ones Growth Fund for him," he said. "He said you tried very hard to discourage him from buying the fund. He said you even intimated that the fund might not be on the up-and-up."

"I only said I didn't feel the change was in his best interest."

"His or yours? As my sister-in-law tried to explain to you a few days ago, there is a demand for this fund. This train is leaving the station whether you choose to be on it or not. It's not too late. We will forget your error this time. Attribute it to inexperience or lack of facts. You can still be part of our team. It's up to you. You can also still be custodian of CANDO's 401-k, but that won't be the case unless you are considered a friend. Get my drift? By the way, there will be an ACAT account transfer coming through on his other accounts. Think about what I've said, and think next time before you speak. A wise man confines his opinions to subjects he understands."

The phone went dead. Jock would not return his phone calls.

CHAPTER 28

Will had learned not to be thin-skinned. He had learned long ago that a broker can't control everything, whether it was markets or client psychology. He knew often clients listen; often they don't. He was also keenly aware that he could only do so much to keep some clients from being their own worst enemies, and that sometimes their farfetched attempts at hitting home runs actually defied the odds and succeeded. This he could accept. He was not always right. After all investing was a qualitative science which involved making risk decisions about the unknown. But the nature and tone of his conversation with Bobby Perez really rankled him. He wasn't used to losing face and then having another sales person call him and rudely rub it in - and even in a subtle way threaten him. The more he thought about it, the more irate he became.

He finally gave Guy Walsh in Vero Beach a call.

"Got a second for me to vent?" Will said. He then reviewed his meeting with Jock Jacquette and repeated his conversation with Bobby Perez. "I'm not used to being treated like that jerk treated me."

"You know me well enough to know I'd be livid if I had been on the receiving end of that phone call," Guy said. "I guess their strong-arm tactics are to be expected. They fall right in line with their investment methodology I described to you at the Square Grouper. These bums have a small amount of money with which they are using to make big bets on illiquid over-the-counter stocks...not what you and I consider a prudent investment strategy. The fund's biggest position is a multi-level marketing company named CANDO."

"We were so busy talking about other things that night at the Square Grouper, I neglected to tell you that CANDO is headquartered out of the lower Keys," added Will. "If it's not a pyramid scheme, it's remarkably similar. Reminds me of Ramway. You remember their landmark case don't you?"

"Sure" said Guy. "It was a precedent-setting case. The Supreme Court ruled that Ramway was not a pyramid scheme because it had a product to sell."

"Exactly. CANDO is using the same strategy. They are staying legal by selling skin care products," said Will.

"I've been researching CANDO further since we spent the weekend with you," Guy continued. "Some of its financial ratios are frightening. Their EBITDA is very low translating into almost no earnings per share. This renders their price-earnings ratio into one that is stratospheric. The return on assets and return on capital are both extremely low despite their low tax bracket. It doesn't get any better when you run a risk adjusted return on capital. The cash ratio sucks. I would have a hard time sleeping if my debt to equity ratio mirrored theirs. The only ratio that seemed under control was their average collection period on their accounts receivable."

"In other words, they may not be able to pay their bills, but they sure know how to collect if you owe them money," said Will laughing. "Are you trying to say their accounts receivable manager is Guido with the broken nose and brass knuckles?"

"Could be more validity to your observation that these guys may be knuckle draggers than you think," Guy said. "Ralph Ness's group, 21st Century Securities, sponsored an investment seminar on the Chosen Ones Growth Fund at Costa d'Este in Vero that was complete with a sit-down lunch and door prizes. Had two out-of-town experts named Talbos and Chamberlain as keynote speakers. I understand they really put a one-sided hard sell on those attending. Dick Jackson and one of his golfing partners decided to attend just as a lark."

"You've had Dick's account for years," Will said.

"Sure have, and I never once worried about somebody snaking him from me. If Dick has a weakness, it's that he has analysis paralysis. He studies everything to death. It has always been frustrating when I tried to convince him to do something that was time sensitive."

"I know the type," Will said. "Ultra-conservative and ultra-cautious."

"That's Dick. Well, he went to the seminar and then scheduled an appointment with me to discuss the material. He even left it with me, and we were scheduled to reconvene the next week.

"The next thing I know I'm getting transfer forms on the account, an account I've had for over twenty years. I tried to call him to find out what was going on. The ACATS said it was going to 21st Century Securities."

"I definitely would have followed up on that situation," Will said.

"He wouldn't return my phone calls," Guy said. "This

is the guy I moved heaven and earth for after he and his wife Rachel got their clocks cleaned in Hurricane Clarice."

"He kept ducking me and ducking me. Finally I ran into him at Fresh Market. I reminded him of the relationship we had had and told him I thought he owed me an explanation. I don't think I've ever seen anyone look more uncomfortable. All he wanted to do was get away from me. Mumbled that he couldn't talk about it."

"I thought he was a bigger man that that," Will said.

"I ran into him again about a week later. I again asked for an explanation. He finally admitted he had bought Chosen Ones Growth Fund after the seminar. A religious mutual fund - shit! Dick Jackson has never seen the inside of a church since he was christened. He always played golf on Sundays. I kept pushing. This was so out of character. I asked him point blank why he had bothered to bring the sales material to my office if he had already decided to buy it. He finally admitted that his son Chip had been found a few days later with crack cocaine in his car, and Rodney Chamberlain at 21st had made the problem disappear. He wouldn't say any more. He only said that friendship was one thing but blood was something else. Can you believe he actually cried?"

"Wow! Maybe I have underestimated these shysters," was all Will could manage to say.

"I think we both have," Guy replied.

CHAPTER 29

Living in Monroe County, Florida, is rarely dull. Many adjectives have been used to paint a word picture of it - tolerant, permissive, odd, uninhibited, insane, decadent, corrupt, utopian - but dull has normally not been one of them. Keys disease is very real and readily explainable.

A story in the News-Barometer illustrating this fact caught Will's attention one morning.

Nudity Gets a Look on County Beaches

Topless women and unclothed tourists in this subtropical region called the Florida Keys have long been relegated to extremely remote areas where prying eyes cannot see.

For to show that much flesh anywhere else, outside the party zone of Fantasy Fest in Key West during a week in October, always results in a strong reprimand from the local constabulary, and sometimes results in spending time behind iron bars in these islands.

And that has flabbergasted many of our foreign tourists for whom topless, clothing-optional and nude beaches are simply a way of life.

Yes, Will sensed, a new debate was about to be added to the long list of queer debates endemic to this tolerant, uninhibited yet sometimes prudish archipelago.

It had all started with a discussion at the Monroe County Board of County Commissioners about upgrades to Higgs Beach. Lash Blutarsky, a Key West mayoral hopeful, suggested that the county make part of that beach a clothing optional beach, arguing that it was rarely used in its present form and therefore a wasted asset. Two county commissioners agreed to the proposal in principle, pointing out that such beaches were common in Europe and would attract European tourists to the Keys. Another commissioner pointed to the success of Haulover Beach in Miami as a clothing optional beach. The board instructed the legal staff to begin researching how and if the county might permit a topless or clothing optional beach.

Soon the prospect of a nude beach was the talk of the county. The concept was not entirely foreign to Monroe County. It had long been known by insiders that the dead-end of Old Boca Chica Road had been used for that purpose and that a small privately owned nude beach existed on Long Beach Road on Big Pine Key. A debate raged. Opponents maintained it would corrupt the county's youth and attract perverts. Proponents said it would promote tourism and bring much needed revenue to Monroe County.

Sun Raye waged into the fray. She stated in a newspaper interview, "There are a lot of adults out there that believe that mere nudity isn't offensive to a child. A lot of people are only nude when they're taking a shower or having sex. That's what they've got to learn about naturists - it's non-sexual nudity. More people than you can imagine would love to be able to live out their naturist fantasies. I know I would. A public nude beach is the only way most people will ever be able to participate in this healthy life style."

Bill Becker on U.S. 1 radio was soon airing shows on

the hot topic. On one show he interviewed a multi-million dollar lottery winner who planned to open up a nude dude ranch in Hernando County, Florida.

The argument took a bizarre keys-like twist at the Hometown Political Action Committee's first candidate forum at Saluté Restaurant. Will and Betsy were standing, drinking a cocktail as candidate Lash Blutarsky began to speak. He jokingly told the crowd that he had contemplated bringing a topless hula dancer to the meeting as a visual aid to emphasize his pitch to bring a clothing optional beach to the Southernmost City, but he resisted the temptation. He finished to polite applause, and one of his opponents, a nervous first-time mayoral candidate, attempted the first speech of his campaign.

Suddenly an *AHHH* arose from the group assembled at Saluté. From each direction came a young female bicyclist with a bikini top. On a prearranged signal the cyclists simultaneously popped their tops and began to leisurely ride in circles around the open-air restaurant. Blutarsky let out a whoop and began to laugh. His nervous opponent dropped both his drink and his speech notes.

All semblance of order immediately vanished, and the meeting was over. Hometown's leader tried to moderate, but the meeting had dissolved and quickly became an impromptu discussion about nude beaches.

"This should uplift things in the Keys to a new level," Will said.

"I disagree, my dear," Betsy replied. "Some things may sink to a new low."

"Are you trying to say 'show me your tits' may become 'please put it back on'?" Will asked teasingly.

Will gestured towards a large hairy fat man helping himself to the chips and dip across the room and whispered, "Imagine him without any clothes on."

"I don't even want to imagine that gorilla shirtless, and pantless gives me the shivers," Betsy said. "With Mr. Blutarsky's help, plastic surgery and liposuction may become a new growth industry in Monroe County."

CHAPTER 30

Adolfo Soltero was enjoying his breakfast and reading the paper. He broke a piece off his tostada and dipped it in his café con leche. He then took a bite of his ham croquette and washed it down with a sip of café con leche. He found the reports about the nude beach controversy to be as entertaining as most other county residents. *Americans,* he thought, *can be so provincial.* Then he saw an article of more than passing interest. It was Sun Raye's interview on the subject of nudity.

More people than you can imagine would love to live out their naturist fantasies. I know I would.

At first he was a little upset that she would call attention to herself on such a controversial topic since controversy was not good for business. All he needed with all the ventures he had going because of CANDO was Sun Raye bringing unwanted attention to herself. But then he started thinking. If she was determined to be a nudist, maybe he could use this penchant to his advantage.

The cartel owned a private island one mile east of Summerland Key that had seemingly outlived its usefulness. It was originally named Money Key; he had renamed it Melody Key so its true purpose would be less obvious. On the five and a half acres were two octagonal structures surrounded by airy verandahs. It had a state-of-the-art boat dock which moored two discreet looking but very fast boats. The house had luxury amenities and a swimming pool. It also had a cleared vacant canal-front lot on Summerland Key that had its own boat launch and room to park five cars. Perfect for moving either drugs or people.

The island was custom made for drug smuggling. Not only were there no neighbors, but the house had 1,500 square feet of screened verandahs on the second floor. The cathedral-ceilinged great room on the third level and its sprawling 35 foot glass balcony gave a 360 degree view of anyone approaching the island. Giving an even more complete view was the crow's nest that went up from the kitchen to a fourth level. The visibility with binoculars gave the island an unbelievable advantage if encroachers needed to be avoided or dealt with.

Unfortunately the property's anonymity had been compromised with the DEA and with the immigration officials when Ike and Jake Blanchard had been arrested. It was now dangerous to use and unfortunately almost useless to the cartel. As he sat eating breakfast, a thought suddenly came to mind. Maybe he could rent the villa to Sun Raye. This would serve several purposes. First, it would give Sun Raye a private place to indulge herself in her nudist fetish that would be out of the limelight. Also he wouldn't have to keep sending maintenance and cleaning crews to the house on an ongoing basis. Third, the rental income would create some cash flow from the investment, and he could pick up a depreciation deduction that would result from its now being a rental. But best of all, it would create a cover so that he could resume using this ideal location for its original intended purpose - occasional smuggling. It would be perfect since Sun Raye wouldn't be living there full time but instead merely using it as an occasional weekend retreat or second home. When she and her guests weren't there, he would have the complete run of the island for his nefarious purposes. Why had he not thought of this before?

He would plant a seed and see what happened. That estúpido Bobby Perez would be a perfect conduit.

Soltero waited for Bobby and Billy to come to Casa Camilio Sur for their morning key lime pie and coffee.

"How are things?" Al asked Bobby. "Mind if I join you?"

"Of course not. It is always an honor."

"I read your mother-in-law's interview in connection with the nude beach controversy. Is she a nudist?" he asked innocently, already knowing the answer.

"I think she would be if she thought she could get away with it," Bobby said. "We've sure seen more of my mother-in-law than most son-in-laws have." He winked and laughed. "Don't look half bad for a cougar."

"I think it would be wise if she discreetly confined this practice to some place where her privacy was assured. It would be better for business. I've got an idea."

He then told them about the rental property on Melody Key.

"Why don't we take Sun Raye out there on your boat, and I'll give you all a tour of the property?" Al said. "I'll let you set it up."

Sun Raye's only request was that Luis Bernstein accompany them.

Not unexpectedly, Bobby Perez owned a hot muscle boat. His boat was a 32-foot Sunsation 322 with twin

Mercury 496HO engines with bravo one drives. He had spent $20,000 just on the yellow gelcoat custom paint scheme. It had a full cabin with a separate galley and had port and starboard jump seats as well a rear bench seat. This boat was meant to be noticed, but mostly it was meant to get places fast.

This was the first time either Adolfo, Luis, or Sun Raye had been out on Bobby's boat. Bobby was determined to show off the boat's capabilities. He set the Garmin GPS and in almost no time they could see the trees lining Melody Key.

The island had been left natural with the exception of the area cleared in its middle to build the house and amenities. A long dock ran perpendicular to the shore on the island's west side. The other side of the island was mostly shallow and non-navigable. Bobby tied the boat up at the dock, and they all got off.

A secluded path led through the brush and trees to an opening covered with pavers. In the middle of this opening was an unscreened marcite pool and spa with a tiki hut nearby. Sun Raye was impressed and told Adolfo so. They continued to walk up to a large brown rustic octagonal structure. Soltero took them into the ground level where they found a large anteroom and a staircase leading to the living quarters above. On the second floor were three bedrooms and three full baths. French-doors led to a balcony that overlooked the pool. From there he took them to the third level and showed them a great-room with a fourteen-foot beamed ceiling. Sun Raye was mesmerized by the view of the Atlantic from the massive balcony. Standing out there feeling the breeze, she felt she could fly.

She had a hard time tearing herself away from the 300-gallon piranha tank. Lastly, Soltero took them up to the crow's nest.

"So what do you think?" Al asked.

"Magnificent," was all Sea Raye could think to say.

"Uh huh! Now let's sit down and talk," Soltero said, pointing to the rattan chairs in the great-room. "How would you like to rent this island? I can make you a deal on it."

He gave a brief overview of the rental arrangement he had in mind.

"I don't know what to say," said Sun Raye.

"Say yes. This would be a perfect place for you to use as a personal retreat as well as a place to hold high-level conferences and meetings where discretion is vital. We can structure a lease so the lessee is the corporation and it is deductible as a business expense. As I said, I can make you a good deal. My motive, in case you are wondering, is to have someone using the property and keeping it up. Also having a resident, even a part-time one, discourages vandals."

Sun Raye sat and dreamily looked around. She could visualize what a marvelous location this would be to conduct her religious meetings and séances. She could also see the pool area as a naturist paradise and imagined communing with her maker. Soltero's words forced her to refocus.

"Here is what I am prepared to do," Al said. "The rule of thumb with luxury rental properties is a monthly charge of between one half of one percent to three quarters of one percent. This means the market rental rate on this house and island should be between $20,000 and $30,000 per month based on its appraised $4,000,000 value. I am prepared to rent it for $12,500 per month on a triple-net-lease basis. A triple-net-lease leaves you responsible for utilities and upkeep. Does that sound fair?"

For once Sun Raye did not have to consult a higher authority. She was too wrapped up visualizing herself sunning in the buff out by the private pool on Melody Key. She glanced at Luis. He nodded his approval.

"Yes," she said with no hesitation.

CHAPTER 31

To bare or not to bare? And if so, where? Those were the questions.

Will had often told his friends in Vero Beach that Keys news was a spicy gumbo for news-junkies even in dull times, and when things occasionally heated up, the gumbo became even more rich and flavorful. Zany is an over-used adjective, but there are times when it fits just perfectly. And sometimes what might start out as a completely improbable proposal can become a serious consideration.

The scope of the nudism discussion had broadened. Whereas the original proposal was to use Higgs Beach for that purpose, other propositions soon emerged since naked Higgs Beach sunbathers and swimmers would be difficult to conceal from the children who used neighboring Astro City Park. One group began pushing Simonton Beach; another group wanted the more secluded area between the West Martello Tower and the Atlantic Ocean. The proposal with the most legs seemed to be the idea of using a portion of Smathers Beach instead. Soon the Key West community was divided not only over *if* but *where* as well.

The Key West business community was surveyed. Eighty percent of the tourism-based business owners surveyed supported the concept of a clothing-optional beach.

As each side drew their battle lines in the sand,

intriguing stories on other topics that normally would have caught the public's imagination were relegated to the back pages. One unexplainable story about a young Japanese man who flew into the Key West airport disguised as an elderly white male barely got any attention at all. When he was taken into custody by perplexed authorities, his carry-on contained a remarkable silicone mask. He had boarded his flight in New York as an elderly man who seemed to have young looking hands. During the flight he went to the restroom and then re-emerged as a Japanese man who appeared to be in his twenties. He gave Key West authorities no explanation why he had attempted the ruse. This story was noted by only a few because on that same day most people were riveted to reports about a topless protest to the nude beach that took place with women protesters on Duval Street.

The President of Florida Keys Free Beaches, Leigh Tracy, decided this presented a golden opportunity to make a statement about gender equality. Her group contended that women should be able to go top-free any place a man could – such when going to the beach, riding their bikes, or walking down Duval Street. Despite losing a lawsuit in Brevard County on this same issue, the women contended that going top-free was a protected form of expression under the First Amendment. When asked if the Monroe County State Attorney would vigorously prosecute the demonstrators, its spokesman said, "I'm not going to put my attorneys down on Duval Street to watch people. We've got other things to do. That's up to Police Chief Walter Wanderley. All I do is prosecute." Police merely chose to ask the shirtless women to comply with local law.

The only person arrested at the protest was arrested on an unrelated charge.

A man wearing only a tie-dyed G-string loincloth detracted from the group's political statement when he declared he was there just so he could see breasts. The march got the seal of approval from the Southernmost City's resident homeless population when one homeless man commented to another as he popped the pop-top on a spewing beer, "Oh, my God. Did you see those tits?" His companion replied, as he popped the top on his own beer, "I maybe homeless, but I'm not blind. Course I saw those honkers. Man, I love this. The good old days is now. I don't even have to say 'Show me your tits' anymore. They just fuckin' do it."

A middle-aged male protestor followed the women down Duval Street with signs saying "America Is Doomed" and "Too Late To Pray." He yelled at them, "You ought to think of people's children." A protester shot back, "Boobies feed babies." In general, passersby reactions varied from parents steering their children to the other side of the street to apathy. One man on a scooter called the protestors "a bunch of derelicts" and shot a marcher in the stomach with a small paint-ball from a pea shooter.

Undeterred, the following day Tracy announced that she was planning another march and her plans to affiliate with a national group, gotopless.org.

Despite the objections of her daughters, Sun Raye participated in the demonstration. She brought some of her flock with her. She wore red, white and blue pasties until one finally came off as she walked down the 1100 block of Duval Street. A cruise-ship passenger off the

Carnival Freedom grabbed it to keep for a souvenir. Another tourist tried to pluck off Sun Raye's other one. Sun Raye kicked him soundly in the groin and then shot him a bird. Adolfo Soltero cringed when he got the report back the following day. *I can't believe this dizzy dame. I hope Cartagena doesn't hear about this.* He had a meeting with Bobby and Billy Perez and demanded that they insist that their mother-in-law confine her naturist activities to the site he had provided at Melody Key.

Within days a Geiger Key man exposed his buttocks on Simonton Street. An officer on patrol saw the man begin to pull his shorts down, exposing his butt. When the officer approached he began to crouch behind a large concrete post and when questioned, he said, "Well, if the women can do it, I don't see why I can't." The officer asked for identification. When the man reached for his wallet, three small white cocaine rocks fell out.

A harried Walter Wanderley dropped in on Betsy at the bank.

"I'm starting to think the only people left around here with good sense are you and me," he said with a sigh as he drank a big swig of coffee.

"President Taft once made a statement that I think is appropriate," Betsy said. "He said 'Enthusiasm for a cause sometimes warps judgment'."

"Very true. You will read about the latest shoe to drop in tomorrow's paper," Walter said. "I had to fire one of my female police officers today. Thank God she was still in her one-year probationary period so I could fire her without cause."

"So what did she do?" Betsy asked.

"Oh, she just published nude photos of herself and some of her male companions on her MySpace page."

"Speaking of poor judgment ..." Betsy commented.

"She knew damn good and well we have a section in our manual that deals with unbecoming conduct. I've known this girl since high school, and now I've had to fire her. It wasn't easy. To my knowledge, she's never done anything like this before. I have no idea if her actions were stimulated by all this nude beach controversy, but I can tell you, infractions concerning nudity are on the rise."

~ ~ ~

At Will's office Jason Pearson was expressing similar sentiments about how irrationality seemed to ratcheting up to a new level. He had stopped by to say thank-you since Betsy had recommended that Sun Raye use him for maintenance and repairs on Melody Key.

"I think time has stopped like in "Groundhog Day" and left us with a permanent full moon," Jason said.

"Why's that?" Will asked.

"Just the way people are acting. I got called out on a run yesterday that's definitely going down in my top five when I write my memoirs," Jason said. "I got called out on one of the strangest car wrecks of all time. Some woman who lives in Marathon had been up on the mainland shopping. When she got back to Homestead she accidentally hit a four-foot gator while trying to text-message her daughter about a sale at Bed Bath and Beyond. With every good intention in the world, she loaded it into the back seat of her Honda Accord, hoping to rescue it. By the time she got to Leyton it revived and started thrashing in the back of her car causing her to crash her car into that empty police car permanently parked on the shoulder of the Overseas Highway. She then got scared because she was driving with a suspended driver's license and hauled ass, leaving the injured alligator in the back seat of her car."

"My God. What a dunce."

"When the sheriff's department caught up with her, she was arrested and charged with possession of an alligator – in case you don't know, that's a felony in the state of Florida. She also got charged with driving with a suspended license and also leaving the scene of an accident. We had to take her to the hospital since she had a concussion, and then she spent the night in the county pokey."

"I've never known anyone who has been charged with possession of an alligator," Will said laughing.

~ ~ ~

The press coverage for a nude beach continued over the next few months. It was decided that the matter should be put on a ballot for the voters to decide. Florida Keys Free Beaches, a group formed to lobby for the nude beach, began holding town hall meetings to answer questions and address concerns on the issue. They also began making appearances on local talk shows like Bill Becker's show on US 1 radio.

Their opposition, the American Decency Association, weighed in fervently. The ADA leader stated, "What a shame to even contemplate having such a beach - we are to be dressed in modest clothing, as spoken by our creator. When you meet your maker, you will have to answer for this kind of decision. May your choice be one that honors

God." They called for a boycott of Key West businesses.

Bartenders and waitresses at the Garden of Eden, Key West's only clothing-optional bar, got their patrons to sign a petition supporting the beach. Another group began circulating vintage pictures of Bettie Page, Key West's iconic 1950's pinup girl known around the world for her bondage photos and fetish films. Betsy laughingly reminded Will over cocktails one evening that this was certainly a strange icon since shortly after Bettie Page had moved to Key West, she had found God after listening to a preacher on White Street.

Sun Raye came up with the most memorable campaign of all. She convinced fifteen middle aged and older women to pose for a calendar in the buff. She got the idea from the 2003 movie *Calendar Girls*, in which older women posed nude or nearly nude for a calendar to raise money for leukemia research. One woman posed under a waterfall; another posed in the moonlight by the post at the Key West Tropical Forest and Botanical Garden. One of the most interesting pictures was taken with its two older nude models holding hands around a tree. The caption said, "Don't just hug a tree. Make out with it." The first run of 500 calendars was a quick sellout, raising $8,000 for the nude beach cause. Public demand caused a second run to be printed.

Bobby Perez came into Casa Camilio Sur waving a copy of the calendar.

He held up a copy proudly for everyone to see. The cover photo had a picture of a topless grandmother with body-paint on both sagging breasts doing a deep throat imitation as she sucked on a giant peppermint stick. A liberty bell was painted on each breast. On her stomach it said "Let Freedom Ring." The photo was taken in front of Casa Camilio Sur and clearly showed the restaurant's sign. There was also an advertisement on the back for CANDO products.

"You can't buy this kind of advertising," Bobby announced.

Miguel Valdes snatched the calendar away from him and grumbled, "That's for goddamed sure. This is serious, moron. We gotta stop this fuckin' loony-tune. She wants to show her tits, but all she's showing is her ass. I'm going to send her a warning, and if that doesn't work I'm going to hurt the flaky bitch. You know, she's not indispensible. The organization can arrange for her to be replaced if she becomes a threat."

He shook his fist at Bobby and said, "And don't you say a fuckin' word to Al about this conversation. I can take care of things by myself."

He began thinking of ways to do so. After giving the matter much thought, he finally hatched a plan and conscripted a subservient, confidential yet unwitting accomplice.

CHAPTER 32

"Sometimes I wonder about you two," Jason Pearson said. "You seem so straight and businesslike, but I've met some of the strangest people through you."

"What in the world are you talking about?" Will asked.

"I mean that maintenance job out at Melody Key. It turned strange right off the bat. That is one really far-out group of people."

"Well, don't just leave us hanging. Tell us what you're talking about," said Betsy.

"Most of my work out there has been outdoors thus far," Jason said. "The place is a jungle with a lot of nuisance plants - Brazilian peppers, Australian pines, things like that. Since no one is there most of the time, I usually have the run to the place to myself. I just get over there whenever the weather permits and I don't have to work at the fire department. It was working out pretty well."

"Until?" Betsy said.

"Until the other day." He then described the events that occurred that day.

~ ~ ~

Sun Raye was very anxious to hold her first meeting at her new digs on Melody Key. She thought about it for days. Finally she had the excuse she needed. WILDO had totally revamped their line of sunblock — a new formula, new packaging and new sizes. She decided to hold a naturist/

clothing optional swimming party for some of her successful distributors and prove how effective the new improved product was. It would give her a chance to show off her new house as well as give her an opportunity to do a motivation speech. She would put out food and drink. Yes, this was going to be a premier function that would also make the rank-and-file jealous that they had not been invited and encourage them to work harder to make her "A" list. In her excitement, she forgot to check with Jason and tell him not to work that day.

Sun Raye made up a guest list of people she did not think would be offended by a naturist function. She sent an e-mail to Bobby Raye telling him to get her a couple of cases of the new sunblock. She made arrangements for food and refreshments. She even chose special music for the occasion.

The day finally arrived for Sun Raye's soirée. Her guests began to arrive. She welcomed them by playing Sister Sledge's "We Are Family" over and over on the outdoor stereo system. Soon the whole group was gathered around the pool - some sans clothing — enjoying themselves, eating the sandwiches, munchies and chicken wings Sun Raye had bought for the occasion.

Not knowing of the event, Jason and Kevin had run a small barge up to one of the few deep spots on the other end of the island. They planned to off-load the debris they had created the day before onto the barge and take it back to Summerland Key for transport it to the county landfill. They had every reason to think they were alone on the island. And they were stunned when this did not turn out to be the case!

Once her guests had all arrived, Sun Raye raised her hands towards Abraham's bosom as gravity pulled hers down towards the netherworld. She began to speak.

"Welcome my friends to my tropical Garden of Eden. You are here because your beautiful minds have made you some my most successful distributors. Your mind is like the garden you see before you. In this garden it is my mission to grow beautiful plants. It is also my mission to plant your minds with beautiful thoughts. If planted with beautiful plants that are carefully nurtured and tended to, lovely delicate flowers will result and make it a place of comfort, beauty and peace. If this garden is neglected, weeds will creep in and destroy the beauty and yield thorns, destruction, and harshness. Sadly enough, some twisted or strange gardeners actually plant weeds and unpleasant plants, but we never will.

"It is the same with your mind. If we plant beautiful, healthy thoughts into our minds, we will reap a harmonious, healthy life. If we plant negative thoughts, we will reap destruction and despair. If we neglect to feed our minds healthy thoughts and are not constantly vigilant about protecting our minds from negative thoughts, the weeds of destruction will creep in and choke us. The power of positive thinking will yield good results in the same way that negative thinking will insure a bad outcome."

As Sun Raye spoke, Johnny Nash's "I Can See Clearly Now" played in the background. She then began her presentation on the new improved sunblock.

Jason and Kevin heard the commotion and silently slipped through the brush towards the sounds. When they saw twenty nude or almost nude people seemingly engaged in a business meeting, they couldn't wait to silently observe and to see what would happen next. They rationalized that there was no use making a lot of noise cutting up tree limbs and spoiling Sun Raye's big day. Besides that, they wouldn't miss this outrageous to-do for the world. It was a hell of a lot more fun than hauling plant debris to the dump.

Sun Raye also had no way of knowing that Miguel Valdes had inadvertently picked this occasion to have his agent get even for the embarrassment Sun Raye had caused the cartel with her nude calendar project. He also vividly remembered the bougainvillea scratches he had suffered at Sun Raye's Kingdom Hall séance. He had been planning vengeance for weeks. God, he was looking forward to this. The bitch had embarrassed him in front of the entire lower Keys with that God-forsaken calendar. His only thought was putting the fear of God into Sun Raye. He had no way of knowing the distress and embarrassment he would be causing her guests as well.

Valdes' objective was a simple one. He would discourage Sun Raye from wanting to run around naked anymore...ever...by giving the vixen a skin irritation she would remember for years. The knowledge needed to implement his prank went back to his daughter's days at Florida Keys Community College.

His daughter had had an extreme reaction while mixing an agent called Benedict's reagent in one of her lab courses. A solution of Benedict's reagent was sometimes used to test for the presence of glucose in urine and determine if the patient was diabetic. It was a non-regulated powdered substance that could be easily purchased from a chemical supplier. If a person got it in the eyes, it caused redness, tearing, itching and burning. If a person swallowed it, the agent would burn the mouth and throat, cause vomiting, and impart abdominal distress. If it were inhaled, it caused irritation of the mucous membranes, coughing and shortness of breath. If it were gotten on the skin, an itching rash would result. This stuff was nasty shit. Yes, it was perfect. The bitch would rue the day she had exposed his restaurant and business to taunting and ridicule. And best of all - she would never know he was the one who shafted her or how it was done. He would dust her lawn with Benedict's, put some in the bin where she kept her beach towels and dump some in the swimming pool. He could hardly wait.

Bobby Perez, as he had been instructed by Sun Raye, brought a case of sunblock out earlier that week in his boat. She had no way of knowing he was inadvertently Valdes' secondary agent of retribution as well. He had not paid a lot of attention to which case he grabbed in the warehouse. Sun Raye did not know it, but one of the side benefits Tango got from packing and distributing CANDO skin care products was that certain cases contained a false bottom to hide and distribute cocaine. These cases were numbered for identification with a coded numbering system known only to a few and shipped only to distributors who worked for the cartel. It had worked out very well up until now. Sun Raye didn't have the least suspicion that her company was being used for this nefarious and illegal purpose. All she knew was that since Valdes had started to manufacture and distribute her products, sales had soared. Bobby never thought to look at the numbering on the case because he didn't think a new product such as the reformulated sunscreen was being used yet by the cartel to ship dope. This oversight would prove costly.

As Sun Raye continued her Melody Key talk, her audience became more and more fidgety and distracted. One woman's eyes began to tear. A second man's nose began to run. A third woman raised her hand to ask a question. Her hand suddenly shot to her mouth, and she ran to a nearby pedestal planter and began retching on its flowering bromeliad. Some of Sun Raye's guests began to break out in a rash. Soon most were jumping around scratching their bodies. Modesty was not a consideration as they scratched, dug into their unprotected crotches or scratched their nude asses as well as anything else that seemed to be on fire. They then began to scratch each other in places they couldn't reach themselves. They reminded Jason of a pack of dogs who had stepped in a fire ant bed.

A couple of people jumped into the swimming pool thinking this would put out the fire. Others soon joined them. For these people the fire only got worse. One man lost control of his bowels and let a load go into the pool. A woman watching him threw up. The scene had ceased to have any decorum.

Sun Raye panicked. She had never seen anything like this before. She thought that maybe sunblock would alleviate their pain. Maybe if she slathered it on her guests, she could ease their distress.

In her haste to cut open the case, she punctured the bag of cocaine hidden in it. When she hurriedly ripped open the box, she and the people adjacent to her were covered with white powder. After she cleared her eyes and throat, Sun Raye began to talk rapidly and run her sentences together. She became even more attuned to the panic going on around her. She began to tap her feet and then dance and sing to "I Can See Clearly Now". This had unexpectedly become the grooviest song she had ever heard. Funny she'd never noticed its poetry and nuances until now. She was now covered with sweat.

Sun Raye remembered a poem her father used to recite in a fake Italian accent on Mallory Square when he got totally shit-faced. She hadn't thought about the poem in years. Every word came back to her, and she suddenly wanted the group to hear it. She looked through the crowd, and she could see him in the distance encouraging her to proceed.

> *Lasta night as I starta closa da place*
> *Dere was a Wop come in wid a smile on his face*
> *He's a say "Christa, Mike, shes a hot around here*
> *Joosta make hurry and getta da beer.*
> *So I maka da hurry and filla da cans*
> *But I wasna so busy, I looka da mans*
> *He no drinka da beer, he joost stans and stans*
> *And by Jesa da Christ, he's gotta no hands.*

Sun Raye began to squirt sunblock onto a fat woman standing in front of her. The stranger next to her vigorously rubbed it all over her torso. She squeezed the plastic bottle again. This time she missed both of them and a huge dollop went on the ground. As the woman turned, she stepped out of her flip-flop and into the slick puddle.

Down she went on top of her benefactor.

Sun Raye laughed and continued to recite from the ground.

So, I take da beer and hole to hess mouth,
And you betcha my life, he make da beer go south.
Then hes a say to me, "Dat beer shees slick
Joost reecha in my pocket and getta da nick.
So I gotta da nick, and hes a say to me
"Have you gotta da place to maka da pee?"
An I points to da door and he joosta stands,
He no can open, cause he gotta no hands.

Jason and Kevin were in the bushes not believing what they saw. This was the funniest damned scene they had ever seen in their entire lives. They began to laugh out loud. Kevin tripped over a log. No one noticed them except Sun Raye who just stared since her eyes by now were dilated. She continued to sweat profusely and her nervous energy made her even more hyper. Two of the guests who had been sprayed with cocaine started cheering for her to finish the poem. It seemed like the appropriate thing to do, so she climbed up on a table and continued.

So I opa da door, and still he stans and stans.
He no can take out cause he gotta no hands.
Now, I no lika dees, but I taka da chance
I go to da man and unbutton his pants.
He maka no pee, and he stans and stans
He no can puta back, cause he gotta no hands.
Now, I no lika do dees too, but I take chance.
I go to da man and unbutton hees pants.

With the exception of the small group high on cocaine, no one was paying Sun Raye one bit of attention. They were too busy running around trying to scratch what itched. Her rapt audience was not to be deprived of the conclusion to her story. One woman began to shout "Olé!" loudly as she rubbed her body up against a gumbo limbo tree. At last with a satisfied look she stopped and belched. Sun Ray wiped her nose and launched into her grand finale.

And da thing he getta hard, swell up like brick
And he says to me, "Come kiss me quick."
And I getta mad, and I giva da kick -
"You son of a beech, wat you want for a nick?"

Sun Raye's small spaced-out audience stopped scratching long enough to break out in wild cheers. One woman grabbed the flaccid penis of the man standing next to her. In the distance Sun Raye saw the image of her deceased father, the Silent Screaming Silver Swabbie, giving her a thumbs-up with one hand as he chug-a-lugged a brew with the other. She began to curtsy. When she did, she slipped on sunblock and tumbled into the pool.

Miguel Valdes didn't have the pleasure of seeing his revenge, but he had clearly won this latest skirmish.

CHAPTER 33

Will's administrative assistant, Barbara, brought some papers in for him to sign. Will chuckled as he read a newspaper article.

"Barbara, got a second for me to read you something bizarre?" Will asked.

"Sure, BiZorro, I'm on your clock," Barbara said smiling.

"A man who bought a foreclosed Key West home discovered a body in the garage, and it may be that of the former owner, authorities report. The man went to the home on United Street on Thursday, a day after buying it, according to Andrew Walters, spokesman for the Key West Police Department. He found the body in a car in the garage. Walters said it it's unclear how long the body had been there, or how the person died. An autopsy is underway.

"The body in the Key West house is believed to be that of a woman," Walters said. "Investigators think it may be the home's previous owner, because she hasn't been seen for a while. She went through foreclosure earlier this year. Mortgage lender BB & T sold the home Wednesday."

"Some people will do anything to keep from paying their bills," Barbara said.

"I think this woman was dead-right not to pay," Will said back to her. "After all, she wasn't living there anymore."

Before Barbara could think of a come-back, Will heard a gentle rap on his door. He looked up to see Felicia Fox, the wholesaler for Nuveen, standing there.

"Good morning, doughnuts are in the kitchen. Got a second for me to show you something exciting?" she said.

"Oh, hi, Felicia. Come on in," Will said.

Felicia sat down and quickly whipped a fact sheet out of her rolling briefcase.

"We've got a new focus product this month, the Nuveen Build America Bond Opportunity Fund. It's a wonderful opportunity for you and your clients," she began. "I assume you are familiar with BABs."

"Yeah, sure. Build America Bonds. Taxable munis," Will said.

"Right on. BABs are munis that are mostly investment grade, have strong call protection and give your clients a competitive current income. Some are even general obligation bonds."

Before Will could comment, Ms. Fox launched into the next phase of her carefully-rehearsed, canned presentation.

"Through Nuveen you can now take this enticing new medium and make it even more exciting with our closed-end fund. Using this format, Nuveen will be able to lower your client's risk to the point where it will be appropriate for pretty much anyone. It is truly a widows and orphans product. Do you know what the default rate is on Baa3 or higher munis?"

"I know it is low," Will said.

"Right again. Much less than AAA corporates, and with this fund we'll be able to get them the same cash flow as a AAA corporate in a diversified professionally managed portfolio. And best of all we'll give you 4% to sell it. A definite win-win."

"Leveraged or non-leveraged?" Will asked.

"Leveraged, but we'll employ sophisticated hedging techniques with derivatives to dramatically lower the interest rate risk. And our portfolio will have a finite life to help us further control risk."

"Let me read the prospectus, and I'll see if I can do something with it. Thanks for coming by," Will said.

"Don't forget. I left doughnuts in the kitchen."

Within ten minutes Will heard another rap at his door.

"May I come in?" the wholesaler said. "Bernie Macomber, Blackrock. You remember me, don't you? I used to be with Lord Abbett."

"And with Pacific Life before that...And Can-Am drilling programs back in the old days. How are things?" Will said.

"Never better. Having a great month. By the way, I left some Klondike Bars in your freezer in the kitchen. And you'll soon be having a great month too after you see what our focus product is this month. I guess you know BABs are all the rage."

"So I've heard," Will said.

"Well, we're once again answering the need of the investment community by putting together a closed end fund for you to sell. Other firms may try to enter this market, but we are the only Blackrock. We know this market. After all, we manage more than $4.5 billion of BABs. "*Our* Build America Bond Trust will be the benchmark product other people will be measuring themselves against. Products like this a few years ago were only available to institutions, but now the man-on-the-street can have the same opportunities as 'smart' investors controlling billions.

"We have assigned two of our best portfolio managers to this deal. They each have over twenty years experience. Our goal is to maintain interest rate risk in a defined range relative to that of the Barclays Capital BABs Index while using an integrated leverage and hedging strategy to seek to enhance both the fund's potential current income and longer risk-adjusted returns using a perpetual fund that will allow us to manage a longer duration portfolio."

"Boy, that was a mouthful. How long did it take you to memorize that and not trip over the words?" Will said smiling.

Bernie did not acknowledge Will's cryptic remark but plowed on full speed ahead.

"And I saved the best for last. We'll pay you 4.5% to sell this product. You'll have to admit, it doesn't get this good very often any more. Things aren't as sweet as they were in the old days."

"Let me read the prospectus, and if it seems a fit, I'll get back to you," Will said.

"If you need some compliance-approved client material, call my internal, Theresa Menz. She'll take care of you. She's good and a real pro. We're a team who's here for the long haul."

"Well, I guess I can throw Paul Samuels' Blackrock card away."

"Yeah, He moved on to other opportunities, but *I'm* here for good."

When you were in here a few months ago, wasn't your internal named Andrea Barlow?"

"She was a good girl, but she moved on to other opportunities too. Don't forget there are Klondike bars in the freezer," Bernie said as he turned to leave.

Will's next visitor was even more interesting.

"Mr. Black, my name is Claude McRaines. I hope you can be of assistance to me."

"I'll do my best, Mr. McRaines," Will said.

"Mr. Black, I'm in Key West from Columbus, Ohio to look for my daughter," McRaines continued.

"What makes you think I can be of assistance?"

"Jacqueline is a fragile young lady psychologically. To be frank, she is manic depressive. Until recently she was a student at Ohio Wesleyan in Delaware, Ohio. She left the college one weekend recently and simply never came back. She's a good girl, but sometimes when she's not on her medication she does irrational things."

"You have my sympathy, but I still don't see where I fit in," Will said.

"I'm going to level with you and put all my cards on the table," McRaines said. "Not long ago Jacqueline's aunt Beth died, leaving her quite a few blue-chip stocks. These stocks were in a brokerage account in Delaware. Not long before she disappeared, Jacqueline went to see the broker and had him issue her all the certificates."

"I still don't understand why do you think I would have encountered her?" Will asked.

"I'm sorry. I guess I'm so torn up I'm not putting things in a logical sequence. When I searched her dorm room, I found propaganda from a religious organization in the Key West area. It calls itself the Cosmic Ray Scientific Church of Prosperity. I found audio tapes as well as printed brochures. I think she might have possibly come to Key West. Mr. Black, I'm a widower, and Jacqueline is all I have. She may have her problems, but she's still my only family," he said, starting to sniffle slightly. "I know this is a long shot, but I thought she might possibly deposit the stock certificates with a broker in Key West or she might have sold one of the stocks because she needed money. I haven't heard a word from her since she disappeared. I have nightmares about some cult getting its clutches into her and taking her to the cleaners - or worse."

"Mr. McRaines, I wish I could help you, but I have had no dealings with your daughter. You have my complete sympathy. I'm a father too, and if my daughter were in danger, I'd be doing the same things you are to try to find her."

"May I leave her picture with you as well as my contact information?" McRaines said. "I plan to be in Key West for awhile until I can either find Jacqueline or satisfy myself that she isn't here."

After McRaines left, Barbara brought Will a telephone message. "While that guy was here, Paul Peterson from Invesco called. He was wondering if you might go to lunch with him today. Said he wanted to tell you about BABs. Am I supposed know BABs? Is she a client of ours?"

"Oh sure, you know BABS. She's Bob's dysfunctional sister," Will said.

Barbara looked puzzled and then just shrugged as she turned to answer the ringing phone.

That evening as he was mixing his and Betsy's first

happy-hour toddy, Will mentioned his unusual visit from Claude McRaines. Betsy told him she had also had a similar visit from Mr. McRaines wondering if his daughter had set up a bank account at WB and had told him she didn't know the girl.

"I feel so sorry for the man," Betsy said. "He seemed like a lost puppy. Can you imagine if that was Lexie?"

"Lexie would never put herself in that position," Will said emphatically.

CHAPTER 34

The day after the fiasco at Melody Key Sun Raye didn't know what to think. She had never experienced such a wide range of emotions in such a short period of time. At first she was confused. What in the world could have gone wrong? She had planned the ill-fated meeting for a week. At first things had seemed to be going so well. And then without warning ... she had never in her life seen so many people go into distress in such a short period of time at such a seemingly nonthreatening setting. What was on that island that could cause that kind of allergic chain reaction? Was the island an old Navy dump site? Surely if there were some poison plants on the island, Jason and Kevin would have given her a heads-up. Now she was afraid to go back out there, and she certainly wouldn't invite anyone else to visit until she got to the bottom of what was going on.

And how in the world did cocaine get out to the island? Once Sun Raye came down off her drug-induced high, she recognized the substance she had been exposed to. She remembered it well from her doping days. The slurred rattling speech, the illusions of grandeur, the paranoia. It all brought back memories. She had sworn to Luis that those days were gone forever – and she had meant it. Had the substance possibly been left behind by the previous tenant? Was someone trying to get her hooked again? Was this a power grab to try to take her company away from her? Maybe the toxic substance had just blown in – kind of like a red tide.

Her emotions next turned to anger? Had someone purposely sabotaged her outing? Was this *the* dirty trick of all times? Who could possibly want to do something like that to her – and why?

Was it a competitor? In her frustration Sun Raye thought about throwing or kicking something, but realized this would accomplish nothing. No, she had to think this problem out logically. And she couldn't bring the authorities in on it – not with cocaine involved. She shouldn't even trust her inner circle – she was all alone with this quandary.

About that time another thought occurred to her as her mind raced for answers. Maybe someone wanted to hurt her or possibly even murder her? And if so, maybe they would try again. But for what reason? Was she a threat to someone? Was this someone's idea of a joke or just pure old-fashioned meanness?

Sun Raye was totally dysfunctional for most of the morning as her mind tried to assess each of these possibilities and assign a probability to each of them. She had a single recurring thought. Was this a one-time attempt, would there be others? Every time she thought of one question, several more would jump into her mind.

She was afraid to discuss matters even with Luis or her daughters. Finally she decided to look online to see if there might be a resident expert at Florida Keys Community College. She found that they had a professor with biochemical credentials. This seemed like it might possibly be someone who would have the knowledge she needed so she called and scheduled an appointment.

The FKCC professor made time to see her as much out of curiosity as any other reason so Sun Raye drove down to Stock Island after lunch for their meeting.

"Dr. Doats, thank you for seeing me. As I said on the phone, my name is Sun Raye. I own several enterprises here in the lower Keys. I would be interested in possibly hiring you to solve a dilemma for me."

"Please call me Merci," she said.

"Merci Doats?" Sun Raye said with a slight giggle. "Reminds me of a song we used to sing as kids."

"I know," Dr. Doats said with a sigh. "Mairzy doats and dozy doats and liddle lamzy divey. Sometimes I feel like the rhyme is tattooed on my chest. Ms. Raye, we all have our crosses to bear. That's why I usually sign my name M. C. Doats."

"McDoats — sounds like a McDonalds sandwich of the month."

"Better than the alternative. By the way, my maiden name was Havv."

"What's wrong with that?"

"Picture it in a teacher's grade book," Dr. Doats said.

Sun Ray thought for a second. "Havv Merci. I see what you mean."

Sun Raye then proceeded to recount to Merci about her unexpectedly eventful afternoon at Melody Key. Merci was intrigued by the situation and volunteered to take her boat out to the island.

When they arrived at Melody Key it was still in pretty much the same condition as it had been left after Sun Raye's aborted conference. Upturned chairs remained upturned. Parts of bathing suits and other clothing parts littered the ground. Ants seemed to be everywhere eating the spoiled food that had been dumped on the ground or left on the unbussed folding tables. Several opened cases of sunblock remained. Towels littered the ground. It looked like a college New Year's frat party on the day after. All that was missing were balloons, confetti, and paper hats.

Sun Raye was paranoid about touching anything. She remembered too well the events of the previous day. Dr. Doats suggested they both don rubber gloves as a safety precaution. Dr. Doats had brought brushes for dusting surfaces, containers for samples, cotton swabs, and other tools to use for information collection. The job seemed overwhelming to Sun Raye, but Merci divided the area into sectors and began to methodically collect specimens. She dusted furniture, got soil samples, retrieved selected items of clothing, and got water samples. Soon they were both hot and sweaty from working the site.

Things were going well until they turned and saw Bobby Perez standing there.

"Hey sexy mama-in-law! What's going down?" Bobby said.

"What are you doing out here?" Sun Raye asked.

"Oh, I just came out here to do you a favor and get any unopened cases of sun-screen so I could return them to inventory," Bobby said and plopped down in a deck chair, making a cloud of noxious dust fly. "Who's your friend? A new distributor?"

A breeze caught the dust Bobby had created and sprinkled it on all three. It stuck easily to Sun Raye's and

Merci's sweaty bodies. Within moments their eyes began to water, and they began to itch. Bobby sneezed and then he too began to feel the effects of the Benedict's powder. They all began to cough and wheeze as their mucous membranes became irritated. Bobby began to gasp for breath. He grabbed a towel to wipe, but wiping only intensified his pain.

"You fool!" Sun Raye screamed. "Why did my daughter have to marry a meddling fool?"

She tried to sock Bobby, but since she couldn't see, hit Merci instead. Merci stumbled backwards, trying to keep her balance and not fall in the pool. Bobby reached for her arm but instead tore off her blouse. He reached again and this time accidentally snatched off her bra. In a reflexive move, Merci popped him in the balls, causing him to swing and release the bra as he tried to grab his crotch. The fasteners on the bra hit Sun Raye in the face leaving a cut on her cheek and a C-cup on her head.

Sun Raye lost control and began to scratch Bobby with her long fingernails. He howled as the scratches opened new places for the Benedict's powder to sting. Sun Raye then swung an opened case of sun-screen downward and hit him with it, coating them all in cocaine. Bobby did the only thing he knew to do. He did a belly-flop into the pool.

A topless Merci, tears flowing down her cheeks, oblivious to her nudity, took off scampering for the surf and the relief she hoped it would provide. Sun Raye followed. By the time they reached the water, they were both feeling the effects of the cocaine blast they had been breathing and their pupils were beginning to dilate. With limited vision, they ran into each other. Both tumbled into

the water. Merci began to laugh and sing,
  Mairzy doats and dozy doats and liddle lamzy divey
  Kiddely divey too, wooden shoe
Sun Raye laughed like it was the funniest thing she had ever heard and joined in. They soon had a duet going. Sun Raye laughed and corrected Merci, "It's not wooden shoe, fool; it's *a kid'll eat ivy too, wouldn't you.*"

Merci laughed back. "Who's the fool, fool? How would you know? It's my anthem."

In the meantime, Bobby was left floundering in the pool, itching and clawing himself, wondering what in the hell was going on.

CHAPTER 35

"I think you should come over to my office," Merci said in a call to Sun Raye. "We need to talk."

"I'll be there," Sun Raye said.

When she arrived at Merci's office, Sun Raye asked, "Have you recovered from the other day?"

"I think so. How about you?"

"I just keep having recurring thoughts about killing my son-in-law," Sun Raye said.

"Oh, I think he paid for his misdeed out at the island," Merci said with a giggle. "Now, let's get down to business. One substance we were exposed to was easy to identify."

"Yeah, I know. Cocaine."

"Be honest with me, Sun Raye. Are you a drug user?"

"Absolutely not. I will admit that I used cocaine when I was younger. That's why I recognized it, but I gave it up years ago. I promised one of my employees that I was going to go straight, and I have. I will never be a recreational user again, but understand me - I don't want the authorities brought into this matter. The repercussions could be too great. That's why I came to you."

"I'll take your word for it, but you do need to find out where the coke came from. I'm pretty sure it came out of one of those cases of sunblock. It covered us when you hit Bobby in the head with the box," said Merci.

"I fully intend to learn more," Sun Raye said through gritted teeth.

"I hope so. Now, the other substance ... It's called Benedict's powder. Benedict's powder is used to detect the presence of glucose in urine in diabetes tests. It is not a controlled substance. It can be bought from any chemical company. However, it is an agent that must be handled with kid-gloves. A person coming into contact with it experiences burning eyes, redness, itching, burning sensations in the mouth and throat, vomiting, and abdominal pain plus other symptoms. In other words, this miracle drug when used incorrectly in an uncontrolled situation can be very unpleasant if it is unleashed. I also might add ... it is water soluble as well as odorless and tasteless. The residue was all over the lawn furniture, the ground and it had been put into the swimming pool. That was not an accident. Someone purposely sabotaged your meeting."

"I suspected as much, but now I don't know what to say," Sun Raye admitted.

"And I don't know what to tell you," Merci said. "You're lucky someone wasn't seriously injured or killed."

"Thank you," said Sun Raye. "I guess I'll have to figure this conundrum out from here."

"Maybe there's some way you can find out if a large quantity of this substance was sold recently by a chemical supply house and to whom," Merci said.

Sun Ray was scared as she drove back to Little Torch Key. She now knew this was not simply an unfortunate accident, but a deliberate attempt to scare or harm her, maybe even murder her. The most daunting fact was that she was no private investigator and truly didn't know where to start.

Luis caught her the moment she walked back in Kingdom Hall's door. "I just got a call from Jennifer Jacquette's husband. He was pretty upset. It seems that she had to go the hospital after attending your meeting on Melody Key. She ended up in the hospital. Couldn't breathe. Her windpipe almost closed up from swelling. She's in ICU and apparently has had a very allergic reaction. The only thing the hospital has eliminated as a suspect is food poisoning. I'm sending her some flowers and a card. I tried to defuse the situation, but I'm not sure how effective I was."

Jennifer could die. Sun Raye was now even more determined to find out what was going on.

By lunch, Sun Raye had only come to one conclusion. She had two substances she needed to trace back to a source. She reasoned that she should prioritize her work by taking the easier project first - locating the source of the cocaine, and maybe that would lead her in the direction of identifying the source of the Benedict's powder.

Another trip to Melody Key enabled Sun Raye to retrieve the cases of sunblock. She tasted some of the white powder. It was definitely cocaine. She put a generous sample in a trash bag for the trip back. Before she hit the dock she had convinced herself that it must have somehow come from Miguel Valdes' packaging plant.

You sorry piece of shit! I am will get to the bottom of this matter, she thought and decided she'd surprise Valdes to assess his true reaction.

Sun Raye drove in a mental fog to Casa Camilio Sur. Fortunately Valdes was there. He seemed mildly surprised at her visit and invited her in with his usual courtesy and panache.

"So what do I owe the honor of this fuckin' visit?"

"I need to talk to you privately," Sun Raye said.

Valdes motioned for her to follow him. When they entered his office, Sun Raye closed the door.

"So what's up in the world of religion?" Valdes said. "Collection plate broken?"

Sun Raye opened the trash bag and put the cardboard box on Valdes' desk.

"Do you know what this is?" she asked.

"It's fuckin' sunblock," Valdes answered.

"And the white powder coating the inside of the box?"

"How the hell should I know?"

"I think you do know," Sun Raye said. "It is a high grade of cocaine."

Valdes said nothing but looked uneasy and nervous. He recovered in a few seconds and said, "What does this have to do with me? You're the ex-dope head."

"Don't try to throw this back on me. I'll make you sorry. This is the way Bobby delivered this case to me and another one just like it."

Valdes became defensive but immediately more accommodating. "I'll get to the bottom of it, Sun Raye. I promise. Now you just promise me in return that you'll keep this under your hat while I'm trying to find out what's going on."

"Don't try to jerk my chain, Miguel. I *will* call the cops. I kept the other batch in case I need it. If I don't hear from you by tomorrow..." she sputtered. "I just don't know what I'm going to do...but whatever it is, I know you won't like it."

With that she turned to leave. "How could you? You sleaze!" she said.

As soon as Sun Raye's car had left the parking lot, Valdes called Bobby Raye on his cell phone.

"Get your sorry fuckin' ass over to the restaurant right this second," he screamed into the phone.

"I'm getting a haircut right now," Bobby began.

"I don't care if you're getting a goddamned vasectomy. Get your goddamned sorry ass over here right now."

When Bobby entered the restaurant, Valdes grabbed him by the shirt and shoved him towards his office. He slammed the door so hard a picture fell off the shelf.

He pointed at the cardboard case on his desk. "Did you deliver some sunblock to Sun Raye?"

"Sure," Bobby said. "She asked me for several cases for a distributor meeting she was having. What's wrong with that?"

"What's wrong, you moron, is that you gave her two of the cases full of dope. Did you bother to look at the goddamned lot numbers on the boxes?"

"Well, I was in a hurry, and I thought all the dope was in cases of suntan lotion, not sunblock," Bobby blurted out.

"No, you fuckin' idiot. We've been packing them in both. That's why we put a special code on the cases, so they will only go to *our* distributors. I've got half a mind to blow your worthless brains out, but they're so small I probably couldn't hit them."

"I'm sorry! I'm sorry! So what do you want me to do to make up for the damage?"

"You've done enough damage," Valdes screamed. "I'll

straighten this mess out. Now get the fuck out of here, and don't let me see your dim-witted face for awhile. And go to a goddamned dermatologist, pizza-face. That rash on you makes you look like you've got some kind of contagious disease."

He threw his stapler at Bobby as Bobby turned to leave. "And you can be goddamned sure I'm not taking a fall for your sorry ass with Soltero. I'll make sure he knows exactly who the fuck-up is in this outfit."

After Bobby left, Valdes sat brooding behind his desk for a few minutes waiting for his blood pressure go down again. He called Sun Raye and in his most civil tone told her he was on his way over to Kingdom Hall.

His plan was a simple one. He'd do what he did best – lie.

By the time Valdes got to Kingdom Hall with the help of a double rum-on-the-rocks he was somewhat composed again. He vowed not to curse one time as he tried to put out the fire Bobby Perez' carelessness had inadvertently lit.

"I promised you I would get to the bottom of this situation, and I have," Miguel began. "I swear by the Virgin Mary that I was as shocked as you were to find out that cocaine was in your sunblock. I have investigated and found it was put there by some fuc-, I mean rogue employees. They have been fuc- ... excuse me I mean severely dealt with. You have my word that this was a one-time problem and there'll be no fuc-, I mean no reoccurrence."

Sun Ray sat there and glared at him skeptically.

"I would never lie to you. I have too much respect for you to do that," Valdes said. "Now you must promise me that this fuc-, I mean this matter will go no further. You do not need to call law enforcement. We deal with our own fuc-, I mean dirty laundry. Look at the big picture. Any indiscreet action on your part can only hurt the organization as a whole, and you might get hurt as well. You don't want to do that, do you?"

"Of course not," Sun Raye said.

"Then let me handle it," Valdes said. "Fuc-, I mean, trust me."

Valdes' tone changed after he got back in his car. *The fucking bitch had better play ball,* he thought to himself, *so I don't have to break her legs or worse. There's too much money at stake here to have her fuck it up. Maybe I need to scare the dog-crap out of this dizzy dame so she'll learn to mind her own business and not stick her nose where it don't belong.*

CHAPTER 36

Sun Raye understood Miguel Valdes' veiled threat very well. She knew he was capable of both violence and intimidation. She vividly remembered how he had muscled his way into becoming both her manufacturer and distributor. He had had her over a barrel then because of her drug dependence problem, but she was capable of dealing from a much better position of strength now. She assumed she could count on Bobby and Billy Perez as muscle if the need arose. After all, they were now family. She also doubted if Valdes was telling her the truth about this being a one-time problem created by rogue employees and about his statement that he had already dealt severely with them. She was still scared. The filthy-mouthed thug gave her the willies, but she was far from the paralyzed state she had been in after her initial encounter with him.

It didn't take long for her to decide that her best defense might be to not deal with this creep one-on-one. Also her best defense would be a good offense, and if she didn't accomplish anything else, she'd try to make sure that if she went down, he would go down as well. She needed to have a strategy session with her daughters. She sent each an e-mail that she wanted to meet with them privately the following day.

Blue Raye was the first to get to her office.

"Mama, I've been so worried about you. The incident at Melody Key is absolutely bizarre. Do you know yet what

211

happened?"

"Yes and no. I partially do. That's why I've summoned you for this meeting," Sun Raye said.

About that time Sea Raye walked in. "Oh, Mama ..." She rushed over to hug her mother.

"Sit, my precious darlings," said Sun Raye. "We're about to have a confidential family conference."

Sun Raye paused to organize her thoughts before she began.

"You can't imagine all the scenarios I have replayed in my mind since that horrid day at Melody Key. I've even considered the possibility that I'm not just paranoid but that I could be the target of a voodoo curse. I'm convinced we have an enemy in our midst. What happened to me last week was not a fluke or an accident. It was a carefully orchestrated plot to either disrupt the proceedings or possibly worse yet, to harm me and my guests."

"Oh, mama, who..." Sea Raye began.

Sun Raye held up her hand for silence. "I don't know who it is, but hopefully I will know more soon. The toxic substance my guests encountered is a powder called Benedict's powder. It is a powder that is legally available to diagnose diabetes and has toxic side effects when it is either ingested or rubbed on the skin. It is odorless, tasteless and water soluble and in large doses can be fatal. This is not a chemical found in nature. It had to be planted there. Certain items on the island were dusted with it. Before you ask, I have no idea who the culprit was or why he did what he did, but with your help, we're going to find out. God help the bastard when I do."

"The second chemical present is something I do know

a bit more about. The cases of sunblock that I took to the meeting for samples contained cocaine. This contaminated product had to originate with Tango Products. I paid a surprise visit to Miguel Valdes and think I caught him flat-footed. He didn't know how to respond to my accusations. He reported back to me claiming he did an investigation and isolated the source of the problem. He says it was rogue employees and that he has dealt harshly with them. He vows it will never happen again. I think the odds are good that he's a lying sack of shit. Which is why your mom needs your help. If something ever happens to me, I want you to drive a stake in his black heart."

"Oh, I'm sure they would never ..." said Blue Raye.

"You never know what could happen," Sun Raye said. "These are some pretty rough people, but I don't care what kind of hoodlums Valdes' people are. I *will* uncover the truth no matter how long it takes, and I *will* make the culprits pay. I'm counting on being able to depend you and your husbands as well to win this war."

That night at home Blue Raye mentioned to her husband Bobby the meeting she had had with her mom, and her mom's determination to identify her persecutors. He winced but said virtually nothing to his wife. He silently listened and prayed she never found out his part in the fiasco or his level of involvement in Soltero's drug smuggling operation.

The following morning as Bobby and Billy were having their morning key lime pie and coffee at Casa Camilio Sur Bobby casually related the details of Sun Raye's meeting with her daughters to Valdes. Valdes almost came unglued.

"And you say the dizzy dame is determined not to let the matter drop? That is not good. I thought she bought my bullshit story. I must be losing my fuckin' charm. See what you've done, you dumb turd? This operation was going smooth as glass until your screw-up," he said and backhanded Bobby.

Valdes conveniently had selective memory about his own role in the Melody Key affair. It never once crossed his mind how ill-advised and unnecessary his vendetta against nudism had been. A consolation was that he was the only person who knew of his juvenile prank, and it was going to stay that way. Soltero didn't even suspect. He sure as hell wasn't going to risk discovery by confiding in this muscle-bound moron. He refused to acknowledge that the Benedict's powder probably been as big a factor in putting Sun Raye on the war-path as much as the cocaine.

"You say the whacked-out religious perra thought some voodoo vendetta may have played a part in it all. I can let it be the red-herring that takes the heat. She's going to be convinced when I'm through. I'm going to scare her shitless too, and she'll be only too glad to stop this witch-hunt. Then I can get back down to business," Valdes concluded. "Haven't I heard you say you know some of these voodoo types? I'm sure you either know one or can find one. You seem to know every weirdo in the Keys."

Bobby just nodded dully, finished his pie and wiped his mouth on his sleeve.

"Did you read Garfield this morning? Garfield kicked Odie in the air and then looked up at the sky and then when Odie hit the ground he said 'Someday we'll achieve orbit.' Isn't that a scream?" Bobby said.

"Yeah, a real scream," said Valdes. "Maybe one day we'll see if you can achieve orbit. Now get your asses out of here and tell your voodoo buddy I want to talk to him. Tell him I'll make it worth his while."

That afternoon a strange black man walked in the door of Casa Camilio Sur. He had a wad of unruly dreads tucked into a yellow, red and green striped knit cap. He wore a faded t-shirt and jeans. The T-shirt said "Zombies hate fast food." Valdes' eyes were instantly drawn to his feet. He was barefoot.

Before he could introduce himself the man's cell phone began to play Marley's "One Love, One Heart". He checked the text message and then put it back in his pocket.

"Mr. Valdes? Bobby Perez says you might need my assistance. My friends call me Burning Spear Chunker. Close friends call me Chunky," he said with a Boston accent.

Valdes rolled his eyes, sighed and thought to himself, *Christ, Bobby really does know every screw-ball in Key West.*

"You don't sound like no fuckin' voodoo priest, Chunky," Valdes said. "What does the phone company call you?"

"I'm an obeah man. And actually I'm listed in the directory under Elmo Levy."

Valdes stared at him like he was wearing a Speedo on the tundra.

"My father was a follower of Abraham, which is where my interest in religion originated. You see I have a master's degree in world religions from Brown. My thesis compared the beliefs of scientologists to Sikh," the man said.

Valdes sighed again. *Where does Bobby fuckin' find 'em.* But, hell, he just had a job that needed to be done. He wasn't adopting this oddball, just hiring him. So he took Spear Chunker in his office and explained the assignment he had in mind.

~ ~ ~

Early the following morning before anyone was awake, Spear Chunker drove his scooter to Kingdom Hall. He took a whole fish he had gotten on Stock Island and hung it from the sill over the front doors along with a Star of David.

This should scare the woman, he told himself. *If she is the novice to voodoo Mr. Valdes described, she'll interpret this as some kind of curse but won't know what kind.*

Chunky didn't know what kind either.

After Chunky left, it didn't take long after Chunky left for a feral cat that lived behind Kingdom Hall to smell the hanging fish. He climbed the door and began to claw at it and chew on the rope holding it up. The cat finally caused the fish to drop and began to devour the feast it had earned. It ate until it was joined by a hungry raccoon, at which time a fight ensued. Soon shredded pieces of stinky fish covered the doorway. Guts littered the sidewalk. When both creatures' appetites were satiated, they left the remainder to the ants.

Blue Raye was the first to arrive at work. She immediately thought the fish was something that had been dragged up by a wild animal and proceeded to clean up the mess before her mother could see it. She got Bobby to throw the residue into the dumpster.

Later that morning when Bobby was having his usual pie and coffee at the restaurant, Valdes casually asked, "Anything unusual going on at Kingdom Hall?"

"We had the damnedest mess to clean up over there this morning," Bobby said between bites. "Some wild animal dragged a fish up to the front door, but my wife and I got it cleaned up before the boss saw it. As it was, when we did tell her about it, she had a hissy-fit."

Valdes was upset that Spear Chunker's half-ass efforts had accomplished nothing, but he said nothing in front of Bobby. Instead he just gritted his teeth and drummed his fingers on the counter. After Bobby left he called Spear Chunker and vented his frustration.

"The bitch barely even knew the fish had been there. Try again, Mr. Obeah man."

The following morning Spear Chunker killed a Key West rooster and again drove to Kingdom Hall. Once again he hung it over the door. *This will get the woman's attention,* he told himself. Bobby came by a short time later and saw the chicken hanging. He walked up and felt it ... *This thing ain't road-kill. It's fresh.* He checked it for signs that it had been eaten-on. *It is still a beauty. You don't get them this fresh at Winn-Dixie. It would be criminal to let this go to waste.* Bobby got a sudden thought. *I'll surprise everyone with some chicken soup.* He pulled it down and took it to the kitchen to clean and prepare his windfall.

The following morning as Bobby was having his usual pie and coffee he laughingly told Valdes about his good luck the day before.

"I don't know where that chicken came from or why it was there, but there wasn't a damned thing wrong with it. It made a marvelous lunch," Bobby bragged.

Valdes wanted to get another chicken out of the cooler and beat Bobby to death with it, but all he could do was grit his teeth and drum his fingers on the counter.

Valdes certainly wasn't a practitioner of voodoo and he certainly wasn't an expert, but he felt like he could learn enough to hold his own. He Googled some ideas and found a ve-ve sign which appealed to him. He was tired of getting screwed because both animal and human chowhounds kept eating Spear Chuncker's symbolic rites. He called the voodoo man and screamed that he had better get his goddamned incompetent act together or Valdes was going take a damned burning spear and stuff it up his ass. He ordered him to try again to rattle that crazy bitch, and this time he said it was going to work because Spear Chunker was going to follow his instructions.

He told Spear Chunker to use a ritual ve-ve. He chose the Iwa Ogoun and showed Spear a picture. All Chunker had to do was draw it on her sidewalk where she couldn't possibly miss it.

Surely Ogoun Feray would terrify that crazy puta since Ogoun was a very powerful and vindictive warrior who was particularly fond of machetes. Chunky was to draw the ve-ve design out of the traditional materials of cornmeal, flour and coffee grounds. Directly on the ve-ve he would place Ogoun's favorite things: two machetes, rum, cigars and red beans and rice. Then he would encircle the design with the red and blue lines that were Ogoun's favorite colors. By God, she wouldn't be able to miss this, and the machetes should scare the hell out of her.

He didn't want to take any chances again so he dubbed a copy of a Haitian song about Ogoun on a CD.

Ogoun bebe a fawo
Ogoun bebe a fawo
Sa ki fo mwen byen, bay yo lavi pou mwen
Sa ki fe mwen mal, lese sang yo koule.

He ordered Chunky to break into Sun Raye's car and plant this recording in her stereo so that it would be the first thing she heard the next time she drove the car. Yes, this would definitely shake her up. She'd think some evil voodoo priest was after her and she'd let this whole matter drop and go into hiding before Ogoun could decapitate her with his machete. She'd never suspect it was this dipshit Rasta-wannabe Boston half-Jew Burning Spear Chunker.

Spear Chunker assembled the needed ingredients, packed the Ogoun sketch Valdes had given him, and took off on his scooter for Little Torch Key early the next morning. There was a brisk breeze coming in from the south when he arrived. He found a clean spot on the sidewalk and started drawing the ve-ve. He used corn meal, coffee grounds, and flour as he had been instructed. However, the wind kept blowing his artwork away. He tried several times, but the results continued to be the same, an unrecognizable mess. Then he got an idea. Five Brothers 2, less than a five-minute ride away, opened at six each morning for the early breakfast crowd. He would go to Five Brothers and buy some hair spray. This should hold his masterpiece together.

Chunky soon returned with several cans of hair spray. While he was in the store he decided on an impulse to reward himself with a bottle of wine when the job was done. With his wine in the cargo pocket of his shorts he returned to Kingdom Hall, quickly drew a section and sprayed it to hold it in place. This worked perfectly. He drew another section and quickly sprayed it. Now he was making progress. In short order he completed the ve-ve. He then placed two crossed machetes, a bottle of Wray and Nephew rum and some Dutch Masters cigars on it.

Chunky stepped back to admire his finished product and to see if it needed embellishment. When he did, he stepped in a bed of sand spurs. The sand spurs felt like thumb- tacks penetrating his bare feet. He instinctively jumped, knocking the bottle of wine out of his pocket. The wine hit the sidewalk and smashed. Before he could regain his composure, Chunky stepped on the sidewalk and into the broken glass. His masterpiece was now marred with big bloody footprints. He howled as he stubbed his toe on the rum bottle and hopped down the sidewalk cursing and leaving bloody footprints everywhere he stepped.

Hop! Hop! "Ouch! Shit! Goddamn!"

Hop! Hop! "Ouch! Shit! Goddamn!"

After the second set of hops, Chunky's personal supply of cocaine fell out of his shirt pocket and splattered in the blood and cornmeal.

Hop! Hop! "Ouch! Shit! Goddamn!"

Chunky fell down onto the pea-rock and started to pull the sand spurs out of his bleeding feet. He felt the CD Valdes had given him and suddenly remembered he was supposed to put it in Sun Raye's car. When he pulled it out of his pocket, it stuck to his hand. When he tried to sling it off, he stuck his finger in his eye.

"Fuck it!" he said as it came unstuck and sailed towards the door. "I've been here three times now. This woman must be a priestess herself. Her magic must be stronger than mine, and she's protecting herself with a curse. I better drag my Rasta-kike ass out of here before I get hurt worse."

In his panic to get the hell out of there, Chunky knocked the scooter over and skinned his knee. He got the bike cranked and ripped out of the driveway. After about a quarter of a mile he suddenly did a U-turn and returned. He reached down and snagged the Wray and Nephew bottle and took a deep burning swig. *Hell, I might as well get something out of this.*

When Sun Raye arrived at the building she was terrified. The voodoo sign covered with blood really shook her up.

So I was right after all. The events at Melody Key were voodoo inspired. I really am in trouble, Sun Raye thought.

CHAPTER 37

Claude McRaines was true to his word. He stayed in Key West and made it his mission to learn more of his daughter, Jacqueline's disappearance. He had flyers printed with his daughter's picture and began to spread them all over town. He posted them in public places and handed them out to anyone who would take one. He methodically interviewed people from all walks of life to see if anyone could remember meeting her. Days stretched into weeks, and his resolve did not lessen. He was convinced that the days before her disappearance had been spent in this island paradise. If discouragement was setting in, he never let it show as he continued his quest. He would often leave a flyer at a place of business and then return a few days later after it had had time to circulate among the staff.

On his second trip to Turtle Kraals he finally hit pay-dirt. The manager told McRaines that one of their fry-cooks thought he might recognize the girl in the photo and that the fry-cook would be working the evening shift later that day. He immediately jumped on the chance to return, and when he did, he was able to speak to the fry-cook.

"Mr. Hillhouse ..."

"Please call me Toby," Hillhouse said.

"Toby, then, my name is Claude McRaines. I am looking for my daughter. Your manager told me that you might possibly have recognized her picture."

"Maybe. I was off work on Memorial Day weekend," said the fry-cook. "That was when they had the Minimal Regatta here at the Bight. Turtle Kraals entered a team in the competition so I came to cheer them on. A queer woman invaded the race and almost caused some people to get hurt. She was talking out of her head. The cops picked her up and took her to the hospital. I think she may have been this girl, but I can't be sure because in this picture of your daughter the girl has long hair. The girl at the regatta had a completely shaved head. I remember her face because the girl seemed familiar. She reminded me of a customer that our bartender had been hitting on awhile back. Once again, I can't be sure because the girl he had the hots for had a completely different hair style from either the picture or the girl in the bar."

"Is that bartender working here today?" McRaines asked.

"He doesn't work here anymore. Management let him go when they caught him doing a line of coke in the restroom."

"What's his name? Do you know where he lives?" McRaines asked.

"His name is Ian Greenwood. I don't know where he lives."

"Thank you very much, Toby. You have been a big help."

The following morning Claude McRaines visited the Key West Police Department. He explained to the sergeant on duty who he was and the nature of his mission.

"One of Turtle Kraal's employees told me that he thought my daughter might be the girl who caused the big uproar at this year's Minimal Regatta."

"That girl was a Jane Doe who we have never been able to identify, but if she is your daughter, Mr. McRaines, I have some bad news for you. The girl at the Minimal Regatta died at Lower Keys Medical Center of a heart attack brought on by a cocaine overdose. It is called cocaethylene poisoning and results from ingesting a combination of cocaine and alcohol."

"Would the body still be available for me to see?"

"No, unfortunately. The county normally keeps a body for two to four weeks. Then it is required by Florida law to bury it. She would be buried in Key West Cemetery since we are not allowed to cremate unidentified bodies. The Medical Examiner, however, makes photos, takes fingerprints and dental impressions, and takes DNA samples before the body is interred. We also keep partial information here. I will be glad to look and see what we have."

McRaines wiped away a tear and said, "Please."

The sergeant came back a few minutes later with photos of the girl who had disrupted the Minimal Regatta. He spread them out on the desk. McRaines picked up the pictures of the girl with the shaved head one by one and looked at them in silence. He wiped his eyes as the tears began to flow and mumbled in a strained voice, "My God, my God, Jacqueline, what has happened to you? Where did I go wrong as a parent?" He stared at the pictures for several minutes and then pushed them back across the desk to the sergeant. He croaked in a barely audible voice, "Thank you, officer. I won't keep you any longer. We'll let her rest in peace here in Key West." He turned to leave. "I will deal with paperwork at another time."

McRaines went back to Schooner Wharf and just sat and stared. He stayed in a trance for the rest of the afternoon, saying nothing to anyone. Finally, he got the energy and resolve to trudge back to his hotel.

The following morning McRaines looked in the phone book and found the address of the former Turtle Kraals bartender, Ian Greenwood. He called Ian on the phone and arranged a time to meet him.

"Mr. Greenwood, do you recognize the girl in this picture?"

Ian became nervous and defensive.

"Mr. Greenwood, please. I do not want to cause you any trouble. I am not a policeman. This girl is my daughter, my only child Jacqueline. Please help me if you can."

"She looks like a girl I took out a few times, but the girl I knew was not called Jacqueline. She called herself Mona Wooten."

"Do you know where Mona lived?" McRaines asked.

"An apartment over on Eisenhower. We used to party there. Now that I think about it, I haven't seen her for a good while. I don't know the address, but I can take you there."

"I would be eternally grateful. What else can you tell me about my daughter?"

"I know she worked for a company named Tango Products. She told me so. After I got laid off at Turtle Kraal, I tried to get her to get me a job there."

McRaines put his hand gently on Ian's arm. "May I ask you one more question? And I promise whatever you tell me will never go any farther. Was my daughter a drug user?"

Ian looked down, said nothing, and slowly nodded.

Ian took Claude McRaines over to the apartment on Eisenhower and left him there. Claude talked to the building manager, showed her a picture and confirmed that his daughter had been living in the apartment building. He also learned that his daughter's rent had recently become delinquent, and the manager was looking for her. McRaines offered to bring the rent current if the apartment manager would allow him to look around. The manager resisted at first, but McRaines suggested he call the Key West Police Department and talk to the sergeant. The sergeant satisfied the manager enough to both sympathize and cooperate with him and left him alone in the apartment.

McRaines went through the apartment and in a drawer found the stock certificates Jacqueline's aunt had left her. They were in envelopes from Reynolds Smathers and Thompson Securities. The delivery receipt cited an account number. McRaines put the certificates into his briefcase. The remaining items in the apartment were of little interest. Since it was a furnished apartment, they consisted of a minimal amount of clothing and personal items. When he was finished he closed and locked the door and returned the key to the apartment manager, not mentioning the certificates. Before he left, he asked the lady if she knew where his daughter had worked. She told him she thought the company was on 11th Avenue on Stock Island.

His next trip was to Stock Island. It did not take him

long to locate Tango Products and

Miguel Valdes.

"Mr. Valdes," he said, pulling out a picture. "Do you recognize this girl? I am told she worked for you. I'm her father."

Valdes looked at the picture and returned it to McRaines.

"Yeah, I knew her. She worked here for awhile. She quit months ago. I don't know nuthin' about her. People come; people go."

McRaines attempted to quiz Valdes about his daughter. He wanted to know what she did at Tango, if she had been friends with any other employee, or if Valdes could tell him anything else. Valdes was evasive and not very helpful. After a few minutes he told McRaines he hated to be abrupt but he was very busy.

When he left, Valdes called Soltero. "Mind dropping by? It's important."

"I'll be there."

"I just had a surprise this afternoon. Remember that twerp Mona Wooten who used to work here," Valdes said after he had taken Soltero back to his office and closed the door.

"You mean the one who discovered the cocaine we were packing in CANDO products?' Soltero said.

"Yep, The fuckin' junkie who ended up stealing coke from us," Valdes said.

"I told you to take care of her," Soltero said. "I don't like the idea that she stole from us. Making her pay would send a signal to others. But worse yet we don't need someone out there who could be a potential source of information or a possible witness for the authorities."

"I put the Perez boys on the project, but she got scared and gave them the slip. We were not able to recover any of the product she stole. I'm sure it went up her nose. They've been looking for the bitch all summer, but it's like she dropped off the face of the earth. We thought that possibly she had blown out of the Keys," said Valdes.

"And now her father is down here stirring the pot?" asked Soltero. "This is not good. What do you think he's learned? There's no telling what he might do next. Desperate people are unpredictable. We cannot risk the problems that a loose cannon could cause."

"I understand," Valdes said. "We will monitor his activities and will take care of him if it becomes necessary."

"If you do, make it look like an accident. And Miguel, put one of your better men on this project. There is too much at stake to risk a foul-up," demanded Soltero.

"You mean assign Billy Perez rather than Bobby."

"Precisely."

~ ~ ~

The following day, McRaines revisited Will Black.

"Mr. Black, I found the stock certificates my daughter inherited from her aunt. They were shipped to her by your firm," he said accusingly.

"May I see what you have, Mr. McRaines?" Will asked.

McRaines handed over everything he had found.

Will instantly saw that the envelopes were indeed RST envelopes, and when he opened one of them, he found a delivery receipt. It had the account number of an account in the Delaware, Ohio office.

"I can readily see why I did not know your daughter dealt with our firm. Her account was with our Delaware, Ohio office. We do not have access to information about accounts in offices other than our own. It is a security, privacy and compliance matter," Will said.

"I can understand, but can you rebook the certificates in the account?"

"I can put them in safekeeping, but I can't put them in a street name without your daughter's endorsement. They are non-negotiable in this form and can never be sold without a valid stock-power. I'll tell the broker in Delaware to prepare stock powers for her to sign."

"I'd rather that no one in Delaware learn about this situation."

"I can't open a new account here since she is not here to sign the new account documents, but since the old account is flat, the broker will not object if I do an inter-office transfer and move it down here," Will said.

"I would appreciate that."

"But if you don't want the broker in Delaware to see the securities being booked in, you will have to wait until the account has moved to this office to deposit the stocks."

"How long will that take?"

"A few days, but I'm still going to need to get your daughter to sign the certificates before they can become negotiable instruments," Will said.

"Mr. Black, I'm afraid I'm going to have to level with you. That's not going to be possible since my daughter is dead."

"Dead? I'm so sorry to hear that. When and where did it happen?"

"She died of a heart attack Memorial Day weekend at the Lower Keys Medical Center brought on by substance abuse. She was in some sort of disruptive incident at what you locals call the Minimal Regatta."

"My God! She was the girl with the shaved head who collapsed on Schooner Wharf. My wife and I were there and saw that happen. I am so sorry," Will said.

"Thank you for your condolences. Do you understand now why I don't want word of this leaking back to Ohio, and why I don't want the stock certificates deposited there?"

"Yes, I do," Will said.

"I'm going to have to hire an attorney to find out where I stand on this matter, Mr. Black. My daughter did not have a will. Who ever thought she would need one at her age?"

"I understand. My daughter doesn't have a will either, but in her defense I will have to say she doesn't own several hundred thousand dollars worth of stocks either," Will said.

"I will tell you something else in confidence too, Mr. Black. The reason for my daughter's death was that someone hooked her on illegal narcotics and was providing her with them. I will not rest until I identify this person and make him pay for his crime."

"Do you have any leads as to who this could be?"

"She was working for a company named Tango Products on Stock Island. It is owned by a man named Miguel Valdes. I've been led to believe that her pusher may have been one of her co-workers there."

"Mr. McRaines, I want to give you some friendly

advice off the record. I would not advise you to proceed on this matter alone. I know Mr. Valdes. He has a reputation for being a very unsavory and dangerous man. I think you should go to the police."

"Thank you for the warning, and I'll take it into consideration, but I hope you understand – I am determined to make the people responsible for my daughter's death pay. What day do you want me to return with the certificates?"

"Try Friday, but call first. I'll tell you if there has been a delay."

"Thank you Mr. Black." With that Claude McRaines left Will's office.

Billy Perez watched him leave RST and wondered why McRaines would visit a stock broker. He reported McRaines' activities back to Valdes and Soltero.

~ ~ ~

The following day McRaines paid another visit to Toby, the ex-bartender. He learned the names of more of his daughter's party friends and interviewed them. All were uncomfortable talking to this stranger and told him little. Billy Perez stalked him wherever he went and would interrogate each person after Claude left. McRaines tried to no avail to find out who Jacqueline's pusher was. Finally one of her former companions admitted that his daughter had been providing cocaine for their whole group. He wasn't totally sure where she had been getting the coke but had the impression it may have been at work. Another search of Jacqueline's apartment finally revealed hidden drug paraphernalia. At first McRaines cried when he found it. Then he saw red and was more determined than ever to get to the bottom of this whole dirty affair that had caused his daughter's death. All of his activities continued to be monitored and reported by Billy Perez.

In an absolute out-of-control snit, McRaines drove back over to Tango Products. Valdes had just pulled out of the parking lot. He followed Valdes over to Casa Camilio Sur and marched into the restaurant. The place was empty. Valdes had just poured himself a cup of coffee and was sitting at a table to go over some invoices. McRaines walked up and threw the drug paraphernalia down on the table. He hovered over Valdes and shook his fist.

"I know either you or someone else at Tango was responsible for my daughter's death, and I'm going to take you down. I have the proof to do it," McRaines bluffed.

Valdes stood, got in McRaines' face and punched him in the chest with his finger.

"Look muthafucker, I didn't even know your piece-of-shit junkie daughter was dead. Back off, or I'm gonna hurt you bad," Valdes said.

~ ~ ~

On Friday, McRaines called Will's office and inquired if he could deposit his daughter's stock certificates. Will said 'yes,' the account had been transferred with no problems. When McRaines came in, he told Will of his showdown with Valdes and reiterated his determination to find the person responsible for his daughter's death. Will repeated his previous warning.

A few days later Will was reading his morning paper. A headline caught his attention.

Hit And Run Rampage:
Police Looking For Perpetrator

Key West police are searching for a man responsible for carrying out a Monday morning rampage in a Nissan Rogue SUV in which he mowed down four pedestrians crossing the 400 block of Truman before grazing a light pole and driving away.

The man, who is thought to be an unidentified Hispanic man in his twenties, has eluded capture thus far. The SUV was found but turned out to be a stolen vehicle belonging to a resident of New Town.

The victims have been identified as local resident Kevin Fagan, his life-companion George Cascón, cruise ship passenger Potrero Hill, and Claude McRaines, a tourist from Ohio.

Police have not established a motive for the rampage. Anyone having any information that could help police solve this crime should call the Key West Police Department at 305 809-1000.

He read the article to Betsy, and they agreed he should call Walter Wanderley as soon as he got to his office.

"Walter. Will Black. I'm calling about those pedestrians who were mowed down on Truman."

"That was really strange," Walter said. "We still don't know for sure whether it was an accident or done on purpose, but regardless, whenever we find this twisted perp, we're going to put him under the jail for a long, long time. Personally I would like to pull the switch on him as he fries. Witnesses say it appears that the driver targeted these people and just mowed them down."

"The reason I'm calling is I know one of the victims. He has been to my office several times recently," Will said.

"Oh! Which one?"

"Claude McRaines, the man from Ohio. He came down here to find his missing daughter. It turned out she's the bald-headed woman who disrupted the Minimal Regatta this year."

"Best I remember that woman died; we never could identify her," Walter said.

"McRaines positively ID'ed her. She was a RST client in Ohio. He transferred her account to Key West and brought me a number of stocks to book into her account that he had found in her apartment. He had turned into a zealot obsessed on finding out who was providing his daughter with cocaine."

"This is interesting news. I never thought about McRaines as being the target," Walter said. "I thought it was probably the two gay guys who got killed. You know, some homophobe or possibly a jilted lover."

"This guy's daughter had worked for one of Miguel Valdes' companies called Tango Products. He seemed to think someone at Tango was his daughter's pusher and was determined to get to the bottom of things."

"He's fooling with some tough characters there," Walter said. "We've never been able to pin anything on Valdes, but I still have hopes."

"In the meantime Claude has left me with a mess," Will said. "An account full of non-negotiable securities, and I can't even establish who owns them. The girl's dead. Her dad was a single father. Now he's dead. She had no will. She was an only child. I don't know if she has other relatives or not. Her dad said something about getting a local attorney, but I don't know if he did or not. And if he did, I don't know who the attorney is. Do me a favor, Walter, if you get a line on any other family members, let me know who they are and how to contact them."

"Of course. In the meantime, I'm going to follow up on what you've told me, but it's still not going to be easy. The SUV was stolen and had been wiped clean. The witnesses can't identify the driver because he had a hat pulled down over his face."

CHAPTER 38

Sun Raye's conscience would give her no peace. Day by day she felt more guilt. Even though she knew it was illogical, she blamed herself over and over for Jennifer Jacquette's extreme allergic reaction to the Benedict's powder. She also asked herself repeatedly about the presence of cocaine at her meeting and what role Miguel Valdes or one of his associates might have had in it. She was frustrated by her inability to find a way to deal with it and began to lose sleep as a result of her preoccupation.

Finally after three fitful nights in a row, a totally exhausted Sun Raye fell into a deep troubled sleep, which soon led to a vivid dream.

At first she had a strange feeling that her bed was pitching and rocking. She began to fantasize that she was no longer in a bed but instead was nude in a boat on a turbulent sea. The boat had no motor or any paddles or oars for her to guide but was instead drifting aimlessly. Suddenly an island appeared out of nowhere and the boat ran aground. Since there was no reason to stay on the boat she went ashore.

She wandered all around and could find no one so she sat on the beach and drank water from the ocean. Even in her dream, she was shocked to find it to be fresh water. Then she stood and began to yell, thinking someone might hear her, but instead she couldn't even hear herself. She was mute!

The sky became overcast behind her, but in front of her it was blue. Through a coconut palm hammock she saw a large white mansion. The house began to sway as she approached it. The palm hammock was extremely dense around the house, and she found herself walking through a wide assortment of bromeliads, all of which were in bloom. All were like nothing she had ever seen before.

She walked along a wall made of coral rock trying to find an entrance to the door-less house. She heard voices. They were talking in strange tongues. A hooded man seemed to be calling to her. Although she didn't recognize him, she was drawn to him. He began to speak English and said over and over, "Wait for the door to open." She kept circling the house until she saw a door. It was small but growing and seemed to beckon to her. She ran towards it but stopped when she remembered the man's message, "Wait for the door to open." It began to open slowly on a single frozen hinge, and she entered.

Inside she found other nude people stumbling and wandering around. CANDO promotional material was everywhere. No one seemed able to see her. It suddenly dawned on her that all these people were blind. She approached a man and asked him where she was. He turned to face her but said nothing. She approached a woman who did the same thing. She suddenly realized these people were deaf as well as blind. She turned to run but now realized she herself made no noise. She was deaf as well.

She looked up and saw a bright orange iguana highlighted against a crimson ceiling. It had gigantic tusks, butterfly wings, and bat-like ears. Its slanted red eyes glared at her. It opened its mouth, a black tongue shot forth, and sunscreen poured out, drowning all the people in the room. They attempted to hold on to floating furniture, but each time they grabbed a piece it would dissolve in their hands.

As strange as things seemed, she was not afraid until the iguana spotted her and moved towards her. She ran and ran but it came increasingly closer. She fell down, and it flew over a cliff where mangroves reached out, encircled it and squeezed it until it was limp. Its lifeless form then fell into a bottomless diamond quarry.

Sun Raye awoke trembling and sweating, convinced the dream was sending her a message that she shouldn't fear her tormenter and could defeat whoever had sabotaged her meeting at Melody Key. She was more determined than ever to get to the bottom of the sordid matter. Since her only suspect was Miguel Valdes, it did not take Sun Raye long to decide that she could get into his facility on Stock Island.

CHAPTER 39

Sun Raye was nervous and uncertain about the upcoming foray. She had never initiated or participated in a break-and-enter. She chose Sunday morning since she figured it to be the least likely time anyone would be working and probably when she was least likely to encounter a passing patrolman.

Sun Raye parked a block away and made the short walk to Tango Products. She wasn't sure what her game plan was. She thought she would simply play things by ear. The door, as she had expected, was securely locked. She walked the perimeter of the building, shaking each window to see if one were either open or unlatched. Finally she hit pay-dirt. Whoever had been using the bathroom left the window up a tad to freshen the air. It only took a moment to push the window open all the way, find something to stand on, and squeeze through headfirst. *Good thing I'm a woman,* she thought. *A man would never be able to squirm through that opening.*

Sun Raye came down headfirst on the restroom floor. It was disgustingly dirty, and the whole place smelled like a cheap gas station urinal. The sink hadn't been cleaned in months. *No wonder they left the window cracked,* she thought. *The only way they could stand it.* When she came out of the bathroom she was in a big open room. At one end were mixing vats. Not far away were 55 gallon drums and piles of bags filled with raw ingredients. On the other side of the room was a bottling operation and the other end was a loading dock with pallets of finished cases of product. Near the bottling area on pallets were stacks of flat cardboard boxes. More boxes were on a rack a few feet away. *Nothing unusual here.*

Sun Raye found a utility knife and cut open one of the filled cases. The contents looked perfectly normal. She rubbed her finger on the inside of the box. *Nothing.* She found a tape-gun and taped it shut again. She tried the same thing with another case. *Once again, nothing.* A third produced the same results.

She walked over to the bottling area. She saw both 6 ounce and 8 ounce empty bottles. *Funny,* she thought, *I didn't know we made 6 ounce bottles. My shipments have always been 8 ounces. They must have had some special requests.*

She noticed a small Spartan office near the bathroom. The door was unlocked. Inside were two rusting metal filing cabinets. The first one was unlocked. When she opened the drawer she saw files with familiar names on them. They seemed to be legitimate folders labeled with the names of distributors she knew very well. The contents showed the ordering history of each distributor. She found the folder for shipments going to Kingdom Hall. *Seems like the ordinary course of business,* she thought.

She tried the other filing cabinet. *Locked.* She wondered why. *Maybe someone just forgot to lock the first one.* She saw a letter opener on the desk. She tried unsuccessfully to jimmy the lock. There was a magnetic paperclip container on the desk. She took one out, bent it, and stuck it in the keyhole and wiggled it. The lock turned and popped out. *Eureka!* Inside were folders with the names of distributors she did not recognize. Nothing seemed unusual at first. After all she didn't know the name of every distributor. Something unusual she did notice, however, was that the case numbers that had been recorded used a whole different numbering system than the ones she had looked at in the first filing cabinet. She went back to the first filing cabinet and selected a file at random. Yes, they were using a dual numbering system. *Unusual but there must be a reason.*

Sun Raye noticed another door going off the back of the office. It was securely locked with multiple dead-bolt locks. She tried to see if she might get lucky and be able to jimmy them, but they held it secure.

She walked back out into the warehouse wondering. *No red flags anywhere.* Then she noticed some flat pieces of cardboard on the box rack. She picked one up. It was partially perforated such that when the perforations were torn and it was folded, it formed a tray that stood about two inches high. *I wonder what these are used for.* Then she noticed that the boxes on the same rack used the numbering system of the shipments recorded in the second filing cabinet. She also remembered that the cases she had used to confront Valdes with after the Melody Key incident had contained these false bottoms. *False bottoms.* A light went off in her head. *Of course, false bottoms. The cases at Melody Key had also had false bottoms but so what.*

She pulled an empty case down and squared it up. She then took down one of the flat panels, folded it, and put it inside the box. It fit perfectly.

Sun Raye looked at her watch and decided she had been here too long. So she put everything back like she found it, slithered back out the restroom window, and put the window back down again. She still wasn't sure what she had found out. She had found no coke, but something told her that things at Tango weren't as uncomplicated at they appeared.

The one thing Sun Raye didn't notice as she roamed Tango were the security cameras that had been observing her from the moment she first left the restroom. They had been turned on by a motion detector. A red light blinked discreetly in Valdes' office each time they were activated to inform him that the tapes needed examining. Miguel Valdes would not see the footage until the next day. He would be livid when he finally did.

~ ~ ~

"You need to come over to the restaurant, Al," Valdes said through the phone Monday. "We got a fuckin' problem. I'll tell you about it when you get here."

When Soltero came in, Valdes motioned him back to his office.

"We had visitor at Tango yesterday," he said. "Watch this."

He played the tape.

"What do you think she learned?" Al said.

"Hopefully nothing she'll ever put together," Miguel said. "But the filing cabinet where we keep our preferred customers was breached, and the bitch was playing around with the special cases we use for certain shipments."

"Let's just keep this matter between the two of us," Al

244

said, "but let's begin keeping our religious friend on a shorter leash."

"I think we ought to take that goddamned leash, wrap it around her scrawny neck, and strangle her to death with it," Valdes said.

"I don't want to start a public disturbance if I can avoid it," Al said, "but if she becomes a threat, we may be forced to choose the ultimate resolution."

The unimaginable then happened. Jennifer Jacquette died from allergic complications to her exposure to Benedict's powder.

People at the bank were saddened and shocked. She had been one of their most popular tellers for many years. Jennifer baked as a hobby and generously brought an assortment of goodies to the bank. She had also just been a fun person to be around, dressing in costumes for various bank promotions. Only rarely did she choose not to participate in the wide array of fundraisers and charity events like walkathons that the bank chose to sponsor.

Reactions to her death ranged from "Why does God take the good ones?" to "She was too young to die."

Her husband, Jock, was devastated. He retreated into a world of his own creation not knowing how, when or if he would heal. He suspended his accounting practice temporarily while he built a do-it-yourself coffin in his garage from a kit he bought. He put Jennifer's arrangements at the funeral home on hold while he worked long hours for several days assembling the pieces. The coffin had a distressed look when he finished because every once in a while the grief would consume his thoughts, and he would whack his work-in-progress with his hammer out of frustration. When Jock was finished, he decoupaged pictures from their marriage on the top and sides. Then he just sat and stared at his creation as he looked at each photo and thought of their time together.

The time not spent working on the coffin was spent on his computer. He changed Jennifer's Facebook page to one that would memorialize her life. He made arrangements for her funeral to be filmed and put online so that mourners would be able to participate from a distance in her final eulogy in case they were unable to attend the service in person. He set up a virtual memorial on the Internet. He thought of the concept of releasing butterflies at her funeral service but couldn't find out how to implement his obsession. He found a web site selling custom "In Loving Memory" decals and ordered one with Jennifer's name and date of death for the back window of his car. No matter what he did, however, Jock could not shake the depression that completely overwhelmed him and sapped his will.

These distractions turned out to be a temporary refuge. Jock needed a more tangible reminder of Jennifer. He decided he wanted a death mask to remember her. He wanted to be sure it was done right and knowing very little about such things he approached his dentist for assistance. He chose his dentist because he knew the dentist made dental molds from plaster of Paris. The dentist balked on getting involved so Jock offered to pay double his going rate for some pending dental work if he would help. The reluctant dentist researched the available materials and suggested they use alginate, a flexible, malleable, extremely light material made from seaweed. The dentist explained to Jock that the mold he would be making was not reusable so he would need to be careful with the finished product.

The funeral director thought the whole matter was very strange, but he couldn't think of a reason to deny Jock's request. After all, Jock wasn't mutilating the body. The funeral director's only request was that they put a cardboard shield around the facial area to keep from making a mess on his table. The casting went well despite the fact that the dentist had to get drunk to face the gruesome task, and Jock got the plaster cast he wanted. Jock took it home and spent hours alone looking at Jennifer's face and remembering their married life.

Jock still felt a void. Finally he decided to demand restitution for Jennifer's death and use the money to set up a foundation in his wife's memory.

Many of Jennifer's friends and colleagues from the bank attended her service. Will and Betsy were both present. A tearful Jock announced his intention to set up a foundation in her memory, though he neglected to mention the details of how it would be funded. With all that was going on, very few people gave the matter much thought. Jock, however, had a plan in mind.

The day following the service he made a call on Sun Raye and her inner circle at Kingdom Hall. They were sitting at the conference room table having breakfast when he arrived. Jock carried the death mask wrapped in butcher paper.

Bobby was eating a big bag of Cheetos. An open one-liter bottle of Dr. Pepper sat on the table. Billy was eating a bowl of Fruit Loops in milk. The ladies ate fruit cocktail.

"What you got there? You bring us some fresh bagels?" Bobby asked. Jock did not answer but carefully placed the package on the table.

"Jock, that was a very touching service yesterday. We will all miss Jennifer greatly," Sun Raye said.

"I can't believe she's gone. She was my whole life. She was not only my wife but my best friend as well," Jock said, choking out his words. "I want to establish a foundation so she won't be forgotten."

He slid the unopened package across the table.

"I heard you say that at the service yesterday," Sun Raye said. "Is there anything we can do to help?"

"Since my beloved died from attending a CANDO function, I think CANDO should fund her foundation," Jock said.

"We're certainly willing to contribute," Sun Raye said. "But we can't be expected to fund it in its entirety."

"I believe you are somehow responsible for my wife's death, and I'm willing to proceed with legal action if you shirk your responsibility."

Bobby unwrapped the package. Jennifer's dead eyes stared back at him. Bobby was visibly shaken and jumped back slightly.

"What kind of money do you have in mind?" Bobby asked when everyone had recovered his composure. He flexed his muscles for emphasis by pressing his fists together.

"Oh, I would settle on half a million," Jock said. "You're getting off easy. I'm sure I would win more than that if I had to sue."

"Bull-fuckin'-shit! The only settlement you'll get is

when I bounce your ass on the pavement," Bobby growled and pushed the package back at Jock. As he rose and pushed the death mask, Bobby's wife swatted his massive arms down and pushed him back into his chair. The mask hit the Dr. Pepper, sending it careening into the bowl of Fruit Loops. This amalgamation covered the death mask in a sticky goo. Trying to save the situation Billy accidentally dumped Bobby's bag of Cheetos on the whole mess. The Cheetos stuck to the death mask like orange worms giving the mask a creepy Medusa-like quality.

"Get outa here!" Bobby yelled.

Jock shrieked and reached for the wet sticky death mask. When he did, it slipped from his hands and hit him on the toe. It bounced and broke off Jennifer's nose. Jock squealed painfully again and fell on his knees to look for the broken proboscis. It was broken into little pieces.

"You're going to be sorry you didn't deal with me willingly and fairly," Jock said after he regained his composure.

"Is that a threat, weirdo?" Bobby growled.

"I'll let you interpret my meaning any way you want, but you will be sorry," Jock said and turned to leave. He slipped in the milk and almost lost his footing. He limped out carrying his damaged effigy, favoring his sore toe.

After he left, Sun Raye turned to Bobby and said, "Do you always have to act like an animal?"

"I don't take no shit offa nobody and certainly not a jerk-wad with a broken Halloween mask," Bobby said.

Sun Raye needed to find out more than ever just who was behind the horrible activities that had marred that day at Melody Key.

CHAPTER 40

Barbara told Will that Jock Jacquette wanted to come in and talk to him.

"You're kidding," Will said. "He moved everything out of here."

"Go figure," Barbara said. "Maybe things aren't going well for him where he is. I told him eleven."

Jock was in Will's office promptly at eleven. After offering him some coffee and a brief minute of unsuccessful small talk Will asked him the nature of his business."

"I want you to take my accounts back," Jock said.

"Why the change of heart? Are the returns not up to your expectations?" Will asked. "I thought your expectations were unrealistically optimistic. As I told you before we do not have the ability to be the custodian for Chosen Ones Growth Fund. There's a good chance you'll lose money if you sell it."

"It has nothing to do with returns," Jock said emphatically. "And I don't give a damn if I lose money. I want out of there. I am going to sell it regardless … And then I'm going to get my revenge against the bastards."

"Jock, you're starting to scare me. I don't know what you're talking about, but please don't do anything you'll regret."

"Oh, I'll have no regrets. My life ended when Jennifer died."

Jock then ranted about the fateful day at Melody Key. He turned red as his blood pressure rose and at one point had trouble catching his breath. Will knew more about the story than Jock did from the account that Jason and Kevin had related, but he just silently listened. Jock raged about his meeting with Sun Raye and the others at Kingdom Hall. He even told Will that he and Jennifer had been trying to start a family. Finally he exhausted himself and seemed to shrink into an empty shell. He left looking like a beaten man.

Will told Betsy later that he had wondered if Jock might be suicidal or homicidal. They debated about whether they should share their feelings with Walter Wanderley but finally decided to say nothing for the time being. They didn't want to cause Jock any further problems since he had been through so much recently.

CHAPTER 41

Luis Bernstein felt sticky like he needed to bathe. Sweat dripped from his armpits and droplets ran down his side as his fingers were poised above his keyboard. The room in his safe-house felt stuffy despite the window unit humming only a few feet away. In spite of this he felt exhilarated to be back in the game. He hadn't realized how much he missed the action and challenge.

The equipment was partially responsible for heating the room up. He had crammed several servers and laptops into the Islamorada motel room. The processors produced a swelter that pulsed through the room. The remaining heat was caused by the tension and excitement of being back in the saddle again.

After spending five years in a Federal prison for hacking, Luis had vowed never to risk hacking again. When Luis was growing up, he had been a computer geek in a town where the outdoor types typically were the ones to get the girls. By the time he got to Key West High he was dabbling in computer and phone hacking, taking printouts of the hacker zine *bigfish* to class and phreaking free phone calls. He also developed an aggressive streak. He was one of the few geeks willing to stand up to class jocks and bullies who loved to taunt him and his geeky friends. At one point he was even charged with assault with a deadly weapon but was let off with probation and a slap on the wrist since he was a minor.

At the University of Miami he took on a new cyber name, *unlimited vision*. He rented a house in South Miami which he and some of his friends transformed into a geek paradise, pimping it with high-performance equipment, with Cat5 cable being laid down the halls. At night they celebrated at all-night raves on South Beach.

After graduating with a degree in communications, Luis started a consulting business, hiring himself out as a freelance hacker. He earned more than $100 an hour performing penetration tests for corporate clients in Miami and Fort Lauderdale. He also volunteered his whitehat skills for local law enforcement, all the while wanting to be a real hacker. What he was doing was like watching porn when he could be having real sex. Therefore as an avocation Luis began to spend his off-hours cavorting through private networks of the very kind he spent his days defending his clients against.

Finally his double life collapsed when Internet experts found a security hole in his ubiquitous BIND name server daemon. If left unpatched, the security hole would allow attackers to seize control of hundreds of thousands of machines. Luis took it upon himself to break into federal sites and fix the error, and while he was at it, install a small backdoor, thereby leaving himself an entryway into government and military networks nationwide.

Soon Luis's computer screen began to explode with alerts from military bases, nuclear labs, the National Institute of Health, and the US Departments of Commerce, Transportation and Interior. This was dandy fun until one day the FBI with the help of a young Navy investigator traced Luis through his popup notifications.

He then learned what it was like to have all teeth and no shell. Luis was headed for five years in the Federal pen.

Luis hummed "The Thrill Is Gone" as he again felt the old rush that had been a big motivator for him in the old days. He told himself, *No, the thrill never went away. Circumstances just forced me to take an unplanned vacation for awhile. It feels good for "unlimited vision" to be back in the driver's seat where I belong.*

He had never told Sun Raye of his background. It didn't seem relevant to their business and personal dealings together. All it could do was prejudice their relationship. He had quietly used his knowledge to keep tabs on 21st Century Securities as well as Chip Talbos and Rodney Chamberlain. He had gradually figured out their game from monitoring their e-mails which had tipped him off about their stock manipulation efforts and the windfall profits they derived from Chosen Ones Growth Fund. He had also learned much about their interrelationship to Adolfo Soltero and Miguel Valdes. One thing he had not figured out was their relationship to the cartel. If he had known this, he might not have been so brazen. He didn't know everything, but he knew just enough to formulate a plan to enrich himself at their expense.

Luis set up a brokerage account with Direxion Securities, a small Internet trading firm. The broker's daughter was a CANDO distributor.

The plan was a simple one. He would hack into 21st Century's computer and monitor their trading activity and their internal communications. When he saw from their memos that they were about to institute one of their pump-and-dump schemes he would buy stock for himself.

He would then monitor the stock's volume, price action, and their subsequent communications and then dump the stock ahead of 21st Century.

Luis put his plan into action. It worked remarkably well. Within a few months his initial grubstake was up several thousand percent and he was able to buy more and more stock on each trade. This was truly like taking candy from a baby. The excitement he got reminded him just why he had gotten into hacking to begin with so many years ago.

CHAPTER 42

Chip Talbos decided he needed to pay Adolfo Soltero a visit to discuss a problem.

"Al, we've got a problem at 21st Century that I have not been able to get my arms around," Talbos said. "Somebody is beating us at our own game."

"In what way?"

"Every time we have a new investment idea lately, a big block of stock trades and drives the price up. Every time we decide to move on to a new idea and sell the old position, a sizeable block of stock front-runs us and drives the price down. It hasn't caused us to lose any money, but it sure as hell has kept us from maximizing our profits from our research recommendations."

"Is it an employee?" Al asked.

"That was my first reaction too. Now I don't think so. I've made a maximum effort to detect a crooked salesman, and I've come up empty. Besides that, we also have tried to really put the fear of God into our employees."

"Then the problem must be external," Al said.

"Exactly. That's why I need your help. I need someone with more knowledge than I have to find out who this individual is."

"What are the names of some of the securities where problems have occurred?" Al asked.

As Chip filled him in with the list, Al took notes.

"Let me see what I can do. I'll be back to you," Al said.

"Why don't I try to use some of my contacts in Jersey to see what I can learn first," Chip said.

"OK, keep me posted," Al said. "I'll put out some discreet inquiries as well."

~ ~ ~

Al, not Chip, was the person who had a breakthrough in the dilemma. The breakthrough came from Berrios & Aguinaga. One of the accountants casually mentioned that Luis Bernstein seemed to have turned into quite a stock trader. Soltero pressed him for more information. The accountant reported Luis's 1040 tax return had been complicated by a very extensive schedule D that was three pages long. Schedule D is the schedule in which a taxpayer declares capital gains and losses. He was surprised because in past years Luis had not even been required to file a schedule D. Even stranger was that his current schedule D had no losses, only gains, and all the gains were short term.

Al asked to see Luis's schedule D. When he examined it he saw the same stocks Chip had told him were being problems for 21st Century Securities.

He then asked to see the confirmation slips. He noted they were all from a small Internet brokerage firm named Direxion Securities. He made Xerox copies of the confirms for future use and told the accountant that he would be receiving a case of his favorite wine.

When he got back to his office he called Chip and told him of his coup. They made plans to get together for a strategy session. Chip called his friend, hacker "Rambo" Romano and offered him some money for his assistance.

Without the cartel's occasional assistance in relocating

him and providing him with a new identity, Rambo probably would have been in prison. Romano had started out exploiting the Los Angeles bus punch card system to get free rides. Then he dabbled in some phone phreaking, ultimately breaking into Digital Equipment's computer network and stealing their software. His hacking career was cut short in LA when he hacked into a fellow hacker's home computer, leading to his relocation to the New York area where he changed his name.

His claim to fame, however, was when he broke into The New York Times, Goldman Sachs and Apple. He used Internet connections at Kinko's, libraries, and various coffee shops to accomplish his intrusions. These intrusions consisted primarily of penetration testing in which he identified flaws in security systems and exploited them. When he broke into The New York Times' intranet, things got serious. He added himself to a list of experts and viewed personal information like social security numbers on selected VIPs. When things got hot again, he was helped to relocate to Florida where he hacked WFLC radio's phone lines making enough to buy himself a Porsche.

Rambo was very willing to offer his assistance to his friends who had helped keep him out of jail in the past. Al and Chip told him the nature of the problem and who they suspected to be the hacker who was causing their problems. Then Rambo convened with Soltero and Talbos to reconfirm the objectives of the Limited Knowledge Penetration Test and gather sufficient information to ensure that the PT testing would not affect their normal business operations. He began his preliminary research by reviewing all the information he could amass on 21st Century Securities to try to understand what information the hacker was using to disrupt their trading.

During these operations, he confirmed that the violator was a 21st Century outsider. After using nMap to footprint the external network, he focused on a rogue FTP server that was curiously installed outside the firewall. A port scan returned extremely troubling results. He found half a dozen open ports. Port 141 was running Net BIOs and allowing extensive leaking of information via Null Session Enumeration. He identified files being used by the hacker to measure the available bandwidth of their server to gauge the efficacy of using the machine to conduct other attacks.

Rambo reported this information back to Chip and Al and asked for permission to identify the source of the hack. His first attempts to guess the hacker's password were unsuccessful, but returning to the drive, he cracked a password using a using regular expression searching with a cracker he had developed. He then conducted a whois to obtain information regarding the owner. At this point, he knew which host the attacker was connecting from and obtained the identity from his ISP. Finally, he attempted to verify whether his connection was being proxied and discovered that the server wouldn't allow IRC connections from unsecured proxy servers. He had the attacker's full name, date of birth, city of residence, e-mail address and photo. Rambo was now ready to report his findings. They would confirm Adolfo Soltero's suspicions.

CHAPTER 43

"I'm interviewing candidates today to replace Jennifer Jacquette," Betsy said as she sat in the bathroom applying her makeup. "I still can't believe she's dead. I guess it goes to show you how serious allergies can be."

"That's for sure," Will said as he picked out a tie in the closet. "I thought all night about the visit I got from Jock yesterday wanting to move his accounts back to me. He sure blames her death on CANDO."

"I guess he's striking out at anyone and everyone," Betsy said. "After all, I keep hearing he was so devastated by her death he's become irrational and dysfunctional."

"I'd be torn up myself if something like that happened to you. The poor soul not only associates her death with CANDO, he blames them for it and is threatening to retaliate."

"You mean with his foundation?" Betsy asked.

"Hopefully that's all, but he'd better be careful or he may end up in hot water himself."

"Do you really think something's wrong at CANDO?" Betsy asked.

"I don't know."

"Ever think about becoming a CANDO distributor?" Betsy asked.

"Are you thinking what I think you're thinking, Jennifer Hart?"

"Uh, huh, Jonathan."

"I always did want to know more about skin care products," Will said.

"We've both been known to fly by the seat on our pants. Maybe I could mention our interest today to Carson since his wife is a distributor."

"Let's do it. I'd sure love to find out what's rotten in Denmark."

Betsy called Will about mid afternoon.

"What you doing this evening?" she asked.

"I've been dreaming all day you'd ask me for a date," Will said.

"In a manner of speaking your wish will come true," Betsy said. "I'm about to invite you to a CANDO meeting at Kingdom Hall. We're going as Cass Crown's guests. She said she'll meet us there."

"Not the date I had in mind, but I'm game."

When they arrived at seven, Cass and Carson Crown were standing in front of Kingdom Hall talking to some other ladies. Will noticed the remnants of a strange red and blue circle as they walked up the sidewalk. *Vandal graffiti artists* he thought. *Even here in the Keys.*

Cass saw them and waved them over to the group. She almost gushed when she introduced them.

"This is Betsy Black, President of my husband's bank," she bragged, "and this is her husband, Will. Carson owes much of his success to her. The Blacks are both true VIP's in the Key West business community. Carson tells me that they are as big a VIP as he is."

"Well, almost. No one can fill a room quite like Carson," Betsy said as she pursed her lips, exhaled and gave Will a sideways glance.

Will winked back and tried not to laugh. "I'll have to admit no organization in the lower Keys would be the same without Carson's august presence. He's everyone's consummate VP."

Cass beamed at the perceived compliments. Carson rubbed the back of his wife's neck and grinned like a Cheshire cat as well.

All smiles, people began to introduce themselves one by one.

"I'm Martha Jean Flynt ... Hi, I'm Dot Hotten ... I'm Ben Thompson ... I'm Mamie McIntosh ... I'm Laurana Simpson ... Marcellius Robinson. We look so forward to getting to know you better."

Will and Betsy couldn't begin to keep up with all the names as people began to talk to them at once.

Cass pulled the Blacks over to a table selling motivational items of all descriptions. "I want you to meet Larry Challies."

"Quite a table of material you have there," Will commented.

"Yes indeed," Larry said. "Welcome to CANDO. We believe that the right mindset is a key ingredient to putting our distributors on the fast track. We are so blessed to have someone as charismatic as Sun Raye as our general leading our troops into battle. You'll be fortunate this evening to see her in action, and then you can certainly appreciate my admiration. She is truly a self-made woman."

Soon the meeting began. Will and Betsy asked Cass and Carson if it'd be OK for them to sit in the back of the room. They wanted to discretely observe the crowd as a whole. Sun Raye was dressed in flowing yellow robes. She welcomed those attending and asked members to introduce their guests. Will felt like he was at a country church revival and waited for the sermon to begin. It didn't take long for that to happen. The only thing missing thus far, he thought, was taking up a collection and singing "Give Me That Old Time Religion".

Sun Raye spread her arms wide. The voluminous sleeves in the robe made them look like wings. She began.

"Have you ever seen a sunset so beautiful that you hoped it would never end? Have you ever been startled by a falling star streaking like a bullet through the night sky? Have you ever seen a rainbow encircle the Seven Mile Bridge? I have experienced many such moments that left me gasping for a reality check and wondering who I am in the vastness of this great universe.

"Life is so precious and fragile, and as Hebrews 9:17 reminds us, it will end. It is appointed for all people to die at some point. None of us know how many more breaths we will breathe in and blow out.

"If your life were to end in the near future, would you have accomplished all that you have dreamed you would? When you lie down and take your last breath, was your life worth living? These are serious questions that we will be forced to weigh eventually."

Sun Raye paused and took a drink from the water pitcher she had next to her. She winced slightly. The water had a tainted after-taste, but she thought nothing of it and continued her talk.

"We work hard to achieve success and acquire wealth.

We are so caught up preparing a comfortable life for ourselves, we give little thought to what is beyond this life. And then one day it hits us that life is fragile and fleeting.

"Ecclesiastes 2: 10 and 11 reminds us of this when it says 'I denied myself nothing my eyes desired; I refused no pleasure. My heart took delight in all my work, and this is the reward for my labor. Yet when I surveyed all that my hands had done, and what I had toiled to achieve, everything was meaningless, a chasing after the wind; nothing was gained under the sun.'"

Will looked at Betsy. His eyes said *What the hell does this have to do with selling sunscreen?*

Sun Raye stopped to sip water once again and made mental a note to remind herself not to get it from that source again. It tasted slightly like rotten eggs.

"Sometimes it takes a wakeup call for us to recognize what our real values are in life. I'm reminded of a song by the Dave Matthews Band. Listen."

Rock music blared from the house system.
Everything's different
With my head in the clouds
I hit this corner
With my foot on the gas
I started sliding, I lose it
Everything's different just like that
Oh, my God, wait and see
What will soon become of me?
Frozen heart
Screaming wheels
Does that screaming come from me?

The music stopped. The room was silent. The pregnant pause caused Sun Raye to involuntarily reach for the water pitcher again. Just as she touched it, she heard a faint plink and the pitcher disintegrated in her hand. Sun Raye stood there shocked. Her mind resisted registering what had just happened. Luis, who was sitting next to her, however, recognized the sound. A bullet from a silenced rifle.

"Sniper!" he yelled and grabbed for Sun Raye. Sun Raye felt her stomach suddenly spasm from the putrid water and let go with a projectile vomit that splattered people in the first five rows before she passed out. Bobby tried to pull his weapon, but it caught on his waistband and went off. The thunderous noise reverberated throughout the building. He had narrowly missed shooting himself in the foot, but the reaction caused him to kick the lectern. The PA system squealed loudly.

An old man with a black lacquered walking stick in the back of the room panicked and started to limp for an exit. Bobby thought the long cylindrical object was a rifle and started to hobble on his sore toe after him screaming, "Stop that man!"

Carson Crown was the nearest person to the man and quickly caught up to him. When Carson reached for the old man, he grabbed the man's toupee which came off in his hands. Carson stood there holding it like a hairy rat. The infuriated old man stubbed Carson's toe with the stick before swinging at him again. As Carson howled and grabbed for his foot, he knocked off the old man's prosthesis. The one-legged man swung it at Bobby and Carson but lost his balance and instead landed on a woman next to him, sending her newly purchased motivational material flying in all directions. She got up and screamed, "You mother...!" and came out swinging. Her roundhouse punch with her purse hit Will square in the jaw. On her next blow, the old man's glass eye popped out and flew into Betsy's hair.

The would-be assassin disappeared, easing out during the confusion, and was gone by the time the sheriff's deputy arrived.

~ ~ ~

Betsy did not find glass eye until later after she and Will returned home and she was seated on the toilet leaning forward rehashing the CANDO fiasco. The prosthetic eye suddenly came out of her hair and hit the tile floor with a thud. It landed right side up and stared back perversely at her. Betsy shrieked. It was almost as if the eye were winking at her. The eye leered at her, making her feel immodest and feeling like it was seeing something above her panties that it shouldn't be seeing.

Will and the dogs came running at the noise. He almost died laughing when he saw his wife with her panties around her ankles, trapped on the john by a single rascally eye. Coco began to bark at this unwelcome visitor. Lucy and Dexter pounced towards it and then backed up, only to pounce again.

When Will caught his breath he said, "This redefines the term peeping Tom, or should I say, this is one way of keeping an eye on things. And I will admit, this evening certainly didn't resemble any sales meeting I've ever conducted. Next time you want to have a hot date, can't we just go to Mangrove Mama's instead?"

"Oh, hush and just get the lecherous thing out of here," Betsy said.

~ ~ ~

Will and Betsy weren't the only ones asking questions. Luis had to give Sun Raye a tranquilizer to settle her down.

`"I think someone was trying to kill me," Sun Raye said shakily.

"And whoever it was, wasn't taking any chances. I kept a sample of some of the sour-tasting water in your glass to take to Dr. Doats. I bet she'll say that water was poisoned."

"But why would someone try to poison me, and then shoot the pitcher?" Sun Ray asked.

"I've got three possible answers," Luis said. "One – he could have been trying to destroy the evidence, two – he was just a piss-poor shot, or three – there might have been more than one assassin."

"But why me?" Sun Raye asked.

"I don't know, but there's a good possibility it might be the same person who sabotaged you at Melody Key," Luis said. He neglected to mention to her his feeling that she might not have been the target at all. It might have been him.

The more Luis thought about this possibility the more enraged and nervous he became. Who could know about his larceny? Instead of backing off, he decided to redefine and accelerate his activities to make damned sure he had plenty of cash in case he had to disappear. Over the next two weeks he hacked 21st Century's Isle of Mann account and transferred $500,000 to numbered accounts in his own name.

CHAPTER 44

Instead of putting her mind at ease, Sun Raye's break-in foray at Tango Products gave her more uncertainties than ever to worry about. Even though she didn't find the smoking gun she had hoped to find, she had found enough to convince her that Miguel Valdes' protestations had been nothing more than a smoke screen.

A chance trip out to Melody Key gave her the break-through she was looking for. The bottles of sunblock left over from her aborted meeting were all six ounce bottles. A leftover sunblock bottle happened to be sitting on her bathroom counter next to an eight-ounce bottle. She made a mental note that it was approximately two inches shorter than the larger size. *I wonder why Tango didn't simply order cases to fit that size bottle,* she asked herself. Suddenly it dawned on her. *Because they wanted to put something else in the case with the bottles.*

Valdes *had* been lying to her about the cocaine being an unauthorized enterprise by some rogue employees. And that's why the numbering systems were so completely different from the six to the eight ounce bottles. It was so they wouldn't risk getting the cases smuggling cocaine mixed up with the regular cases. *This is an organized effort to smuggle illegal drugs authorized by management.* She had always suspected Valdes had a hidden agenda when he muscled in on her fledgling business a few years back. *My God, I'm a drug smuggler and don't know it, and I can go to jail if Valdes gets caught.*

Sun Raye was in a panic. Who could she trust? Luis had always been straight with her. He had never lied to her. After all, Luis was the person who forced her to get off drugs when she was a junkie, and he always seemed to have the street-smarts to handle delicate, difficult matters. She desperately needed a confidant. But they couldn't discuss her findings and suspicions at Kingdom Hall. They might be overheard, and if Valdes was what she thought he was, she now had no doubt he was a very lethal adversary who would stop at nothing to accomplish his mission.

Sun Raye went into Luis's office and asked him if he wanted to take the boat out. She said it was both a good opportunity to catch up on business and to get some sun. Bobby was present and promptly commented that the boat was way overdue for servicing. He said he worried about her taking it out and insisted that he'd get the Sea Center to take care of it immediately.

The following day Sun Raye and Luis took the boat to Marvin Key. She packed a couple of subs from Joe and Missy's and took a supply of soft drinks. Since it was in the middle of the week there would be very few people, if anyone, at Marvin Key. Sun Raye's assumption was correct. When they got to Marvin Key, they were the only boat there.

As she and Luis sat on the beach eating their subs, Sun Raye finally started to recount her suspicions to Luis. She informed him of the cocaine that had been present on that fateful day at Melody Key. He knew that day had been a total disaster, but this was the first time he had heard all the details. She told him of her confrontation with Miguel Valdes and of his excuses and denials. She then related to him the details of her illegal entry into Tango Products' Stock Island manufacturing plant. Lastly, she told Luis of her recent conclusions and suspicions. She cried when she tried to discuss Jennifer Jacquette. Not wanting to interrupt and distract her, Luis silently listened to Sun Raye's recitation and admissions.

Sun Raye suggested to Luis that the sniper who had interrupted the CANDO meeting might be a result of her meddling in Valdes' and Tango's affairs. Luis did not admit his suspicions that he might have been the target instead of her because he had hacked 21st Century Securities computers and stolen a large amount of money from them.

Luis proposed they do nothing for the time being except snoop around, consider what their strategy would be going forward and revisit Marvin Key in a week to re-discuss their options.

Both Luis and Sun Raye had been so preoccupied, that they didn't notice that while they were talking the tide was steadily falling. When they got ready to depart, it was near low tide, the boat was beached, and they were stranded.

Sun Raye and Luis were not the only ones who decided to take advantage of this marvelous day. Will and Betsy Black had come to the same conclusion. They had decided it would be a marvelous day to take off work and explore the back country. As they approached Marvin Key, Will and Betsy saw the stranded boat.

"Looks like somebody's overstayed their welcome at Marvin," Will commented to Betsy.

"It's easy to do. If a boater gets all the way in there, he has to have high tide to get back out to the channel," Betsy said. "We've almost learned that the hard way a couple of times."

"Let me see if I can roust them up on the radio," Will said. "We may need to help them out."

Will and Betsy were surprised to discover that the stranded couple were not strangers but people they knew. They got as close to Marvin Key as they dared, and Luis and Sun Raye waded out to meet them and boarded. Will offered to take them back to Little Torch Key so they could return with Bobby to retrieve the boat when the tide was higher again. Everyone agreed it sounded like a plan.

Will backed the Grady-White out to deeper water and as he turned into the channel, they were all jolted by an enormous explosion. Sun Raye's boat exploded with a deafening roar that could be heard for miles. A central ball of fire like a movie-footage A-bomb explosion sent a geyser-like orange and yellow fireball screaming three stories into the air. A plume of ash-colored smoke topped the explosion. Each person would later have his own analogy of the scene they had witnessed. To Betsy it sounded like a jetliner taking off; to Sun Raye it seemed more like a sonic boom; to Will it looked like an airplane or air-borne missile had crashed into the ocean; Luis described it as being like a fiery hot-air balloon.

The explosion launched the boat's engine high into the air and it fell back near the boat, landing on the mangled remains of the detached T-top. Will and Betsy's boat was drenched with a shower of salt water and fish that had also been thrown high into the air by the terrible force of the explosion. Sun Raye's ice chest was thrown into the air and landed not far from the Black's boat.

After the explosion they watched the rapid spread of flames as the wind-whipped blaze danced across the water. The blast dislodged the remains of the boat which floated with the current until it lodged itself on a nearby sandbar where the remnants of the bow presided over the black mass like a religious icon which mutely mourned the terrible scene, a silent witness to what it had just seen. The charred remains of the fiberglass hull could be seen, crisped and blackened by the fiery element. Sun Raye shivered as she looked at it and imagined her and Luis sleeping the sleep of death in this watery grave. The fire would rage unabated for almost an hour.

Will immediately called in the explosion and waited for help. He was somewhat comforted when he heard Kevin's familiar voice on the other end of the radio and identified himself. Kevin said he and Jason were on their way. They all then simply stared at the debris littering the ocean around them and waited. Remnants of boat seemed to be everywhere. At first the conversation was limited to inane one-syllable exclamations. Each of them was too shocked by what they had witnessed to elaborate further. Slowly the reality of the situation set in.

Sun Raye was the first to snap out of this shock-induced trance. She hugged Luis and began to sob and shake uncontrollably.

"That was meant to be us," she said. "This was no accident. Someone wants to kill me."

Luis held her, neither agreeing nor disagreeing.

Will tentatively probed her for the meaning of her

statement. Sun Raye began to regurgitate the whole story of recent events. It was as if she desperately needed just to talk to someone new. At first Luis tried to stop her but finally gave up, and she rattled on. She was determined to get everything that had been bottled up off her chest. Luis still said nothing about the possibility the he had been the primary target.

Sun Raye finally collapsed on the deck and began to plead with God, "Help me, Lord! I don't want to die! Please don't let me die! Tell me what to do."

No one volunteered a ready answer.

CHAPTER 45

Luis Bernstein was mildly irritated but mostly bored as he met with Chip Talbos and Rodney Chamberlain for their semi-annual investment meeting. He put on a polite face, but everything about the two had begun to slightly irk him. He didn't care for their expensive clothes and shoes, their luxury car, their carefully oiled back hair, or their condescending way of explaining things.

"Luis, you know what keeps me up at night?" Rodney said. "There's the fact that commodities have a high unpredictable dynamic that most other industries don't – Mother Nature. Nature can be positive or negative, but you have to be aware of the incremental volatility these forces can add to these investments. My biggest concern, though, is the danger of policy making errors that could allow protectionism or price controls to infringe on the marketplace."

Luis stifled a yawn and silently laughed to himself, *You know what keeps me up at night? The possibility that you might figure out my personal investment strategy, making money the old fashioned way – stealing it by the bucket-loads from you pseudo-sophisticated assholes.*

Chip jumped in. "Our goal is to take advantage of the intersection of the replacement cycles in developed countries..."

Both Chip and Rodney rambled on for another thirty minutes while Luis just sat and endured their egotistical diatribes.

After what seemed like an eternity, Chip asked, "Do you have any questions? If not, we need to be going. We promised we'd drive up and make a sympathy visit to the widowed mother of a childhood friend from our old New Jersey neighborhood. She lives in a retirement village in Key Largo. It's sort of a bizarre story. I'll tell you if you have a moment to listen."

Finally they might say something that won't put me to sleep. "Sure, go ahead."

"Louie was a computer genius," Chip continued. "Whereas most of us wanted to play football or hockey, all he ever cared anything about was his computer. When he went to the University of Delaware, he made his way through school hacking blue boxes, the devices that bypass telephone-switching mechanisms to make free long distance calls. He sold long distance calls to fellow students at a fraction of what they would have had to pay the phone company. He could also be a clown. I remember one time he called the Pope and pretended to be Henry Kissinger. His biggest accomplishment, however, was just recently when he reactivated the old Yellow Page numbers for an escort service and then ran a virtual escort agency."

"You have some interesting friends," Luis said, by now finding the story to be interesting.

"Unfortunately when his enterprise was featured on the TV show *Unsolved Mysteries,* the 1-800 numbers for the program crashed, and he was identified by some of the unsavory people in the escort industry he had been costing money. They arranged a little tea-party to get even. He was abducted. His mouth was taped shut, and he was dumped in the trunk his mother's Buick. His penis was hooked by a long wire to the car battery. A ground-wire was shoved up his rectum. When the escort cranked her car, no more Louie."

"That's hideous," Luis said shuddering.

"Shocking is probably a better word." Chip laughed at his own sick joke. "Old Louie always did like to play with fire. You know, if you mess with the bull, you get the horn. His mother simply wanted to go away and forget...you know, too many bad memories. So she left Jersey and moved to Key Largo. We promised her we'd come up and visit her this afternoon." He then winked at Luis and said, "Call us if you need us to defuse any car batteries."

When Chip and Rodney left, Luis called Bobby Perez in and asked him if he had the meeting room ready for the CANDO meeting that evening. Bobby assured him everything was in order. He said he had taken care of things personally. Sun Raye then came by and asked Luis if he would mind opening the meeting instead of her since she might possibly be running a few minutes late.

That evening the room was filled with CANDO distributors. Luis stood in front of the group to open the meeting as he had promised. People were ushered to their chairs, and Luis tapped on the microphone to see if it was live. Will and Betsy sat in the middle of the front row. Even though Sun Raye had arrived on time and was sitting next to the podium, she decided to let Luis open the meeting anyway. He grabbed the mic to adjust the height. When he did, Luis was hit with an electrical shock. It felt like an epileptic seizure, and he couldn't let go. He felt a pop or crack on his left arm and saw a bright spark at the same place. The current that arced across his body was so bright he would still be able to visualize it the next day when he shut his eyes. Even though Luis's left side took most of the shock, the muscles on his right side were badly stunned and in a lot of pain. The microphone glowed momentarily with tendrils of purple light, very similar to a plasma light. Luis's mind had a dull, eerie feeling that the air itself was turning to plasma. He lost consciousness as the electrical shock hit his lower back and tailbone and shot down both legs.

Will jumped up and shoved Luis, breaking his frozen grip on the microphone, and Luis slumped into a limp heap on the floor. Will rushed around the lectern and started to give him mouth-to-mouth resuscitation. Luis partially recovered consciousness and looked at Will through dazed eyes, not recognizing him. It initially felt like two of his left fingers were missing, but the feeling started to come back in patches like someone else's fingers had been attached to his hand. He had been saved from dying by his Crocs. The material in these shoes had decelerated the electricity and kept it from reaching its full potential in his legs and feet. A fireman in the crowd rushed up to say he had called for an ambulance to take Luis to Lower Keys Medical Center.

Lower Keys Medical Center kept Luis overnight for observation. The CANDO meeting was adjourned and Sun Raye rode in the ambulance with him to the hospital. He was too dazed and exhausted to talk to her, but she stayed until the hospital told her to leave.

Later that evening Luis got an unwanted visitor. A large hulking man dressed as an orderly slipped into the hospital. He brazenly came in the front entrance, rode the elevator up to Luis's room, and silently entered. Luis, by this time, had been lightly sedated and was dozing fitfully. He awoke when he felt the man poised over his bed but couldn't focus. The man quickly and silently jabbed a needle of PCP into Luis's arm and immediately left the room.

Now that he was awake, Luis felt the need to go to the bathroom. He groggily stood up and dragged the rolling instrument table with him to the bathroom. He tried to drop a wadded-up Kleenex into the toilet. Instead of going into the bowl, the Kleenex landed on the seat. It seemed perfectly normal to Luis to then try to wash it into the bowl with urine. He laughed as he tried. Soon the seat and the floor around it were covered with Luis's efforts.

Luis stumbled back to the bed and somehow got back in. He saw geometric patterns on the ceiling that kept growing and shrinking. He felt as if he was sinking into the bed, and things started looking far away. He tried to reach the nurse's call button, but his muscles felt like jelly. He just lay there watching himself feeling like he was out of his own body. Time began to slow so much he felt he would get stuck in the present and began to have what he would describe later as a near-death experience where he was immersed in a bright white light and bathed in beautiful music. Time just seemed to space out. He would later tell Sun Raye that he felt his whole life pass before his eyes. He tried reaching the button again, but his arms felt three feet thick. His head felt like it was shrinking until it became the size of a pea. As his head seeped into his arms, they became 10 miles long. He finally successfully mashed the button.

The nurse came in the room, panicked, and called for assistance. Luis's heart rate and blood pressure were both elevated. He was flushed and sweating. Since he did not recognize the nurse and thought it was the same person who had administered the shot, Luis became anxious and paranoid but was having trouble communicating his fears. He could hear the staff talking to him and each other, but it sounded to him like they did not really exist.

The remaining part of the evening was spent stabilizing Luis and trying to decide just what had occurred. It remained a mystery. The imposter orderly, meanwhile, had long slipped back out of the hospital, not knowing his efforts had failed to kill Luis.

CHAPTER 46

Sun Raye rolled over in the motel bed and wrapped her arms around Luis. The sheets were mussed from their bout of frantic love-making. They had made frenzied love like first time sweethearts or last time lovers who would never have the opportunity to experience each other again. As she dozed she felt satisfied physically but her brain was churning. A knot tightened in her stomach as her subconscious rehashed recent events. She replayed the day at Melody Key. She could still see a very dead Jennifer Jacquette in her open casket. The only problem was the face in the coffin kept mutating into her own with a voodoo mark emblazoned on her machete-split forehead. This vision was momentarily blocked out as the body in the coffin shot skyward in a blazing jet of orange and yellow flames, only to explode in mid-air, spreading body fragments in the wind.

"You could have been killed," she blurted out as she awoke with a start. "I've used that mic a thousand times and it was always perfectly all right."

"And whoever it was, wasn't content to give up after one try," Luis said. "He tried again at the hospital. Despite the dim light, I know it was a large man. I remember waking and seeing someone dressed like a hospital employee. I assumed he was supposed to be there. Then he hit me with an injection, and he was gone."

"Thank God you were able to punch the nurse's call

button," Sun Raye said with a shudder. "Otherwise you might be dead right now, and I'd be left all alone."

She snuggled him again, and they said nothing for a few minutes.

"Do you think the killer may have been after me?" she finally asked. "Nine times out of ten I would have been the first person to grab that mic, and I wouldn't have hesitated to clutch it. After all Bobby set up the room earlier that day, and surely he's trustworthy. After all, he is family."

"I don't know what to believe," said Luis. "At this point I wouldn't take anything for granted. Keep in mind that Bobby helped you set up your meeting at Melody Key too, and look what happened there. Up until now, these accidents seemed to be happening only to you," Luis said. "But if you were the one they wanted dead, why did I get the follow-up visit from the assassin at the hospital?"

"Another mystery. Do you think Jock wanted to get even with anyone in our organization because of Jennifer's death?" Sun Raye asked. "After all, since she died he doesn't seem to be playing with a full deck."

She grabbed Luis again and kissed him, using him as her security blanket. Luis kissed her back, and the room became silent, both of them momentarily absorbed in their own thoughts and fears. Luis was the first to speak and break the silence.

"I have an admission to make," he said. "Since that day on the beach in which you opened up and trusted me by telling me about what happened to you on Melody Key and also about your Tango break-in and the subsequent confrontation with Miguel Valdes, my conscience has been bothering me about some of my own past activities. I haven't always been totally open with you until now. I hope you will understand and forgive me."

He then told her about his background as a hacker and how he had used his expertise to invade 21st Century's computers and interfere with their trades. He also confessed he had transferred his monies to several off-shore numbered accounts.

Sun Raye couldn't believe what she was hearing. There was a larcenous side of Luis that she never knew existed.

"What else are you keeping from me?" she asked. "I guess next you'll be telling me you're married and have a family."

"Be reasonable, Raye. Have you told me everything about your background?"

"I guess not. Some things just don't seem relevant when you're trying to put your best foot forward and your past behind you."

"Exactly. If you're smart, you don't broadcast your dirty laundry. All I can do at this juncture is to plead for your understanding and forgiveness," Luis said. "We both need to put our pasts behind us, concentrate on the present, and move forward, but that is going to be impossible if we can't be candid enough with each other to put all our cards on the table."

"I know you're right. That was pride talking. So the questions become who can we trust? Also, will they do it again, and if so, when and how? Do we need bodyguards? Should we be hiding out?" asked Sun Raye. "If not, how do we fight back?"

"I don't have all the answers today. One thing that is a certainty, however, is we need to watch our backside.

We've got to think clearly and formulate a strategy," Luis said. "It is not logical to think we can just go into hiding. That is only a temporary solution. As far as who we can trust, I certainly don't know who we can rely on. The enemy could be anyone – including family. We can't be too careful since we're talking about survival."

"As much as it hurts me to agree with you, my gut tells me you're right."

"But let me finish my thought," Luis continued. "If we're going down, we shouldn't go down alone. We need to confide in someone else of our suspicions so the authorities will have something to go on if worst becomes worst. I suggest Will and Betsy Black, the couple who rescued us the day the boat blew. They are totally neutral parties with nothing to gain from our demise. Also they are intelligent, respected members of the Key West business community. I trust their judgment. After all, they are business people used to evaluating options and making decisions. They are also high profile enough to have connections with the right people."

"Sounds logical. No one else is coming to mind."

"Now I've got one other matter. Before we go back to Little Torch Key and pretend things are normal, we need to formulate a last ditch plan in case it becomes necessary."

"OK."

"I think it would be prudent to be as liquid as possible until things are resolved," Luis said. "I want you to liquidate both your bank savings accounts and your brokerage accounts and let me move the funds offshore. I will do the same with mine. We will only leave sufficient funds for the near term in our checking accounts."

"But Will and Betsy are our financial advisors, and I thought they were going to be our confidants. I don't want to insult them. What excuse can I make?"

"We can't afford to be completely transparent with anyone. If the shit hits the fan, we may have to act in a hurry, and we can't leave any unnecessary trails behind. There is only so much anyone can or will do legally to help us without jeopardizing themselves. Remember, in the final analysis, we are on our own, and the only people we can trust are each other. Use the excuse that you have back taxes and need money. If we're forced to vanish, we're going to need money, and we have to be able to disappear without a trace. Understand me, without a trace."

"I do think it's best if I tell Betsy, though, about my break-in at Tango and my subsequent run-in with Valdes," Sun Raye said.

"Whatever," Luis said. "I wouldn't, but that's up to you."

Sun Raye kissed Luis on the neck.

"I feel better now that we have the beginnings of a plan," she said.

"We'll start to deal with these matters tomorrow," Luis said. "Right now I have a more immediate need."

He moved her hand under the sheet. She knew immediately the problem he was describing, and she knew how to solve it.

CHAPTER 47

Sun Raye called Betsy at her office.

"Y'all available for some pizza Friday night?" she asked.

"I think so. Let me clear it with Will, and I'll get back to you," Betsy said.

"I was thinking No Name Pub," Sun Raye said. "Luis and I need to pick your brains. Since we're still on daylight savings time and the weather's nice, we'll use a picnic table out back so we can have some privacy. Let's tentatively say 6:30."

Friday night arrived, and Will and Betsy drove out to No Name Pub. They entered the dark room and had to be careful not to stumble on the ramp. Roberta was working that night and briefly made small-talk with them. They went around the tall rustic bar papered with dollar bills, through the main room, and out the back door to the fenced back yard. Inside, the bar was already buzzing with patrons and the television was going in the background. Most of the tables had already been staked out by regulars. Listening to the noisy patrons, Betsy could easily understand why Sun Raye had wanted to meet out back. Luis and Sun Raye had already arrived and had ordered a pitcher of Michelob AmberBock draft beer. While they were waiting for Will and Betsy, Luis cautioned Sun Raye to let him do most of the talking and reminded her of the pitfalls of becoming a totally open book, i.e. drugs, stock manipulation or computer hacking were off-limits topics.

"Draft beer OK for you folks?" Luis asked when Will and Betsy approached the picnic table.

"A good cold beer with pizza works for us," Will replied.

"Don't you mean 'coldbeer'?" Betsy said teasingly. Will winked knowingly.

They made small-talk before Sun Raye and Luis got into the real purpose for their meeting. Luis was blunt.

"We're convinced someone is trying to kill or maim one or both of us," Luis said.

"We surmised you weren't just accident prone from our discussion the day the boat blew," Will said. "Tell us more. Why would someone want to do that?" Will said. "Tell us more."

"At first we thought these incidents were flukes or accidents, but as they kept mounting up, evidence is mounting to the contrary. We're telling you this because if something dire happens to either one of us, we want to know someone we trust is aware of the danger we were in and will give law enforcement the information they need to instigate an investigation. We would hate to think some lousy bastard could do us in and get away scot-free just because we didn't have the foresight to confide in someone. We don't know who the culprit is yet, but if we're not alive to speak up, we certainly don't want the world to mistakenly think these incidents were a mere series of misadventures or bad luck by two snake-bitten fools."

He paused to let his comments sink in.

"I'm going to be very candid with you," Luis

continued. "We decided to confide in you two for several reasons. First, we trust your intelligence, judgment and discretion. Second, we think you are a neutral party who stands to gain nothing by our fate, good or bad. And third, you have been present when several of these incidents have occurred and witnessed them for yourselves. Specifically, I mean the sniper, microphone, and boat episodes. Other mishaps, like Jennifer Jacquette's death and my unexpected visitor during my hospital visit are ones you would know little or nothing about."

Luis then filled them in on many details about recent events. He included Dr. Doats' findings and conclusions as well as the second incident at Melody Key involving Sun Raye, Dr. Doats, and Bobby Perez. Despite his seeming candor, Luis was careful to be selective in the information he imparted.

"We're honored but somewhat daunted that you chose us to be your confidants," said Will. "We had no idea so many mishaps had occurred."

"Who do you suspect?" Betsy asked as the waitress came over. They agreed on their pizza toppings and ordered.

When the waitress left, Luis continued. "First let me tell you, Miguel Valdes especially concerns us. He is our involuntary minority partner on sunscreen formulation and shipment. It did not start out that way, but let's just say he was both persistent and insistent. Even though I had misgivings at first, I will have to admit that on the surface things have worked out quite well. He seems to be producing a quality product for us and appears to have been instrumental in helping us increase our sales. I do worry that he might get greedy and possibly try to take complete control in the future. I also might add, both our corporate investment advisor and our auditor were introduced to us by Valdes."

"Valdes' strong-arm tactics don't surprise me," Betsy said. "I have dealt with him as a banker."

"We have also thought that Jennifer's widowed husband, Jock, might be a suspect," Luis said.

"I never thought of Jock as being a violent person," said Will, "and I know him pretty well since he's a longstanding client."

"I'm not accusing Jock. I'm merely throwing out some random thoughts," Luis said. "Desperate angry people sometimes do unexpected things."

"Wasn't Bobby Perez your gopher who set things up for several of these meetings?" Betsy asked.

"I had a run-in with Bobby once over a client," Will said, "and he was not what I would term to be 'a scholar and a gentleman'. Pardon me for being frank, Sun Raye. I know he's your son-in-law, but he acted like a strong-arm hoodlum."

"We've taken it for granted he's our ally, but we never thought he was the brightest bulb in the chandelier," Luis said. "I know we can't afford to rule out either him or his brother. After all, if Sun Raye were dead, Bobby's wife becomes one of her heirs."

"You've given us a lot to mull over," Will said.

Sun Raye finally spoke. "I'm terrified. These attempts have failed so far but ..."

She couldn't finish her sentence.

Roberta, the waitress, picked that moment to bring

their pizza.

"Can I get you anything else?" Roberta asked.

After a unanimous 'no' she left them to eat.

"Before we talk about happier topics, there's one other business matter we need to cover," Luis said. "Sun Raye has an extraordinarily large tax bill she needs to satisfy and needs liquidity. Would you both mind liquidating her brokerage accounts and savings accounts? This is only a temporary situation. We'll return the money to the accounts as soon as she catches up and gets her affairs under control."

As she bit into her pizza, Sun Raye nodded in agreement.

"Wow, business must be really good, if you owe that much in taxes," said Will.

"Oh, business has been good, but part of this is to satisfy some back taxes created by a tax audit," Luis said.

They finished their pizza and visited further, but each of them was still primarily preoccupied with the matters they had been previously discussing.

CHAPTER 48

The crusade to get approval for a nude beach in Key West continued to gain momentum and legitimacy. For every argument presented, there seemed to be a counter argument. Both proponents and opponents became firmly entrenched and refused to either budge or compromise. Representatives of Florida Free Beaches and its spinoff, Florida Keys Free Beaches, became increasingly vocal in their demands that the City Commissioners vote on the issue, not have it decided in a voter referendum.

"Did we do a referendum to create Fantasy Fest?" said Lash Blutarsky in his campaign for City Commissioner. "Did it take a vote to adopt the creed of *One Human Family*? Of course not! The City Commission had the guts to vote on it and do it. If you resort to a popular vote every time something comes up, you're not doing what you were elected to do."

An incumbent commissioner agreed with him and said, "I truly believe if we put this issue to a referendum we are being inconsistent on how we treat issues. I would like to see us give it a try for one year. We have nothing to lose."

Sun Raye appeared on Bill Becker's US 1 radio program with Bernadette Jacob, a topless barmaid from the Garden of Eden. They made an appeal to the public.

In a shaky voice, Bernadette said, "I get asked every night at work where Key West's nude beach is. Please give us a chance. Just allow us to open up a clothing optional beach. It will not do Key West any harm. Some of us just don't like clothes."

On the other side, an opposing commissioner pointed out that people would be reluctant to use local beaches for weddings if they were clothing optional which could jeopardize much of the local wedding industry and that it would discourage some people from wanting to walk or jog there as well.

"You're losing money now because the beaches are underutilized," retaliated Leigh Tracy, the president of Florida Free Beaches.

The cause of the emissaries for change was not helped when a nude tourist on LSD ran into traffic from Bobalu's parking lot screaming he was "king of the world." He ran at the female deputy attempting to detain him yelling he was "a beach superman made of steel" and had to be tased three times before he could be handcuffed.

Luis suggested that Sun Raye have a fundraiser for supporters of the clothing optional beach proposal. She would have loved to invite supporters to Melody Key for a day of fun in the sun but was paranoid about doing so after the fiasco she had had there before. Instead she landed on the idea of having a clothing optional cruise to the Caribbean.

She contacted shoesonlytravel.com, decided on a cruise, and blocked off some of the cabins. The cruise she chose was a seven-night cruise of the western Caribbean. It had four ports of call – Labadee, Haiti; Ocho Rios, Jamaica; George Town, Grand Cayman and Cozumel. She was able to secure cabins on the second deck at a significant discount because of cruisers' general reluctance to visit Haiti.

The Caribbean Sun was a medium size ship with 123 staterooms and 31 cabins. It had three restaurants, one of which was a glass-enclosed veranda. It offered passengers sexy games by the pool in the daytime and clothing optional dancing in the evening. The travel agent described sensually themed parties, each with a different theme – *Dipped in Red, Leather and Lace, Sexy on the Seas,* and *White Night.* The ship contained a playroom with exotic, gauzy fabric billowing from the ceiling with wall-to-wall mattresses designed for either individual couples or group play. This cruise was precisely designed for adult entertainment. She smirked slightly when the agent described a late-night special blindfold play time. She happily grinned from ear to ear as she visualized herself conducting nude séances. What an opportunity! The bonding that would happen on a trip like this would certainly galvanize the Florida Free Beaches supporters into an even more cohesive effective lobbying group.

Sun Raye tested the cruise dates and ports of call from a numerological point of view. They both passed with flying colors. She also knew the ship's name was an omen. The trip was a definite go.

CHAPTER 49

It is not uncommon for archeologists to uncover evidence of multiple civilizations on a single location, one interred on top of another. This phenomenon is not as unique as it might seem. In the modern Florida Keys, multiple cultures routinely and spontaneously exist as a matter of course, not on top but side by side with each other. There is a locals' culture obliviously co-existing with an entirely different one inhabited by a wide variety of pleasure-seeking transients. Whereas these short-term hedonists might receive their daily messages and marching orders with "ship's log" or a resort newsletter as they entertained themselves ogling "quit-your-job-and-move-to-paradise" real estate magazines for sticker shock (Mabel, you ought to see what they're asking for this one), the permanent residents get their skinny from more reliable sources like the investigative reports in "the mullet wrapper" or from "the coconut telegraph", which relies often on hearsay, hot tips, exaggeration, emotional blogs, and outright lies.

When Sun Raye did not return from her clothing optional cruise, locals were bombarded with reports and articles leading to a rainbow array of conclusions and speculations.

The Key West Citizen:

LOCAL BUSINESSWOMAN AND ACTIVIST MISSING ON CARIBBEAN CRUISE

The Keynoter:
FOUNDER OF CANDO INDUSTIRES VANISHES IN JAMAICA

The Blue Paper:
FAMILY SEEKS ANSWERS ABOUT MISSING KEYS WOMAN

The News-Barometer:
CRUISE LINE CANNOT EXPLAIN DISAPPERANCE OF A PASSENGER

The Key West Weekly:
TOURIST'S DISAPPEARANCE IN JAMAICA LEAVES AUTHORITIES WITH BAFFLING QUESTIONS

Even *The Miami Herald* carried an article:
DISAPPEARANCE OF LOCAL WOMAN LEAVES UNANSWERED QUESTIONS

The reactions of Sun Raye's friends and acquaintances ranged from curiosity and revulsion to criticism and censure. On their second day at sea, Sun Raye had spent a relaxing day on the nude beach at the Labadee, Haiti port of call. The ship had then travelled to Ocho Rios. There Sun Raye disembarked but never returned, and the ship was forced to sail at 5 p.m. without her. The ship reported her absence to her daughters. Her whereabouts were unknown for several days. Local authorities were of no assistance. Sea Raye and Blue Raye sent Luis Bernstein to Jamaica to find their mother. After several days of travelling around the country, he reported back to them that she had been killed in a hit-and-run accident outside of Runaway Bay. He further said that the corpse had been in bad condition, that he had chosen to have the remains cremated rather than deal with the Jamaican and United States bureaucracies, and he was bringing her ashes back in an urn with a Jane-doe death certificate. He also cited the prohibitively high cost of transporting the body as a factor in his decision. Sea Raye and Blue Raye ran an obituary in the Citizen. The responses were immediate and varied.

As he was drinking his morning coffee, Will read the obituary in the paper and called out to Betsy.

"Sun Raye over at CANDO is dead," he said. "Her obit's in the *Citizen.*"

He read it to her.

"In Jamaica? On a cruise!" Betsy said. "It seems too coincidental that Sun Raye had a premonition that something bad might happen to her, and then almost immediately it actually does. Maybe she wasn't just being paranoid when she came to us."

"Confucius say coincidences normally take a lot of planning," Will said.

Al Soltero was having a whole different set of emotions as he sipped his morning coffee and thought about how to keep any business interruptions as a result of Sun Raye's death minimal and which successor would be the least likely to become a future thorn in his side. *I need to be sure I attend the memorial ceremony,* he thought. *Maybe*

I can identify who the power players will be going forward.

Miguel Valdes was debating a different set of issues. He was simultaneously relieved to have Sun Raye out of his hair but sadistically pissed that he didn't get the pleasure of putting her away himself after he sweated to get what he wanted to know out of her. Now he would have to continue to worry that she had compromised his private files and then had passed incriminating information on to someone else. He also wondered if drugs had played a part in her demise. After all, he reasoned, *everybody knows those fuckin' Jamaicans are all up to their fuckin' asses in illegal dope. I guess I'd better go to the goddamned burial for fuckin' appearances sake.*

Bobby Perez was ecstatic. *The gravy train has finally pulled into the station,* he thought, *and the bill-of-lading has my name on it.* This was the opportunity for him through his wife to take over the CANDO organization and to prove to the world he wasn't just a muscle-bound meathead. He plotted his next move. *It won't take me long to get rid of all this odd-ball religious shit and get back down to the business of making money, and this Bobby Raye shit is going to go away forever. Bobby Perez is back.* He decided that as soon as possible after the service, he'd put that dumb twat wife of his in her place and let her know from now on *he* would be the one really running things.

Jock Jacquette was preoccupied with who now to sue over his wife's death and who he could call to testify if and when he did. *Darn,* he thought. *Sun Raye was the only principal of the firm actually present at Melody Key that day. I was counting on nailing her on the witness stand and getting the seed capital for Jennifer's foundation. Now what do I do?*

Chip and Rodney openly debated what would happen to CANDO's stock price and how to reel in some suckers on a trading opportunity.

Sun Raye's fellow nudists second-guessed why she left the group in Ocho Rios all alone and guiltily rationalized that if they had taken her with them to Dunn's River Falls, she'd still be alive today. They also discussed what media-spin they could put on Sun Raye's death that would give them both good publicity and keep her death from hurting their campaign to secure approval of a clothing optional beach.

Carson Crown spent an entire day calling everyone he knew cheerfully gossiping, joking and speculating. He was having the time of his life. He even came up with a list of bad-taste one-liners for the occasion.

The signs at the nudist beach: *Sorry, clothed for the winter.*

Sign: Senior Citizen Nude Beach Ahead. Watch For Golden Oldies.

Always swim nude. Sharks hate to peel their food.

Nudists are people who wear one-button suits.

A naked man fears no pickpocket.

Burning Spear Chunker a.k.a. Chunky a.k.a. Elmo Levy congratulated himself on his good fortune. After all, would you rather be hot or lucky. He would claim his magic was indeed all powerful after all and as a result, command higher prices and get more respect. He wondered if anyone would challenge him if he began to call himself The All-Worshipful and Powerful Shaman. That title would sound more exotic and convincing than being an obeah man. Who's to say that all shaman had to be from the Caribbean? With a little effort maybe he could shake this Boston accent and become proficient at patois. *Maybe as a shaman I'll be in demand as a guest on TV shows,* he dreamed. Despite the ongoing tenderness on the soles of his feet, cutting them to shreds on those glass shards might have been worthwhile after all. Those cuts could turn out to be a career move. *When I get my act down pat, I'm gonna call some gullible honkies with more money than sense and get some sho' nuff good gigs.*

Dr. Doats renewed her efforts to research Benedict's powder to see if there was some residual effect that could have played a part in the whole equation and mused just who she should now report her findings to if she determined that to be the case.

The emotions that seemed to be ignored in the whole equation for the most part by the living were simple sympathy and compassion.

Billy Perez occupied himself feigning to comfort his wife while putting together a zinger of a memorial service. He rationalized that this is what his mother-in-law would have wanted so she could make a final lasting statement. He also schemed on ways to pad the costs and then skim a little mad money for himself. He finally decided that Kingdom Hall would be the logical setting for the memorial service since it was free, and that he would get Reverend Dub Bootee to officiate. Then they would all adjourn and caravan to the Garden of Eden, get shit-faced, eat hors d'oeuvres and have an ash scattering ceremony over Duval Street. After all, he rationalized, Sun Raye's heritage was on Duval Street since her mother had been a bartender and her father had been a street performer. Plus she used to work for Rainbow Ministries before she became a minister in her own right. It all seemed to be a perfect fit. He conferred with Sea Raye and Blue Raye, putting enough spin on his presentation to sell the deal. They both concurred that his ideas were excellent. He checked, and both the Garden of Eden and Reverend Dub were available. Yes, he was going to make this a service that would become part of Key West folklore. That was the way Sun Raye would have wanted it, to go to heaven with style and pizzazz in a butt-naked blaze of glory. He got with the girls and began to come up with an invitation list. He began to make a list of guests who as supporting players would augment or enhance the performance. Wait until Key West society saw this flock turned out in their Sunday finest birthday suits! Maybe they'd even make the *Conch Color* magazine.

CHAPTER 50

The more Bobby Perez thought about being the CEO of CANDO the more he liked the idea. At last he would be able to prove to the world that he was executive material. At first he was inclined to manage things the only way he knew how –by intimidation. He would simply use macho bravado and push to get his way – i.e. he'd just tell people and if they didn't like it, he'd simply beat the shit out of them. That included his wife.

That evening he happened to see "The Godfather" on TCM. When he went to bed he dreamed about scenes in the movie. In his dreams Adolfo Soltero's face displaced Marlon Brando's as the godfather, and Bobby tried to muscle his way into an enterprise in which the godfather had an interest. In the next vignette, he was being kidnapped by a scowling Omar Perillo and Miguel Valdes and was roughly tossed into the trunk of a car. His hands and feet had been tied, and he had a burlap bag tied over his head. He could hear them laughing as they discussed his fate.

"Soltero said put this arrogant upstart where no one will ever find him."

"We could take him out beyond the three mile limit and weight him down," said Perillo. "The sharks would love him. Bobby always wanted to swim with the big fish."

"I got a better idea. I think dirt fits his personality better. I know where a sewer project is going in. Why don't we bury him under where the pipe is going to be laid. Shit! Al knows the contractor, and the contractor owes him. He'll let me use his front-end loader. Meathead'll be six, maybe eight feet under. Nobody will ever find the dip-shit – like anyone cares anyway."

"It's too bad it had to come to this. All Bobby had to do was show a little respect."

"Oh, well, what's fuckin' done is fuckin' done," Valdes said. "Once a meathead, always a meathead."

They both laughed.

"You gonna miss this worthless ass-wipe?"

"Riiight!" Valdes said sarcastically. "I'll never be able to eat key lime pie again."

Bobby woke up in a sweat. He had to find Adolfo Soltero tomorrow and follow the protocol in *The Godfather*. Then he'd live prove to his detractors that he was CEO material.

Bobby made an appointment through Miguel Valdes to talk to Soltero privately. Valdes demanded to know the reason for the appointment, but Bobby told him it was a matter for Soltero's ears only. As usual, Soltero was very cordial and reluctantly agreed to support Bobby for the CANDO opening. What went unspoken was that this support was only because Bobby was Sun Raye's son-in-law and then it was only to be on a probationary basis.

Bobby was on cloud-nine. He immediately ordered business cards with his new title and began to make plans. One of his first actions was to hire a decorator for his new office.

Not long after, Bobby got a call from Rodney Chamberlain requesting an advisory meeting. Bobby quickly agreed and insisted they meet at his office so he could show off his new desk.

"Bobby Perez," said Rodney as he looked around the refurbished office. "I always knew you were an up-and-comer. I can spot them a mile away."

Bobby beamed.

"Do you like making money?" Rodney asked.

"I'm certainly looking for ideas," Bobby replied.

"I knew when I first met you that you were no common stick-in-the-mud," Rodney said. "I told Chip, keep your eyes on this young man. He's going to be somebody to be reckoned with."

He pulled out a package and laid it on Bobby's desk. Bobby picked it up and read the label, "Ivory Wave Bath Salts."

"So what?" he asked. "What's so special about this?"

"You ever heard of Magic, or Super Coke?' Rodney asked.

Bobby shook his head.

"Or MTV or MDPK or Peevee?'

Bobby shook his head again as he read the ingredients label and tried to pronounce the words.

"Epsom salts, Sodium Barcarbonate, Sodium Chloride, minerals, trace elements, and naturally occurring amino acids," he read. "This is just smellum for women's baths."

"That's where you are wrong, my young friend," Rodney continued. "This is a legal cocaine substitute. You can swallow it, snort it, smoke it, or shoot it up and it gives you the same high as cocaine. Some people even stick it up their asses as a suppository. They stay high three to four hours and unless they use too much, they don't have a painful come-down. For the horny, it acts as an aphrodisiac. For the shy, it makes them social. For students, it's a study aid. For workers, it increases their ability to concentrate, and best of all – it is L-E-G-A-L."

"Shit, sounds like the perfect drug," Bobby said.

"Almost, and if you're not in a mood to party, you can take a bath with it. It does however have one bad feature. It sometimes can be addictive," Rodney said, "but for the seller that's good because we get to sell the user more of it."

"Has anyone ever died using it?" Bobby asked.

"Not that I know of," Rodney said. "That's why it's still legal."

"How do you get it?"

"Simple. I know where to import it legally as bath salts. That's where I got this package. And I have multiple sources. I can buy it under the names of Ocean, White Dove, Red Dove plus a half-dozen other names. I simply go where I can get the best terms on price and delivery."

"Why are you sharing this idea with me?" Bobby asked.

"Distribution, my young friend. Because CANDO is selling personal care products," Rodney said, "you have a distribution network in place, and this is going to bring you into contact with a whole new legion of potential customers. I haven't brought it up before now because I didn't think your former mother-in-law had the vision or ambition that I think you do."

"Wow!" was all Bobby could think to say.

"And think what it can do for your existing distributors," Rodney said. "You're always having these motivational meetings and distributing motivational materials to try to get more productivity out of them. This drug is guaranteed to make them receptive, outgoing, energetic, and alert...and it's LEGAL. What more could you ask? By the way, imagine slipping distributor prospects a mickey when you're trying to close the deal and watching their enthusiasm rise?"

"How much does it take to get someone high?" Bobby asked.

"Five to twenty megs," Rodney said.

"Well, shit this package is 500 megs," Bobby said.

"But we don't sell them this package," Rodney said. "We package it in baggies in smaller amounts, re-label it, and mark it up accordingly. I've even got a name. "We'll call it Sno-White Bath Salts."

"You may be on to something," Bobby said, "and your timing is excellent. I'm looking for ways to take this business to the next level."

"I've got two conditions," Rodney said. "First never ask my source, and two, this is your deal and my deal to split fifty-fifty – our side enterprise. Nobody else. Comprende. Nobody else. We don't need to share the gravy with anyone. You and I will wholesale it to the company, and we will make the mark-up."

"Not even my brother?" Bobby asked.

"Not even Billy," Rodney said. "And I've got one further suggestion. Now that Sun Raye's gone, find some excuse to dump Luis Bernstein. He's the one person in the organization who is probably smart enough to give us problems at some point and try to horn his way in."

"What excuse do I use?"

"Maybe if you just make his life miserable, he'll leave on his own. You don't need him anymore. If he doesn't quit on his own, we'll think of something else. Ciao, pard. To new highs."

CHAPTER 51

Bobby Perez decided to take Rodney's advice. Luis Bernstein had to go. His thoughts went back to *The Godfather* again where whenever someone became a threat to Marlon Brando or Al Pacino, he was efficiently removed. It might be merciless Bobby rationalized, but good management techniques were often ruthless. *Like Alice Cooper said, No more Mr. nice guy. Maybe I'll make Luis an offer, he can't refuse. Nah, that might get back to my wife. I'll just make Luis want to be somewhere else.*

Bobby was a self-made homophobe and proud of it. First of all, he was an inherent sadistic bully, and he had found gays often easy to bully. Second, familiarity with gays from living in Key West had given him the justification he needed in his own mind to be contemptuous. Third, since his self-esteem had been questioned on multiple occasions by people who thought he was a meathead, he relished the illusion of superiority. Last, a specific incident a few years back reinforced his prejudices. He conveniently forgot that he had created this embarrassing situation himself.

Bobby thought back. His gym had been used by a wide spectrum of people. An outgoing popular regular there was a former Fantasy Fest king named Harry Dickman. Harry had come out of the closet years before and was accepted for what he was. The rift started one day when Bobby attempted to push ahead of Harry on the treadmill, and

Harry refused to be bullied. Each time Bobby saw Harry at the gym thereafter he would make snide remarks, calling him "San Francisco," "renter," or "light in the sneakers." He often made light of Harry's name in front of others by calling him "Hairy Dickless," "Hairy Dick-A-Man," or Harry Dick-Head." He told other exercisers that it would be more appropriate for Harry to patronize the woman's gym in Key West since this was "a real man's gym." Finally one day Harry had had enough. He stated to Bobby in front of a group that he was as much of a man as Bobby was and could not only match him on the free-weights but surpass him. He issued a challenge and bet Bobby $500 that he could beat him in a two-man competition supervised by the gym's personal trainer. They would compete in five categories: bench press, clean-and-jerk, squat, dead-lift, and pull-up. Whoever could lift the most weight in three of the five categories would be declared the winner. The loser would be required to contribute the $500 to the non-profit organization designated by the winner.

Bobby quickly agreed and bragged for a week how it would be the easiest $500 he had ever made proving to the world once and for all that a queer was inferior to a real man. After all, he said, everyone knew that "all Harry's muscles are in his dick." When the day arrived, in front of many witnesses Harry decisively beat Bobby in four of the five categories. Bobby only managed to barely win the dead-lift. Despite Dickman's being a good winner, Bobby never forgave him for the embarrassment he suffered. To make matters worse, Dickman's choice of a non-profit was the Key West Gay and Lesbian Community Center.

Bobby's humiliation was complete when Dickman wrote a letter to the editor at both the *Key West Citizen* and the *Florida Keys Keynoter* publicly thanking Bobby for his contribution. Bobby seethed for days.

Bobby did not know enough about Luis's job to know if he was doing it well or not. Bobby also knew that if he simply nit-picked everything Luis did, he either would make a fool of himself or it would get back to his wife and sister-in-law. So the solution was simply to make Luis so uncomfortable that he would leave on his own, and what better way to do this than to start rumors that Luis was a raging fag. Maybe he could even plant some evidence in Luis's computer. The campaign was on.

In the meantime, Luis had his own fish to fry. Now that Sun Raye was no longer at CANDO, he began to consider splitting as well. He was still not convinced that he had not been the intended target on some of the recent assassination attempts, and he sure didn't want to give the killer another chance to succeed. So it was time to consider his options.

His short term goal, he decided, should be to write down everything he knew about all recent assassination attempts and to put a summary of both the facts and his suspicions in his safety deposit box at Betsy Black's bank. He also included what he knew of 21st Century Securities illegal market manipulation techniques as well. He conveniently forgot to put anything in the box concerning his own illegal activities. He decided he should surreptitiously give a key to the Blacks. Then he would quickly amass as much capital as possible in his off-shore account in one last attack on 21st Century's corporate account. He determined it would be safest if he did this after he left CANDO and went underground. He began to make his preparations.

Bobby began his attempts to undermine Luis by dropping hints that Luis had a secret life in the closet. Luis, however, was so involved in his own affairs he was apathetic about Bobby's smear efforts, and even when he was aware of them, they only served as a minor irritation. After all, he had his own fish to fry. When Luis chose to disappear, Bobby congratulated himself on his campaign's success.

But Luis who really didn't give a damn, just for fun after he left turned the tables on Bobby by sending his wife an anonymous e-mail telling her that Bobby had an illegitimate half-breed child in Miami. He attached a dummy birth certificate to his e-mail.

On his last day Luis had begun to clean out his desk. He found a cotton bag in his desk drawer containing the glass marbles he had played with as a child. He had totally forgotten the marbles were in the drawer. He opened the sack and reminisced. There were cat's eyes, milk glass marbles, aggies, devil's eyes, beach ball marbles and of course, toothpaste marbles. He even found his old shooter. As he began to dump his treasures on his desk, the old cloth bag tore and released marbles everywhere. Luis gasped as his treasures bounced off the floor and began to roll in many directions. Soon he was on his hands and knees retrieving his childhood treasures. At that moment the door opened, and Bobby entered to tell Luis he was on his way to the gym. His foot hit the loose marbles, and he lost his balance. He skidded into a bookshelf toppling a glass vase on a high shelf. Luis lurched from his knees to try to save the doomed vase and in doing so was accidentally head-butted by Bobby. Luis's nose shattered and blood soaked them both. Bobby grabbed a gym towel and let Luis use it until the blood subsided. After apologies were offered by both sides, Bobby threw the towel into the back of his truck and headed to his workout.

A few days before his accident, Luis bought a foot-and-a half braided Malabar chestnut or "money tree" at Home Depot. He took the safety-deposit key, double wrapped it in small baggies along with the number of the safety deposit box, and buried them both in the repotted plant. He bought a tasteful white ceramic pot so it would not need repotting again for a long time and took his offering to Betsy's office.

"Mrs. Black, I just wanted to bring you this as a small token of my appreciation for not only rescuing us the day the boat blew but being a sounding board for us afterwards," he said as he presented it to her. "This plant belonged to Sun Raye. I thought this would be appropriate for a banker, and I know how you like plants. Many people have nicknamed this plant a 'money tree.' Feng shui believers think it will bring you good luck."

Betsy laughed and said, "Well, thanks. The leaves make it look like a marijuana plant. With everything that happened, I guess Sun Raye needed something to bring her luck. It's frightening to think that she thought someone was out to get her here in the Keys, only to die not long thereafter in an accident abroad."

"Well, you know what they say, sometimes if a person didn't have bad luck, he wouldn't have any luck at all,"

Luis said. "I really miss her. I guess you know we had grown quite close. Traveling to Jamaica and making all the arrangements for her was probably the toughest thing I've ever done. Anyway, I hope you enjoy the money tree. Take good care of it so it will always bring you good luck. I hope it gives you something to remember her by."

With that he said goodbye. He would only tell her about the safety deposit key if the need arose. He made sure to prepay the box rental before he left the bank.

Luis's next task was to find a safe-house out of the county. Then he began his illegal hacking activities in earnest. He began to wonder if someone at 21st Century Securities had traced his IP during his last raid on them, and took measures to keep it from happening this time.

When Luis checked, he found that they were running Netscape Enterprise and that Port 8088 was open to allow the server administrator to look after, edit and manage the account details of its various users. This was all Luis needed to edit and change his own account details. When he connected with Port 8088 he was greeted by the HTTP authentication screen. This screen contained details of the target machine's name and asked for a username and password. Not knowing either of these facts, Luis left both lines blank and clicked OK, bringing up another HTTP authentication screen that looked the same except the realm field now said "unknown prompt." So Luis typed in his own user name and password and was taken to the Netscape Server Account page. Once on this page he changed all of his ISP contact details to a false name, address and phone number.

Luis leaned back in his chair and smiled. *Now let the*

assholes try to find me. Even if they suspect who I was the first time, they'll never be able to prove that I'm back. Fuck you, Jack, and the horse you rode in on.

Within two weeks Adolfo Soltero got a phone call from Chip Talbos.

"The hacker is back," he said curtly.

"How much this time?" Al asked.

"$800 grand."

"He's worn out his welcome. I'll get him out of our hair permanently."

"I already called Rambo. He says the ISP account details are different this time."

"Please explain," Al said.

"I mean a different name, address and phone number."

"My gut tells me it's our nemesis at CANDO again."

"Mine too," Chip said, "but I can't prove that."

"We have methods of persuasion," Al said.

"You'll have to find him first," Chip said. "He hasn't worked at CANDO in two weeks."

"Even more reason to suspect him. Call your buddy, Rambo, back. Tell him to find him," said Al. "There will be a nice bonus for him if he succeeds. We're going to stop our boy once and for all this time."

Luis was taking no chances. He shut down his safe house and went deeper underground. He also decided not to get greedy. He would hit them one more time and call it a day. He could always do it again down the road if it became necessary. This had given him three million dollars. This should be plenty of seed money for now.

CHAPTER 52

Betsy called CANDO on bank related business and asked for Luis.

"He doesn't work here anymore," said the receptionist. "Can someone else help you?"

"Doesn't work there anymore?" Betsy responded. "He was just in my office a couple of weeks ago."

"I wish I could tell you more," she said. "If you would like to talk to Mr. Perez, I'll transfer you now. Bobby is in. Billy is not in yet."

"Bobby Perez," said a voice.

"Bobby, Betsy Black. I was just told Luis no longer works for you."

"Yeah, we came in one morning and his letter of resignation was on my desk."

"Do you know where he went?"

"I don't have a clue," Bobby said. "You know how flaky these pantywaists can be. Probably holed up with a new squeeze. I'm just as glad the fag's gone."

"I didn't know Luis was gay."

"He always seemed to me like the type who could swing both ways," Bobby said. "Now, can I help you with something?"

Betsy told Bobby the original nature of her call.

When she hung up, she called her husband.

"Will, did you know Luis Bernstein quit his job?"

"Something doesn't sound right about that," Will said. "He just came to see you two weeks ago with that plant, and you told me he seemed perfectly normal."

"Seemed like it to me. He was still somewhat distraught over Sun Raye, but it didn't seem like it had made him dysfunctional."

"You've got his address on your bank records," Will said. "Give it to me, and I'll ride by there and see if anyone's home."

Will rode by Luis's rental house. No one was home. He knocked on the door of Luis's next door neighbor. She said she hadn't seen him in a couple of weeks. When Will got back to his office, he reported his findings to his wife.

"Do you think something's happened to him?" she asked. "Maybe he is in trouble after all. I'd hate to think Luis is dead too."

"I think we ought to tell Chief Wanderley our suspicions," Will said.

"I think you're right," Betsy said. "Since I haven't seen Walter this week, I think I'll call him and suggest he stop by. Just one more strange event. I'll tell him what you found ... or didn't find out ... about Sun Raye while he's here."

"I concur completely. No use holding back."

Betsy called Walter. Walter told her he was dealing with a crisis at that moment, but he'd be over before the bank closed and that he'd fill her in on his situation when he got there. Betsy told him hers would hold until he got there.

Walter walked in about mid-afternoon.

"So what fire did you have to put out?" Betsy asked.

"Honey-buns," Walter said.

"Is that a term of endearment, or is it what you brought for our afternoon coffee?" Betsy asked.

"I might never eat one again," Walter said. "As you may know, we sell honey-buns at the jail. The prisoners crave sweets, and they make the ideal snack. They're a lowly but sturdy comfort food; they're big; they're cheap; they have long code dates; you can mash them up in your coat pocket and they're still fit to eat. Some prisoners even use them for birthday cakes. We sell more honey-buns each month than we do cigarettes, envelopes or even Coca Colas. The only thing we sell more of is freeze-dried coffee and ramen noodles."

"OK, so they're nature's perfect food. So what's the problem?"

"Well, it has come to our attention that some of our scheming inmates have been offering detainees in the drunk tank an irresistible deal. They'll exchange honey buns for the drunk's social security number. Then using these numbers, they've been filing tax forms with false information. The IRS tells us that their calculations show they've paid out over $1 million in fraudulent refunds," Walter said.

Betsy had to stifle the chuckle that had inadvertently worked its way into her throat.

"You can laugh," Walter said, "But this is a real mess. So what's your problem?"

"Not as entertaining as yours, honey-bun-snookums," Betsy teased. "I knew life would have been more interesting if I had become a cop."

"So what's your problem today?" Walter asked.

"I hope it's not a problem," Betsy said, "but Will and I thought you should decide. Luis Bernstein has suddenly resigned his job and dropped out of sight. We sincerely hope he's OK."

She then gave Walter a summary of all the prior accidents or attempts on either Sun Raye's or Luis's lives. She related to him about the voodoo graffiti that had been scribbled on CANDO's sidewalk as well as the dead fish someone had hung from their doorway. She told him about Sun Raye's and Luis's insistence they get their assets liquid and their macabre paranoia shortly before her death. She told him what little she knew about Sun Raye's breaking-and-entering at Tango. Last she related her seemingly innocuous visit from Luis shortly before he disappeared.

"I'm like you," Walter said. "I don't know if a problem exists or not either. He may just be on vacation, but it wouldn't be prudent for me to just ignore all these coincidences. By the way, I will leave you with something to ponder regarding coincidences. Erma Bombeck concluded that Thanksgiving dinners take eighteen hours to prepare. They are then consumed in twelve minutes. Football half-times last twelve minutes. Do you think this is a coincidence?"

"Cute. I'll leave you with a thought. Once is an accident. Twice is coincidence. Three times is enemy action. One last thing," Betsy said. "Will went on the Internet and brought up the *Jamaica Gleaner*, the newspaper out of Kingston. He could not find any news stories about Sun Raye's hit-and-run accident. Wouldn't you think an unsolved hit-and-run involving a tourist would be newsworthy?"

"I would certainly think so," Walter said. "Let me put out an APB on Luis Bernstein and see what happens. I'll just say he's a person of interest wanted for questioning."

"By the way, Luis also has family in Key West. They own Bernstein's Down Home Cuban Grocery Store."

The following week Betsy looked out her window and saw the police chief's car pull into a parking place. She waited for him to enter the building.

"Well, if it isn't the exalted ruler of the honey-bun realm," she joshed. "Walter, I found myself wondering after our last visit, do you think there should be a check-off on the tax forms allowing a person to request his tax refund in honey-buns?"

"I used to take it as a compliment when my wife called me honey or honey-bun. I also thought the song in *South Pacific* with Mitzi Gaynor and Ray Walston was adorable," Walter said. "Now I hope I never hear the expression again. You wouldn't believe the latest."

"Try me."

"First, I have also discovered that some of our inmates are mixing honey-buns with orange juice and making home-made wine. I also had two very interesting meetings with the common-law wife of an inmate accusing me of running a correctional facility out of compliance with state nutritional guidelines. We are required by the state of Florida to provide each inmate with a daily diet of 2750 calories that limits both fat and sodium. We have always come through our inspections with flying colors. Well, it turns out that her husband, who has been our guest for a little over a year, has ballooned from 120 pounds to 185 pounds, upsetting her greatly. When I checked to try to find the source of his problem, I found that he was spending all the money she was sending him on honey-buns."

"Just remember what Paul Harvey said about in times like these, it's good to remember that there have always been times like these. Now you know why you get the big bucks," Betsy said. "You're a problem solver.'

"Not exactly," Walter said. "I've yet to stop this problem. She insisted that I cut off his honey-bun allotment. I tried to explain that I can't tell him how to spend his money. If she wants his honey-bun ration cut off, she is going to just have to quit sending him money. She didn't like my solution one little bit."

"Speaking of problems," Betsy continued. "What have you been able to learn about Luis?"

"If you're asking, have we found Luis," Walter said, "the answer is no. Bobby Perez acted like he was just glad to have Luis out of his hair. Luis's family hasn't heard from him. He's gone under our radar screen. He hasn't used his cell phone or a credit card. He's turned into the invisible man."

"I hope our suspicions about him being a possible victim of foul play are wrong," Betsy said.

"So do I," Walter said, "but we both know he could be with the fishes. The only thing we've been able to learn so far is that we are not the only people looking for him. One of my undercover men heard rumors of a possible contract out on Luis. Also there was some chat room chatter that seemed to be trying to locate him. All I can tell you is I'll keep trying."

"I wish we'd had a conversation about him before we did," Betsy said. "I hate to think Luis's out somewhere alone in trouble."

CHAPTER 53

Merci Doats was troubled. She could not get Sun Raye's death out of her mind. Attending Sun Raye's memorial service had not given her the closure she had hoped to get. She had gotten quite fond of Sun Raye in the brief time she had known her and admired her for what she had accomplished despite being a high school dropout and a single mom. She was also secretly envious of Sun Raye's panache. Being an academician, she would never have guts to be both as spontaneous or as focused as Sun Raye seemed to be. She still smiled as she visualized Sun Raye and herself caterwauling that nonsense song together at Melody Key. It also bothered her that Sun Raye died so violently shortly after someone had obviously tried to sabotage her efforts.

Rather than considering her job complete, she felt an obligation to disclose what she had learned to someone. She tried to call Luis Bernstein, but he never returned her phone calls. Bobby Perez blew her off. She finally decided that the person who now had the largest vested interest in the whole affair was the widowed husband of the lady who had been killed. She easily found Jock Jacquette in the phone book, gave him a call, introduced herself and offered to go by his office and tell him everything she knew. He gratefully agreed to see her at her convenience.

When Merci arrived Jock immediately invited her into

his office and got her a cup of coffee.

"Thank you so much for taking time to see me," Merci began. "Before we go any further, let me give you my heartfelt sympathy over your wife's untimely death. I was never fortunate enough to meet her, but I have heard nothing but good things about her.

"Sun Raye felt very badly about what happened at Melody Key and hired me to help her solve the mystery. I work for the college. I am also an expert in toxic substances. The substance that your wife was exposed to was a powder named Benedict's powder."

She went on to give him an overview about Benedict's powder and why it was a dangerous but usually not lethal substance.

"Is this a substance that is found in nature?" Jock asked.

"Definitely not," Merci replied. "It had to be purposely spread around by someone wishing to be malicious. I might add, your wife would not have detected it since it is odorless, tasteless and water soluble."

"But who would want to commit mass murder?" Jock asked.

"I'm sure that's not what they had in mind," Merci said. "The powder is normally not life threatening. It is just an extremely harsh irritant. More like something an irresponsible sadistic prankster would use."

"This certainly turned into more than a prank," Jock said. "Isn't that island restricted to the private use of Sun Raye and her organizations?"

"That is my understanding," Merci said, "but that would not necessarily deter an intruder."

"Then the odds are it was someone connected with her company or church. Everyone involved must be held responsible," Jock said, "and I'm not going to rest until I make them pay. Jennifer was my whole life."

"I can't advise you on that," Merci said, "but let me just say this, please don't let this incident make you do something irresponsible that you will always regret."

Jock got emotional and his voice began to crack. He snapped a pencil he was holding. "I am going to get even with anyone and everyone who is even remotely involved in destroying my life, and I don't give a damn what the consequences are."

The meeting with Dr. Doats caused Jock Jacquette to redouble his efforts for revenge. He wrote letters; he visited Kingdom Hall; he brought up his wife's death at CANDO meetings; he visited 21st Century Securities and demanded to see records on Chosen Ones Growth Fund. He seemed to be everywhere as a constant thorn in everyone's side.

Jock visited Betsy at the bank to learn what paperwork would be involved to set up a foundation account once he was successful. She extended to him the same advice Dr. Doats had given him, "Please don't break the law by doing something foolish."

Bobby Perez finally got to the point where he refused to return Jock's phone calls and would not meet with him when he came to the building with a new angle. More than once Bobby contemplated settling the matter his way only to be restrained by his wife and her sister.

One evening as Jock left his office, he felt the presence of another person. As he turned in the dark, he saw a hulking figure in the shadows. What came next was a barrage of blows, one after another that knocked him unconscious. His next memory was briefly waking up on the ground with a broken nose and a dislocated jaw. When he was taken to the hospital his head trauma was so severe that surgeons had to remove a third of his skull to relieve the pressure on his brain. Jock was later told by doctors that if his surgery had been delayed for ten more minutes, he might not have survived.

It would take six months of brain surgeries and months of rehabilitation before he was much improved. Even then he would struggle with intense pain and other health problems, including vertigo and memory loss. His ability to walk and talk would be very limited.

For weeks following his first surgery Jock couldn't recognize any of his visitors. When he finally went home from the hospital, it was with 40 staples in his skull and a tube that drained blood from his head into a bag.

Jock began to struggle with flashbacks and depression. His face was partially paralyzed and his dislocated jaw made it difficult to chew. He was so exhausted that he slept nearly all day, every day for weeks. The medical bills topped $800 thousand.

Jock was left looking freakish with a scar that was a ragged "u" that looped from his forehead to the back of his head and then around to his ear.

The only good news was that he became a celebrity cause for mugging and crime, and some local musicians held a benefit to try to raise money for him.

Since he was no help in identifying his assailant, Jock's beating simply became another cold case. Robbery was ruled out as a motive since nothing was stolen. Some people thought it was a professional job; no one knew for sure.

CHAPTER 54

"Honey, I may be a little late this afternoon," Will Black said as he was leaving for the office. "I'm going to stop by the hospital and take my client Mary McInnis a get-well card after the market closes this afternoon. She just had her left knee replaced. Then I thought I'd also maybe drop by and look in on Jock Jacquette."

"Wish Mary the best for me," Betsy said, "and good luck with Jock. I thought he was pretty much out of it most of the time."

"I guess I'll find out," Will said.

The visit with Mary McInnis was short and uneventful. She was a widow and appreciated Will's thoughtfulness. Then he headed for Jock's house.

Will was shocked by Jock's appearance. The ragged scar that went around his shaved head that ended up around his ear gave Will the creeps. Jock's speech was hesitant and hard to understand as he stuttered and had trouble pronouncing his words. He had lost weight and looked pale and gaunt.

"It'th good to see ... you, W-W-ill," he said. "Tank you...for c-coming."

"Good to see you too. I didn't know what to expect," Will said. "I sure hope they catch the bastard who did this to you. Do they still think it was a mugger?"

"D- dun ... know ... dark. Hard to re-mem-ber."

"What do you remember about your assailant?" Will asked.

"Dunno n-n-noth ..."

Jock gritted his teeth and started to cry as a wave of pain hit him.

"W-water," Jock said and pointed at a glass with a straw just out of reach on his table.

Will retrieved it for him.

"Had dream last n-night," Jock continued after taking a sip. "The fist ... conexted to big arm with pitcher."

"Water pitcher?" Will responded.

"No, pitcher...pitcher...art pitcher."

"A picture on the arm? You mean like a tattoo?"

"Yeth, tattoo," Jock said.

"What kind of tattoo?"

"Skull...fish...swim fish."

"Which arm?"

Jock pointed to his left arm and poked it. "This one...I think."

"White guy...?" Will asked.

Jock nodded sluggishly.

"Do the police know this?" Will asked.

Jock shook his head and said, "No...just have dream last night."

"This could be important," Wills said. "Do you mind if I tell the police chief?"

Jock did not respond. He was already dozing off. Will let himself out. When he got in his car, he called Walter on his cell phone and told him of his conversation with Jock. Walter said he'd get back to Will after he had had a chance to mull the matter over.

Walter came into Will's office the next morning shortly before the market opened.

"Boy, that was fast," Will said. "Want some coffee?"

He had Barbara get Walter a Styrofoam cup of coffee with a dash of milk in it.

"They make better coffee at the bank," he said and smiled.

"I bet a doughnut would improve it," Will said. "It just so happens the Franklin sales rep left some earlier this morning."

Walter pushed a drawing across Will's desk. It contained a design that had an alternating skull and flanked by swimming sharks. The design was over a bed of barbed wire.

"Does this look like what you thought Jock was trying to describe?" he asked.

"Matter of fact it does," Will said. "Where'd you get it?"

"I'll tell you that later," Walter said, "if my suspicions turn out to be correct. Would you mind accompanying me on a visit to Jock Jacquette to see if this is the design in his dream? It shouldn't take long."

"It would be a pleasure," Will said. He called Barbara into his office and confirmed that she could manage things for an hour or so in his absence.

"My car or yours?" Will asked as they were leaving his office.

Walter drove them over to Jock's house. After a short wait while the visiting nurse cleaned his drainage tube, Jock welcomed Will and Walter and slowly walked towards his living room couch.

"You remember Chief Wanderley, don't you?" Will began.

Jock nodded hesitantly.

"I told him about the dream you had the other night," Will said as he handed Jock Walter's drawing. "Is this the design you saw in your dream?"

Jock looked at the picture and said nothing. Finally after a pregnant pause he said, "Yeth, I think so."

"Which arm was it on?" Walter interrupted.

Jock pointed at his left one and grimaced as another pain shot through his shattered jaw.

Walter and Will thanked him, bade him goodbye and let themselves out.

On the way back to Will's office, he asked Walter, "So now are you going to tell me what's going on? Where'd you get that picture?"

"Will, this is confidential," Walter said.

"Of course," Will said.

"That is the same design that the Perez twins have on their arms."

"I thought it looked familiar," Will said.

"Billy has this design on his left bicep," Walter continued. "Bobby has it on his right. They got tattooed years ago so people could tell them apart."

"So that's why it's so critical which arm it's on," Will said.

"Correct," Walter said. "Looks like I need to have a talk with Billy Perez."

"Mind if I tell Betsy?" Will asked.

"As long as she understands that her silence and discretion are imperative," Walter said.

"Hell, she's a banker," Will said with a laugh. "Discretion is her business."

CHAPTER 55

"Life sucks, and then you die," Billy Perez said to himself out-loud as he drove up U.S. 1 to his office. He was tempted to snatch the parking ticket he had gotten in Old Town the day before out of his pocket, wad it up and pitch it, but he knew this wouldn't solve anything. Instead he shot a finger at a Big Pine fireman collecting donations at the intersection of Key Deer Boulevard. This act of defiance didn't make him feel any better. *Buffett had it right,* he told himself, *when he said it's just another shitty day in paradise.*

It had been a hell of a week. It had begun with a knock-down-drag-out with Bobby over some CANDO policies. Then his wife had given him grief for backing down and giving in to Bobby. Then Bobby had found a poem Billy had written and accidentally left in his in-box and then chided him about it in front of some of the people at the gym. Bobby had said only fags write poetry. *If you weren't my brother, I'd show you who's a fag. I'd punch your lights out,* Billy thought. And then this parking ticket.

About that time Billy's cell phone rang. It was the secretary he shared with Bobby calling to give him a heads-up that she'd given out his cell phone number to Sgt. Victor Rivas from the Key West Police Department. *I wonder what that mother-fucker wants.*

He wouldn't have to wait long to find out. His cell

phone rang.

"Mr. Perez, this is Sgt. Victor Rivas with the police department. I would like to extend an invitation for you to stop by the police station at your convenience to see if you might be of assistance to us in the matter of the Jock Jacquette assault."

"Do I have a choice?" Billy asked.

"You always have a choice, Mr. Perez," Sgt. Rivas said.

"Are you trying to imply that I had something to do with it?" Billy continued.

"No, we would like to see if you could help us shed some light on the situation," Rivas said.

Billy agreed to come down that afternoon. When he did, he was shown into the interrogation room.

"Mr. Perez, my name is Sgt. Victor Rivas. This is Sgt. Eyal Goldshmid. This interview is being tape recorded and may be given in evidence if it were determined that you were involved in the crime against Mr. Jacquette. I will be making notes during this interview purely for my own reference."

He then proceeded to get Billy to state his full name, his date of birth and address and confirmed for the purpose of the tape the nature of questioning. He asked Billy to explain the meaning of the word caution and reiterated to him that he had a right to silence, the right to the services of an attorney, and that any information derived from this interview could later be used in a court of law.

"Mr. Perez, you do know Mr. Jacquette, do you not?" Rivas said.

"His wife was a distributor for my company," Billy

said.

"You say 'was'," Rivas said.

"Yes, she is now deceased."

"Is it true that she died as a result of an illness that she picked up at a CANDO function?" Rivas asked.

"That was never proven," Billy said. "Where'd you hear that?"

"No matter," Rivas said. "Isn't it also true that her husband has been disruptive at some CANDO meetings since his wife's death?"

"He's a nut case."

"Isn't it true that he threatened to bring legal action against the company?"

"I suppose. Like I said, he's a nut case."

"So you have ample reason to dislike Jacquette."

"He's not one of my favorite people, but I didn't dislike him enough to hurt him."

Rivas got out the drawing of the tattoo and slid it across the table.

"Recognize this?" he asked.

Billy pealed up his shirt sleeve and exposed his own tattoo.

"It's a drawing of this. So what?" he said.

"We have a witness that says the assailant had this tattoo on his arm," Rivas said.

"So what! I ain't got a patent on this fuckin' design."

"Only one I've ever seen."

"My brother's got one too."

"On his left arm?" Rivas said. "Our witness says the assailant had this tattoo on his left arm."

"Oh, no, you don't. You ain't pinnin' this shit on me,"

Billy said. "I haven't been near that blackmailing weasel."

"Then where were you the night Jock Jacquette was assaulted?"

"I'd rather not say."

"You better say," Rivas said. "Do you realize that a first offense for aggravated assault is five years in Florida?"

Billy said nothing.

"And the prosecution may go after more than aggravated assault. Let's try attempted murder on for size," Rivas said. "Now let's see ... The penalty for that is life."

Rivas looked at Goldshmid and sighed, "Life is a long time for someone in their twenties. Eyal, what do you think this fit young man's life expectancy is? Eighty-five or so! That would mean sixty years of being locked up with hardened criminals. Would you want to spend the next sixty years locked up?"

"I wouldn't," Eyal said. "That's why I'd cooperate so I could try to get a better deal for myself. I'd certainly try to help someone who was trying to help himself."

"I would too," Rivas said. "That's what a smart person would do."

"Up until now, I thought you were talking to an intelligent young man," Eyal said. "Maybe we overestimated him."

"I could use a cup of coffee," Rivas said. "Why don't we go get one and give our young friend a few minutes to think?"

They both left the interrogation room, leaving Billy to fret.

After the two detectives left, Billy began to think. He

remembered a phone call Bobby had made shortly after the incident. He had accidentally walked by Bobby's open door as he was talking to Miguel Valdes. He remembered hearing Bobby say, "Well, I guess Jock the jack-ass won't be a problem anymore." At the time he had just thought Bobby was gloating at Jock's misfortune, but now he realized that the conversation had meant more than that. *Bobby beat Jock to a pulp, and now it's about to get pinned on me. I'm not taking the fall for his impulsiveness, even if we are brothers, but I couldn't live with myself if I turned him in.*

Rivas and Goldshmid reentered the interrogation room. Billy was nervous and undecided.

"I did not commit this crime," he said. "I'll tell you where I was. I attended a poetry reading at My Blue Heaven that night."

"Why didn't you tell us that before?" Rivas asked.

"Because I was ashamed. My brother said only fags go to things like that," Billy said. "I have written some poems. Bobby found one in my in-box and ragged me unmercifully about it at the gym in front of the other guys. I was going to read my poem at the meeting that night, but when I got there, I was too shy to do it. So I just sat in the back of the room and listened to other people."

"That should be easy to verify," Goldshmid said. "A six-foot two muscle-bound meathead would certainly stand out with that bunch of eggheads even if he didn't do anything but sit in the back and keep his mouth shut."

"If you didn't do it," Rivas said, "that must mean that your brother was the perpetrator."

Billy was silent.

"But the witness said the tattoo was on the assailant's left arm," Goldshmid said.

"If someone is facing you, then his left is on your right," Rivas said. "In the victim's addled condition, he simply could have pointed to the direction he saw it by mistake."

He turned to Billy.

"Billy, we are going to check out your alibi," he said. "We'll get back to you if we need you again. Keep your mouth shut about this, or you'll wish you hadn't. I wouldn't want to have to make you an accessory after the fact. You can go now. "

CHAPTER 56

Detective Rivas wasted no time in obtaining a search warrant for Bobby's home and truck. The home search revealed nothing, but the search of the truck was another matter. It didn't take long to uncover the gym towel with dried blood stains. Rivas had the towel tested for DNA. The results shocked even him. He was now ready to interrogate Bobby Perez.

After the standard opening basics, the interrogation quickly got down to the matter at hand.

"I've thought for a long time that I'd eventually nail you for something," Rivas began, "and I guess that day has finally come."

"I don't know what you're talking about," Bobby said. "You're trying to blow smoke up my ass."

Rivas put the drawing of the tattoo on the table and said, "Recognize this?"

"I got one just like it," Bobby said. "So?"

"So I've got a witness who said the person who assaulted Jock Jacquette had a tattoo identical to this one."

"My congratulations to him on his good taste."

"So there's only one other tattoo like this one that we know of in Monroe County – your brother, and he has an alibi for that night that didn't include you."

"You're bluffing if you think you can convince me that Billy would hang me out to dry," Bobby said.

"Maybe not intentionally unless it came down to saving his own ass. Do you know what CYONYB means?" Rivas asked.

No, what?"

"Cover your own ass not your brothers," Rivas said.

"Cute. I guess the city of Key West pays you extra to be their stupid resident clown," Billy said.

"By the way, since you brought up funny and stupid, I found a towel with blood stains in the back of your truck. Bobby, if you're going to commit a crime, you ought to be at least smart enough to get rid of the evidence."

"Shit, cop, you're going to have to do better than that," Bobby said. "I cut my hand, and wiped it on that towel."

"You're not going to be so smug when I tell you what the DNA test revealed about that towel," Rivas said. "The results surprised even me. I found not only your blood on it but Jock Jacquette's and Luis Bernstein's as well."

"That fruit Bernstein had an accident at work."

He explained to Rivas the incident concerning the glass marbles and how he had accidentally head-butted Luis as they both tried to save a falling glass vase.

"So you two overgrown kiddies were playing marbles," Rivas said sarcastically, "but you weren't playing nice. I always thought marbles was a non-contact sport. Didn't you, Sgt. Goldshmid? I'll have to say this, I had heard you were a meathead, but in all my years as a law enforcement officer, I've never heard that story. I'll give you a '9' for creativity and a '10' for imagination. Did anyone see you two children playing marbles?"

"No, we were in Luis's office."

"Figures. So there's no way to corroborate your story. I

guess you know Bernstein has not been seen in Monroe County for weeks," Rivas said.

"So, I'm not his keeper. I fired his sorry ass for pulling no-shows at work," Bobby said. "I'm sure when you find him you'll find he's been off shacking up with some other faggot."

"Bobby, you're a liar," Rivas said. "Do you want to know what I think? I think both of these people's blood is on that towel because of two reasons. You beat the crap out of Jacquette because he had become a relentless thorn in your side. Wasn't he threatening to sue you after his wife died?"

"That was a bullshit threat. Everyone knew that."

"Was it? Do you want me to tell you what else I think? We found open containers of bath salts also in the back of your truck. I know what dope-heads use these bath salts for, synthetic cocaine. I also know they sometimes make people act irrationally. What I think is that you got high on bath salts, went over to Jacquette's house and almost killed him. That's what I think and intend to prove," Rivas said.

Bobby glared at him hatefully.

"Do you know what the penalty for aggravated battery is? I'll make your sorry ass a guest of the state of Florida for five years...and that's if you get off light. We might just go for attempted murder. That will take you out of circulation for the rest of your life. And at this point we're building a pretty damned strong case against you."

Bobby still glared.

"Now let's get to the matter of Luis Bernstein. I think you might have killed him and disposed of the body, and

I'm going to do my damnest to nail you for that crime too."

Bobby shot Rivas a finger.

"Did you ever see the old Paul Newman movie, "Cool Hand Luke"? It had a famous line.

"What we have here is a failure to communicate."

I get the feeling we have the same problem again right here in this room. You can either cooperate now and I'll recommend leniency, or you can roll the dice. Paul Newman rolled the dice in the movie, and he ended up dead. It's up to you, hot-shot. Sgt. Goldshmid, I could use some coffee. How about you? Want to think it over, big-shot?"

"There's nothing to think about. If your case was as good as you say, you'd be snapping the cuffs on me right now. I just want to get the fuck out of here," Bobby said.

"Have it your way," Rivas said, "for the moment. May I give you a word of advice? Enjoy your freedom while you can. It may be short-lived."

CHAPTER 57

Bobby Perez was so mad he had trouble controlling himself as he left the police station. All he could think about was what he would like to do to Victor Rivas if he ever caught him off duty. He saw two police cars. He looked around to see if anyone was looking and when he saw he was alone, keyed both of them. This made him feel just a wee bit better.

He rode through town and when a tourist slowed to show a point-of-interest to his wife, leaned on his car horn and shot the man a bird. He still didn't feel any better. He parked his car over near Front Street and walked down the sidewalk. Just for meanness he toppled a sidewalk display of t-shirts and disappeared around the corner before the shopkeeper could come out. He had almost welcomed a confrontation just so he could punch someone out.

He walked over to Teaser's on Duval Street. Yes, they had what he needed - a few drinks and some tits and ass. One drink turned into two, two turned into three and before he knew it several hours had passed. He paid for a couple of lap dances on the bar, but he still couldn't forget about Rivas and his Jew buddy. Finally he picked a fight with one of the lap dancers, and the bouncer invited him to leave.

When Bobby stumbled back out on the street he was surprised to see that it was now well into the evening. "Fuck 'em," he said out loud to a passing group of college students. "I was tired of that place anyway." The students quickly crossed the street to get away from him.

Bobby knew where he wanted to go next. He headed for Cowboy Bill's Honky Tonk Saloon a few blocks away. This was Wednesday. He was sure to see some tits and ass on Cowboy Bill's mechanical bull. Besides that, he was hungry, and Bill's served cheeseburgers.

Bobby passed a couple of street cops and did have the presence of mind to keep his mouth shut and not cause any more trouble, but when their backs were turned, he pretended they were Rivas and Goldshmid and shot them both a bird.

The music pulsated as Bobby walked into Cowboy Bill's. A band on the stage pumped out a deafening country rock song. They were backed by a red banner proclaiming "Cowboy Bill's Presents," a large Jim Beam sign, and a large inflated Jim Beam bottle. The leader of the band was a shaved-head white man who had painted his face into a snarling horror mask dominated by two rows of enormous fangs. He looked like the band *Kiss* as envisioned by Stephen King. The bass player was a friendlier looking dumpy character in a porkpie hat. Bobby couldn't help but stare at the third member of the band, a thin black guy who played a purple fiddle behind his head. A drummer banged loudly behind the band.

Inebriated people were already riding the mechanical bull that was out in the middle of a padded corral. A tanned barefooted beefcake male rider wearing cargo shorts and no shirt was thrown off the bull seconds after Bobby entered. Bobby went to the bar and ordered a drink and a burger. Two attractive girls in halter tops and short shorts climbed on the bull facing each other and began to kiss as the bull tried to buck them off. As the mechanical bull's bucking became more violent, one girl stabilized herself by grabbing the other by the breasts, almost pulling her top down.

"This is more like it," Bobby announced to the bartender, "but I came here to see tits *and* ass." The bartender said nothing. He just smiled and took Bobby's money.

"Just wait," the bartender said. "This is women's sexy bull-riding night."

"I gotta call Billy," Bobby said to no one in particular. "He'll love this shit."

He dialed Billy on his cell phone.

Within 20 minutes Billy had joined him in the bar. Billy's motivation was not as much tits and ass but keeping his drunken brother out of trouble. By this time the party was in full swing.

A topless blonde wearing a white sundress and cowboy hat gave the bull a wild ride, never getting thrown. When she completed her ride, she lay on the bar while her date drank a jello shooter out of her naval. The crowd cheered an enthusiastic approval. Three topless girls in cut-offs next mounted the bull and attempted to ride as a trio. All three were quickly thrown.

During a lull, Billy finally asked Bobby what had spurred his night out. Bobby told Billy about the interrogation he had endured with Rivas and Goldshmid. He embellished his story with multiple "f" words. Billy then told Bobby he had been grilled in a similar manner.

"That mother is going to pay," Bobby said. "The two of

us together can screw that cop to the wall."

Billy pleaded with Bobby not to make matters worse, but the drunken Bobby was adamant. He was going to get even with someone.

They watched the next rider, a topless girl who wore only bikini underwear. She had a tattoo of the sun on her leg. After she had been thrown, Bobby announced he had changed his mind. His target would be Jock Jacquette instead. His reasoning, Jock couldn't identify anyone if he was dead. Billy just groaned. His brother seemed determined to get them both sent up for life.

CHAPTER 58

Billy was finally able to get his drunken twin brother to leave Cowboy Bill's before midnight. As he drove him home, Bobby continued to talk about how he could make all their problems disappear by finishing the job on Jock Jacquette. Billy pleaded with him to drop the whole matter and hoped when Bobby sobered up the following morning the idea would be forgotten. He called Bobby the next morning and found Bobby as adamant as ever.

He made the mistake of mentioning the incident to Miguel Valdes when he stopped by Casa Camilio Sur for his morning coffee.

Valdes responded immediately. "You've got to talk him out of that and any other crazy ideas he might have. There is too much at stake to have him endanger it all acting like a loose cannon."

"I've tried," Billy said.

"Let me rephrase my fuckin' self," Valdes said. "Either you solve the problem any way you can, or I will. I can tell you right now, you won't like the organization's solution. It's severe, brutal and permanent. I'll also say this. You have an opportunity to earn the respect of the organization if you solve it permanently yourself."

"I hope you're not suggesting that I take out my brother," Billy said, grabbing Valdes by his shirt. "Let me go on record that I don't approve of his plan, but if anyone messes with either of us, he better be prepared to take on the other one. Do we understand each other?"

Later that day Valdes mentioned the conversation to Adolfo Soltero.

Solero's answer was short and simple, "Get Billy to handle Bobby once and for all. He is no longer an asset but a liability."

"He fuckin' refuses," Valdes said, "and he said he is willing to defend Bobby if he has to."

"Then you may have to deal with the matter personally unless you wish to be perceived as a weak manager. That is not an image you wish to project," Soltero said. "I will check with my superiors and get their input on how the situation should be handled. Just remember, *Ars longa, vita brevis.*"

"What the fuck does that mean?" Valdes asked.

"The work is long, the life is short, my unrefined friend," Soltero replied as he turned around and left the restaurant.

Soltero stopped by Casa Camilio Sur again the following day.

"Well?" Valdes asked.

"All matters will soon be resolved," Soltero said. He put his hand on Valdes' shoulder and said "Errare humanum est – sed perseverare diabolicum." (Mistakes are human, but to continue making mistakes is devilish.)"

"I wish you wouldn't talk that shit I can't understand," Valdes said.

"It doesn't matter," Soltero said. "You will understand soon enough. Ut Deus tecum sit."

"Huh."

"All my problems will soon be solved," Soltero said.

~ ~ ~

The day began on a high note. The sun was bright. The sky was clear. The remnants of a full moon could be seen in the sky. The wind was moderate. People's moods were light. It appeared to be a perfect day in paradise, the memorable kind of day tourist brochures led outsiders to believe happened every day. It would turn out to be memorable all right, but these memories would never be mentioned in future tourist brochures. The memories would be the kind locals would like to forget.

Miguel Valdes went by The Restaurant Store on Eaton Street to pick up some things he needed for the restaurant. He parked over by Strunk Ace Hardware. He got the things he needed and brought them back out to his car. He put them in the back seat and pushed the shopping basket back around the side of the building. As he began to get in his car, a man in dark glasses and a baseball cap came up behind him. He stuck a long thin stiletto into Valdes' back and twisted it to make sure it sliced vital organs. He then grabbed Valdes by the hair and slit his throat. He walked quickly without looking back to White Street, rounded the corner and was picked up by a waiting scooter. The scooter rode to Truman, took a left, and was soon lost in the traffic on U.S. 1.

Within 30 minutes Billy Perez received an anonymous phone call telling him that Bobby had been injured at S & S Amusements near Garrison Bight. He rushed over to see what the problem was. All the way over, he envisioned something or someone having sent Bobby into a tirade resulting in his tearing the place apart. He found a parking place by S & S and got out of his car. Things seemed quiet enough. He had expected to find police cars or an ambulance. As he walked toward the building a car sped down Roosevelt and from the passenger side an AK-47 appeared. Before he could react, Billy was riddled with bullets and collapsed where he stood. The car sped away as shocked onlookers scattered.

Bobby Perez received a call from Rodney Chamberlain.

"I need to see you alone about Sno-White Bath Salts ... NOW," he said. "It's important. We need to meet at a secluded place. I'll be down near the end of Middle Torch Road in half an hour. You'll see my car. Keep your yap shut about our meeting. I'll fill you in when you get here."

Bobby had no idea why Rodney was so insistent on meeting him, but the urgency in Rodney's voice was clear. He rushed out of his office and quickly drove to Middle Torch Road.

At the far end he saw Rodney's Mercedes parked on the shoulder of the road with the engine running. The tint on the windows prevented him from seeing in. Rodney must be staying in the air conditioning as long as possible.

Bobby got out of his car and walked over towards Rodney's. A man came out of the brush holding a shovel. Two others walked up behind him. Bobby began to get nervous when suddenly Rodney opened his door and got out of his car. One of the men behind Bobby grabbed him and pinned his arms behind him. Bobby shook him off. Suddenly the man with the shovel swung it like a baseball bat. It caught Bobby in the face, breaking his nose and squirting blood on his shirt. One of the men behind Bobby hit him in the back with the claw end of a hammer. The third produced a baseball bat and went to work on Bobby's legs and knees. The man with the hammer broke his arms. Rodney just stood there watching. When Bobby hit the ground, the man with the bat hit him with a sickening force that broke his ribs. Bobby began to pass out. No one had said a word. The men grabbed Bobby by the legs and dragged him into the brush. Bobby was just conscious enough to realize they were dragging him into a three-foot hole that had been dug by the man with the shovel.

When they got Bobby to the edge of the hole, they kicked him in. Rodney walked over to the edge of the hole and spit on him. The man with the shovel started shoveling mucky dirt back in the hole. The first shovelful covered his face. Bobby tried to scream, but nothing came out since his mouth was full of dirt. He realized he was being buried alive. As shovelful after shovelful of dirt went back in the hole, Bobby Perez gradually smothered to death. The men dragged brush over the fresh dirt to hide the burial site and left.

One man drove Bobby's car. The remaining members of the death squad followed. They drove the car to the Key West Airport, parked it in long-term parking and then dropped Bobby's keys down a sewer.

That afternoon Adolfo Soltero received a phone call.

The caller did not identify himself but simply said, "We have fulfilled our mission."

Soltero said, "Thank you. Have a nice day" and hung up.

CHAPTER 59

"Walter plopped down in Betsy's office. I guess you saw the headlines today. The newspaper is calling yesterday *Bloody Monday*."

"That's all anyone has talked about all morning," Betsy said. "Do we have a gang war going on in our little slice of paradise?"

"Damned if I know," Walter said. "We think it might be a power struggle at CANDO, but we're not sure who the players are. A likely candidate is Bobby Perez. He seems to be missing, and his car was found at the Key West Airport. We started looking for him after his wife called and said he hadn't been home. The car was easy to find since it was covered with some really obnoxious bumper stickers."

"Like what?" Betsy asked.

"He had one that said 'You suck' and another one that said 'It's tourist season. So why can't we shoot them?' plus some others that were equally offensive. He may have taken off for parts unknown, but we can't find any evidence of him boarding any of yesterday's flights. The whole thing has got us buffaloed."

"The paper's descriptions of yesterday's events almost make them sound like professional hits," Betsy said.

"Sure looks that way, doesn't it," Walter said. "Bobby's car was wiped clean. Not a print to be found, not even his."

"Hmmm," Betsy said. "That's certainly not normal."

"There was also no sign of violence having occurred in

the car," Walter said. "I was so sure we were about to nab him for beating up Jock Jacquette. Maybe that's why he hauled it. He sensed that it was just a matter of time until we nailed him."

"Could be," Betsy said. "He may have figured he was on borrowed time here in the Keys. You know what they say, when the going gets tough the tough get going."

"Yeah, right into hiding," Walter agreed. "We had another curious event happen this morning."

"Oh yeah! What was that?"

"We were contacted by LAPD. It seems that a car crashed and exploded in Los Angeles yesterday. The ID's they found in the car were for one Sun Raye and one Luis Bernstein of Little Torch Key," Walter said.

"But ... she's dead already," Betsy exclaimed. "How many times can she die?"

"She's like a cat using up her nine lives," Walter said, "and I've wondered what happened to Luis."

"Do they have a positive ID on the bodies?" Betsy asked.

"No, they were cremated beyond recognition in the fire that followed the crash," Walter said. "The ID's were found in what remained of the glove compartment."

"My God," Betsy said. "Do you think that was a professional hit as well?"

"If it weren't for everything else happening, I would have accepted the crash at face value," Walter said. "Now I wonder. It's just too many coincidences happening to too many people connected with CANDO."

"I wonder what happens to CANDO now?" Betsy asked.

"I guess the daughters will take over," Walter said. "I'm sure the religious part will fold. I think that was pretty much their mom's obsession."

"If after all this they want to see it continue," Betsy said. "I certainly wouldn't blame them for walking away from it all. I guess this closes another chapter."

"Not necessarily," Walter said. "We still need to try to find out who the culprits are, and we still need to try to locate Bobby Perez. I'll admit that I don't have a clue as to where to begin on either one."

"Maybe John Walsh could help," Betsy said.

"There's always the possibility."

EPILOGUE

Rachel Cirilli woke and stretched. She looked across the bed, and her husband, Jerry was still asleep. She got up, pulled the curtains and looked from her 20th floor apartment at the Manhattan skyline. It looked like it was going to be a beautiful Sunday, a good day to go to Central Park. She got up and went to the kitchen to start coffee. The smell of coffee wafting through the apartment soon woke her husband. He dramatically opened the kitchen door and broke into an off-key rendition of *New York, New York.*

I want to wake up in that city
That doesn't sleep
And find I'm king of the hill
Top of the heap

Rachel cheerfully chimed in.

My small town blues
They have all melted away
I'm about to make a brand new start of it
Right there in old New York ...

"You seem to have slept well," Rachel said as she hugged him.

"Good morning, darling," he said. "It looks like it's going to be a marvelous day. Why don't we go out for brunch later?"

"Sounds like a plan to me," Rachel replied. "In the

meantime, why don't you go downstairs and get a Sunday Times so we can enjoy our coffee."

"This sure is the life of Riley," Jerry said. "I like being dead."

"I'm glad you thought of it. Actually I think I'm getting pretty good at it," Rachel said. "It sure beats looking over your shoulder constantly to see if the cartel has found you."

"Practice makes perfect. I couldn't have done it without Reverend LeRoy's help," Jerry said. "He sure has all the right connections in low places to make things happen."

"I know it was expensive for him to arrange that car wreck," Rachel said, "but it was worth every penny of it."

"Plus he knew the perfect person to create a new identity for us," Jerry said.

"I'm going to miss Key West, and I'm certainly going to miss my girls," Rachel said, "but you've got to do what you've got to do if you want to be a survivor. They should do all right for themselves ... even with those crumb-bum husbands of theirs."

"Oh," Jerry said. "I was waiting for the right time to tell you. Billy Perez was killed by a hit man in Key West, and Bobby hasn't been seen since."

"I hope this doesn't sound callous, but I'm almost glad," Rachel said. "I always did have reservations about both of them. Maybe the girls will do better the next time around."

"Especially since they are both intelligent and well-fixed financially," Jerry said. "After all, they are young, and very attractive girls."

"I know it's my maternal instincts, but I sure wish I could be there to hold their hands," Rachel said, "but I also know it's time to cut them loose."

"And speaking of well fixed, we're not paupers either," Jerry said. "The money I was able to make as well as take through 21st Century Securities should be more than enough to keep us in the style we would like to be accustomed for the rest of our lives."

"I sure miss the tropics though. Maybe we could even find ourselves an island retreat," Rachel said.

"All we have to do is decide which one," Jerry said. "In the meantime your yoga school is sure taking off."

"It really is fun, and being chosen to be in one of Wai Lana's videos has sure helped recruiting students … even if I was only background as part of the class she was instructing for the film. It was a real stroke of luck that we were on Maui when she was filming it," Rachel said.

"I was nervous about the exposure when you did it, but you wanted to be on it so bad I wasn't about to deny you the opportunity. After all, Wai Lana is probably the most famous yoga instructor in the whole world. I'm sure none of our former associates would ever watch anything like that. Yoga's not macho enough for them. I can just hear Bobby Perez saying 'that sissy shit is for fags and dykes,'" Jerry said.

"As I said a moment ago, I'll never understand what persuaded my girls to get involved with those crude Perez boys. I never could see their magnetism. Yoga will keep me active and busy, but what do you want to do?"

"Oh, I'll think of something," Jerry smiled. "Maybe I'll set up the IT systems for your yoga school. I am pretty good at that, you know."

"Yes, you are," Rachel said, "but promise me no more hacking."

"You have my word," Jerry said. "It's not worth the risk. Well, goodbye to Madelyn and Luis, hello to Jerry and Rachel."

"I'm glad to hear you say that," Rachel said.

"I can't wait to toast a marvelous tomorrow at brunch today," Jerry added.

"And all the tomorrows after that," Rachel agreed.

Jerry went to the bedroom to change clothes. There was a knock at the door.

"I'll get it," Rachel said.

When she opened the door Will and Betsy Black stood there.

Before she could catch herself Rachel gasped, "Mr. and Mrs. B...."

"Hello, Sun Raye," Betsy said quietly. "May we come in?"

"How did you find us?" Rachel asked, her voice quaking.

"What do you mean — us?" Betsy said. "We thought we had just found only you."

"Luis and I got married," Rachel said.

Jerry came out of the bedroom and stood there dumbstruck.

"Invite us in, and we'll tell you everything," Will said.

The Blacks sat in the living room's upholstered chairs while Sun Raye and Luis sat on the sofa and nervously held hands.

"I'm sorry we ran out, but we were afraid for our lives," Sun Raye blurted out.

"After what happened ... or should I say what almost happened ... to both of you, I'm not surprised," Betsy said, "and you did have us fooled for a long time. We thought you were dead. We even went to your funeral."

"If you'll fill us in on how you managed the ruse, we'll tell you how we found you," Will said.

Sun Raye then came clean on all the details of her faked death and Luis's disappearance. Once she began to open up, she held nothing back.

Will and Betsy listened silently, afraid Sun Raye would get cold feet about finishing her story if they interrupted by asking questions. When they were sure she was finished Betsy said, "Now I'll tell you how we located you. It was luck actually. Our daughter who lives in California has become involved with yoga. She came to visit us in Florida recently. Since she was not going to be able to attend her yoga classes while she was in the Keys, she brought a Wai Lana DVD to work out with at our house. I was watching her one day and saw someone in the background who looked a lot like you. I got her let me replay the DVD several times, and the more I saw it, the more I was convinced it might really be you."

Sun Raye nodded her head, "Yes, it was me. We just happened to be in Maui when Mai Lana was filming it, and when she found out I was a yoga instructor, she allowed me to participate. It was one of the greatest honors of my life."

Luis shook his head and said, "I knew that program might come back and bite us in the butt."

Will took up the story. "Later I called Wai Lana's office and pretended to be an IRS agent," he said. "I convinced one of her office workers I needed your name and address because of some tax matters. They didn't want to give the info to me at first, but I hinted to them that I could make them the target of a tax audit if I so chose. Finally the woman caved and gave me the information I wished. She took it from the disclaimer agreement you signed before they could allow you to participate in the program."

"I remember signing one," Sun Raye said.

"After that it was relatively simple to track you to New York," Will said.

"I know well the power of the internet," Luis said. "It's an amazing tool. So what do you plan to do now that you've found us?"

"Nothing at the moment," Will said. "We just had to find out if we were right first. We truly believe that your lives were in danger. We've had past dealings with Adolfo Soltero. Do you know that Valdes and Billy Perez are dead, and that the police have not been able to locate Bobby?"

"We heard," Luis said.

"I swear to you we had nothing to do with any of it," Sun Raye blurted out.

"And we believe you," Betsy said. "You were long gone when these things occurred."

"Did you know Adolfo Soltero's organization was using CANDO to secretly distribute drugs?" Sun Raye said. "My problems began after I discovered it."

"No, we didn't. Did your daughters know about the smuggling?" Will asked.

"Definitely not," Sun Raye said quickly. "They're good girls."

"So Valdes and Perez got caught in the middle of a

drug war," Will said.

"So it seems," Luis said.

"Please don't set up my daughters to take a drug bust," Sun Raye said. "They're good girls."

"I'm going to guess that Valdes' and Perez's deaths were the Cartel's way of closing down the operation since it was in danger of getting out of control," Will said. "I'm sure they've moved on to greener pastures. They're survivors who know when to not overstay their welcome. We have a friend who is Chief of Police in Key West. We'll explain the situation to him and see what he wants to do about it. If your daughters are as clean as you say they are, he will do everything in his power to protect them."

"And us?" Sun Raye asked.

"We'll just forget this meeting ever happened," Betsy said, "unless we find out you haven't told us the truth."

"Thank you," Sun Raye said quietly. Luis nodded in agreement.

"Though I would suggest you at least change your alias and location one more time," Will said.

"But I'll have to close my yoga school," Sun Ray said.

"A small price to pay for our lives. You're good, my darling," Luis said. "You can start another one. Just think of it as a new challenge. After all isn't yoga a lot about positive thinking."

"It's sure a lot simpler than dying again," Sun Raye said. "I'm running out of creative ways to do it."

"And you'll never be able to top your last funeral," Will said smiling. "It was a real doozy."

Thank you for reading. Please review this book. Reviews help others find Absolutely Amazing eBooks and inspire us to keep providing these marvelous tales. If you would like to be put on our email list to receive updates on new releases, contests, and promotions, please go to AbsolutelyAmazingEbooks.com and sign up.

About the Authors

David Beckwith is a three-generation native of Greenville, Mississippi, with a BBA and an MBA from Ole Miss. His parents owned an independent cash commodity trading firm which also cleared securities trades through Goodbody & Co. David spent 40 years in the securities business, the first half of his career with Bache & Co. and its successors, the second half with Morgan Stanley. He retired as a Senior Vice President with approximately $500 million in responsibilities. For 25 years he has served as an adjunct professor at five different universities.

His first book was a narrative nonfiction work published by the University of Alabama Press in 2009 entitled *A New Day In The Delta*. The Mississippi Institute of Arts and Letters chose it as the runner-up for nonfiction book of the year. The book is often compared to Pat Conroy's *The Water Is Wide*.

David's wife Nancy earned a doctorate in finance and was the largest commercial lender and underwriter for Florida National Bank/1st Union/Wachovia, a member of their President's Club, and a board member. Also she served as the provost of the Brookley Campus for the University of South Alabama.

David and Nancy started writing the Will and Betsy Black Adventure Series in 2010. The protagonists of this series are a married couple somewhat reminiscent of Nick and Nora Charles of *The Thin Man* Series or Jonathan and Jennifer Hart of *Hart To Hart*. Their unique hook was that like the books' protagonists the authors were also a happily married couple.

Moving to Key West, the Beckwiths were tapped to write a book review column for the Key West *Citizen*, which David continues to produce on a weekly basis.

ABSOLUTELY AMA⚡ING eBOOKS

AbsolutelyAmazingEbooks.com
or AA-eBooks.com

www.ingramcontent.com/pod-product-compliance
Lightning Source LLC
Chambersburg PA
CBHW060926030726
47503CB00003B/491